SPARRING
PARTNERS

ALSO BY JOHN GRISHAM

JOHN GRISHAM

SPARRING PARTNERS

DOUBLEDAY

New York

Copyright © 2022 by Belfry Holdings, Inc.

All rights reserved. Published in the United States by Doubleday,
a division of Penguin Random House LLC, New York, and distributed in Canada
by Penguin Random House Canada Limited, Toronto.

www.doubleday.com

DOUBLEDAY and the portrayal of an anchor with a dolphin are
registered trademarks of Penguin Random House LLC.

Book design by Maria Carella
Jacket design by Will Staehle

Library of Congress Control Number: 2022932013
ISBN: 978-0-385-54932-5 (hardcover)
ISBN: 978-0-385-54933-2 (ebook)

Manufactured in Canada

1 3 5 7 9 10 8 6 4 2

First Edition

FRI

Contents

SPARRING PARTNERS

HOMECOMING

(1)

It was one of those raw, windy, dreary Monday afternoons in February when gloom settled over the land and seasonal depression was rampant. Court was not in session. The phone wasn't ringing. Petty criminals and other potential clients were busy elsewhere with no thoughts whatsoever of hiring lawyers. The occasional caller was more likely to be a man or woman still reeling from holiday overspending and seeking advice about unpaid credit card accounts. Those were quickly sent next door, or across the square, or anywhere.

Jake was at his desk upstairs, making little progress with the stack of paperwork he'd been neglecting for weeks, even months. With no court or hearings scheduled for days, it should have been a good time to catch up with the old stuff—the fish files that every lawyer had for some reason said yes to a year ago and now just wanted to go away. The upside of a small-town law practice, especially in your hometown, was that everyone knew your name, and that was what you wanted. It was important to be well thought of and well liked, with a good reputation. When your neighbors got in trouble, you wanted to be the man they called. The downside was that their cases were always mundane and rarely profitable. But, you couldn't say no. The gossip was fierce and unrelenting, and a lawyer who turned his back on his friends would not last long.

His funk was interrupted when Alicia, his current part-time secretary, chimed in through his desk phone. "Jake, there's a couple here to see you."

A couple. Married but wanting to get unmarried. Another cheap divorce. He glanced at his daily planner though he knew there was nothing.

"Do they have an appointment?" he asked, but only to remind Alicia that she shouldn't be bothering him with the foot traffic.

"No. But they're very nice and they say it's really urgent. They're not going away, said it wouldn't take but a few minutes."

Jake loathed being bullied in his own office. On a busier day he would take a stand and get rid of them. "Do they appear to have any money?" The answer was always no.

"Well, they do seem rather affluent."

Affluent? In Ford County. Somewhat intriguing.

Alicia continued, "They're from Memphis and just passing through, but, again, they say it's very important."

"Any idea what it is?"

"No."

Well, it wouldn't be a divorce if they lived in Memphis. He ran through a list of possibilities—Grandma's will, some old family land, maybe a kid busted for drugs over at Ole Miss. Since he was bored and mildly curious and needed an excuse to avoid the paperwork, he asked, "Did you tell them that I'm tied up in a settlement conference call with a dozen lawyers?"

"No."

"Did you tell them I'm due in federal court over in Oxford and can only spare a moment or two?"

"No."

"Did you tell them that I'm slammed with other appointments?"

"No. It's pretty obvious the place is empty and the phone isn't ringing."

"Where are you?"

"I'm in the kitchen, so I can talk."

"Okay, okay. Make some fresh coffee and put 'em in the conference room. I'll be down in ten minutes."

(2)

The first thing Jake noticed was their tans. They had obviously been somewhere in the sun. No one else in Clanton had a tan in February. The second thing he noticed was the woman's smart short haircut, with a touch of gray, stylish and obviously expensive. He noticed the handsome sports coat on the gentleman. Both were well dressed and nicely groomed, a departure from the usual walk-ins.

He shook their hands as he got their names. Gene and Kathy Roupp, from Memphis. Late fifties, quite pleasant, with confident smiles showing rows of well-maintained teeth. Jake could easily picture them on a Florida golf course living the good life behind gates and guards.

"What can I do for you folks?" Jake asked.

Gene flashed a smile and went first. "Well, sad to say, but we're not here as potential clients."

Jake kept it loose with a fake smile and an aw-shucks shrug, as if to say, *What the hell? What lawyer needs to get paid for his time?* He'd give them about ten more minutes and one cup before showing them the door.

"We just got back from a month in Costa Rica, one of our favorites. Ever been to Costa Rica?"

"No. I hear it's great." He'd heard nothing of the sort but what else could he say? He would never admit that he had left the United States exactly once in his thirty-eight years. Foreign travel was only a dream.

"We love it down there, a real paradise. Beautiful beaches, mountains, rain forests, great food. We have some friends who own houses—real estate is pretty cheap. The people are delightful, educated, almost all speak English."

Jake loathed the game of travel trivia because he'd never been anywhere. The local doctors were the worst—always bragging about the hottest new resorts.

Kathy was itching to move along the narrative and chimed in with "The golf is incredible, so many fabulous courses."

Jake didn't play golf because he was not a member of the Clanton Country Club. Its membership included too many doctors and climbers and families with old money.

He smiled and nodded at her and waited for one of them to continue. From a bag he couldn't see she whipped out a pound of coffee in a shiny can and said, "Here's a little gift, San Pedro Select, our favorite. Incredible. We haul it back by the case."

Jake took it to be polite. In lieu of cash fees, he had been paid with watermelons, fresh venison, firewood, repairs to his cars, and more bartered goods and services than he cared to remember. His best lawyer buddy, Harry Rex Vonner, had once taken a John Deere mower as a fee, though it soon broke down. Another lawyer, one who was no longer practicing, had taken sexual favors from a divorce client. When he lost the case, she filed an ethics complaint alleging "substandard performance."

Anyway, Jake admired the can and tried to read the Spanish. He noticed they had not touched their coffee, and he was suddenly worried that perhaps they were connoisseurs and his office brew wasn't quite up to their standards.

Gene resumed with "So, two weeks ago we were at one of our favorite eco-lodges, high in the mountains, deep in the rain forest, a small place with only thirty rooms, incredible views."

How many times might they use the word "incredible"?

"And we were having breakfast outdoors, watching the spider monkeys and parakeets, when a waiter stopped by our table to pour some more coffee. He was very friendly—"

"People are so friendly down there and they love Americans," Kathy interjected.

How could they not?

Gene nodded at the interruption and continued, "We chatted him up for a spell, said his name was Jason and that he was from Florida, been living down there for twenty years. We saw him again at lunch and talked to him some more. We saw him around after that and always enjoyed a friendly chat. The day before we were to check out, he asked us to join him for a glass of champagne in a little tree-house bar. He was off-duty and said the drinks were on him. The sunsets over the mountains are incredible, and we were having a good time, when all of a sudden he got serious."

Gene paused and looked at Kathy, who was ready to pounce with "He said he had something to tell us, something very confidential. Said his name was not really Jason and he wasn't from Florida. He apologized for not being truthful. Said his name was really Mack Stafford, and that he was from Clanton, Mississippi."

Jake tried to remain nonchalant but it was impossible. His mouth dropped open and his eyes widened.

The Roupps were watching closely for his reaction. Gene said, "I take it you know Mack Stafford."

Jake exhaled and wasn't sure what to say. "Well, I'll be damned."

"He said you guys were old friends," Gene added.

Stunned, Jake was still grasping for words. "I'm just glad he's alive."

"So you know him well?"

"Oh yes, quite well."

(3)

Three years earlier, the town was rocked with the scandalous news that Mack Stafford, a well-known lawyer on the square, had cracked up, filed for bankruptcy, divorced his wife, and left his family in the middle of the night. The gossip raged for weeks, with all manner of tales spinning off wildly, and when the dust began to settle it appeared that most of the rumors were actually true, for a change.

Mack practiced street law for seventeen years and Jake knew him well. He was a decent lawyer with a passable reputation. Like most of them, he handled the routine business of those clients who walked through his door, and barely managed to keep his head above water. His wife, Lisa, was an assistant principal at Clanton High School and earned a steady salary. Her father owned the only ready-mix plant in the county, and that placed her family a notch or two above the others, but still a considerable distance below the doctors. Lisa was nice enough but a bit on the snooty side, and for that reason Jake and Carla had never socialized with them.

After Mack disappeared, and it became obvious that he had indeed vanished without a trace, word leaked from somewhere that he had left town with some money that wasn't exactly his. Lisa got everything in the divorce, though the couple's liabilities almost equaled their assets. Mack dumped his files and clients and legal troubles on Harry Rex, who whispered to Jake that he had been paid in cash for his troubles, and Mack left some money behind for Lisa and their two daughters. Lisa had no idea where it came from.

The fact that he had so successfully disappeared only fueled the speculation that he had done something wrong, and stealing clients' money was the most likely scenario. Every lawyer handled his clients' money, if only for brief periods of time, and the quickest and most common route to disbarment was pilfering a bit here and there. There was no shortage of legendary cases where lawyers succumbed to temptation and looted entire trust funds, guardianship accounts, and settlement pools. They usually tried to hide for a while but all were caught, stripped of their licenses, and sent to prison.

But Mack was never caught, nor was he heard from. As the months passed, Jake asked Harry Rex, always over a beer, if he had heard from Mack. He most certainly had not, and among the local lawyers the legend grew. Mack pulled off the great escape. He left behind an unhappy marriage, a dismal career, and was on a beach somewhere, sipping rum. Or at least that was the fantasy among the lawyers he left behind.

(4)

Kathy said, "We got the impression he did something wrong around here, but he never mentioned it. I mean, you gotta figure a guy like him, living in some exotic place down there, using an alias, and so on, had a pretty colorful past. But, again, he didn't give us much."

Gene said, "When we got home we did some digging and found a couple of stories in the local newspapers, but it was pretty general stuff. His divorce, bankruptcy, and the fact that he was gone."

Kathy asked, "Can we ask you, Mr. Brigance, did Mack do something wrong? Is he on the run?"

Jake wasn't about to confide in these strangers, two nice people he would probably never see again. The truth was that Jake didn't know for sure that Mack had committed a crime. He deflected the question with "I don't think so. It's no crime to divorce and leave town."

The answer was completely unsatisfactory. It hung in the air for a few seconds, then Gene leaned in a bit closer and asked, "Did we do anything wrong by talking to him?"

"Of course not."

"Aiding and abetting, something like that?"

"No way. Not a chance. Relax."

They took a deep breath.

Jake said, "The bigger question is: Why are you here?"

They exchanged knowing little smiles and Kathy reached into her bag. She withdrew a plain, unmarked, unstamped manila envelope, five-by-eight, and handed it to Jake, who took it with suspicion. The flap had been sealed with glue, tape, and staples.

Gene said, "Mack asked us to stop by and say hello, and tell you that he sends his greetings. And he asked us to deliver this. We have no idea what it is."

Kathy was nervous again and asked, "This is okay, right? We're not involved in anything, are we?"

"Of course not. No one will ever know."

"He said you could be trusted."

"I can." Jake wasn't sure what he was being asked in trust, but he didn't want to worry them.

Gene handed him a scrap of paper and said, "This is our phone number in Memphis. Mack wants you to call us in a few days and say, simply, yes or no. That's all. Just yes or no."

"Okay." Jake took the scrap of paper and placed it next to

the envelope and the pound of coffee. Kathy finally took a sip from her cup and remained expressionless.

They had completed their mission and were ready to go. Jake assured them that everything would be held in the strictest of confidence and that he would tell no one about their meeting. He walked them to the front door and outside onto the sidewalk, and he watched them get into a shiny BMW sedan and drive away.

Then he hustled back to the conference room, closed the door, and opened the envelope.

(5)

The letter was typed on one sheet of plain white paper, tri-folded, with a smaller envelope stuck in the fold.

It read:

> *Hello, Jake. By now, you've met my two newest best friends, Gene and Kathy Roupp, of Memphis. Fine folks. I'll cut to the chase. I want to talk to you, down here in Costa Rica. I want to come home, Jake, but I'm not sure that's possible. I need your help. I'm asking you and Carla to take a little vacation and come see me, next month during spring break. I assume Carla is still teaching and I assume the schools take their normal spring break the second week of March. I'll arrange six nights at the Terra Lodge, a splendid eco-tourist resort in the mountains. You'll love this place. Enclosed is $1800 in cash, more than enough for two round-trip tickets from Memphis to San Jose, Costa Rica. From there, I'll have a car waiting to bring you here. It's about three hours and the drive is beautiful. Rooms, meals, tours, everything is on me. The dream vacation of a lifetime. Once you get here, I'll eventually find you and*

we'll talk. Privacy is my specialty these days and I assure you no one will ever know about our meeting. The less said about the vacation the better. I know how people love to talk around that awful town.

Please do this, Jake. It will be well worth your time, if for nothing else than an unforgettable trip.

Lisa is not well. Okay to discuss this with Harry Rex, but please swear that loudmouth to secrecy.

I will not do anything to jeopardize your well-being.

Think it over. In a few days, call Gene and say either "Yes" or "No."

I need you, pal.

Mack

The small envelope contained a slick brochure from the Terra Lodge.

(6)

The most dangerous place in downtown Clanton on a Monday was undoubtedly the law office of Harry Rex Vonner. With a well-earned reputation as the nastiest divorce lawyer in the county, he attracted clients with assets worth fighting over. Monday was volatile for various reasons: bad behavior on Saturday night, or too much time in the house arguing over this and that, or even another explosive Sunday lunch with the in-laws. There was no shortage of detonators, and the frazzled and warring spouses rushed to get legal counsel as soon as possible. By noon, the place was a tinderbox as the phones rang nonstop and litigants, both current and brand-new, dropped by with and without appointments. The harried secretaries tried to maintain order as Harry Rex either stomped around, growling at everyone, or hid in his bunker-like office out of the fray. It was not unusual for him, on a Monday, to storm out of his back room and order someone, client or otherwise, to get the hell out.

They always complied because he had a reputation for unpredictability. It, too, was well earned. A few years earlier, a secretary had rushed into his office and said she had just hung up on a husband who was headed into town, with a gun. Harry Rex went to his closet, and from his impressive arsenal chose his favorite, a Browning 12-gauge, pump-action shotgun. When the husband parked his truck near the courthouse and started for the office, Harry Rex emerged onto the sidewalk and fired two shots into the clouds. The husband retreated to his truck and left. The blasts boomed like howitzers over the square. Offices and stores emptied as folks scurried to see what was going on. Someone called the police. By the time Sheriff Ozzie Walls parked in front of the office, a crowd had gathered on the courthouse lawn, a safe distance away. Ozzie went inside and met with Harry Rex. Discharging a firearm in public was a crime all right, but in a culture where the Second Amendment was revered and every vehicle had at least two firearms, the statute was rarely enforced. Harry Rex claimed self-defense and vowed to aim lower next time.

After dark on Monday, Jake eased around the square and, avoiding the chaos in the front, ducked into an alley and entered the office through the rear door. Harry Rex was at his desk, rumpled and wrinkled as always, his tie undone, food stains on his shirt, his hair a mess. He actually smiled and asked, "What the hell are you doin' here?"

Jake said, "We need to split a beer."

It was code for: *We need to talk, and now, and it's top secret.* Harry Rex closed his eyes and took a deep breath. "What is it?" he asked in a low tone.

"Mack Stafford."

Another deep breath, then a look of disbelief.

Jake said, "Meet me at the Riviera at eight."

At home, Jake kissed, hugged, and pestered Carla as she put a chicken in the oven and prepared dinner. He went upstairs and found Hanna busy with her homework. He went to Luke's room and found him playing quietly under his bed. Back in the kitchen, he asked his wife to have a seat at the breakfast table and handed her the letter. As she read it, she began shaking her head and tapping her teeth with a painted fingernail, an old habit that could mean several things.

"What a creep."

"I always liked Mack."

"He left his wife and kids and disappeared. And didn't he steal some money from his clients?"

"That's the legend. He vanished three years ago, but he didn't really leave his wife. They were getting a divorce. Is she sick?"

"Come on, Jake. Lisa's had breast cancer for a year now. You knew that."

"I must have forgotten. There's so much cancer. She was never your favorite, as I recall."

"No, she wasn't." Carla looked at the letter again. "Check those potatoes."

Jake walked to the stove and stirred a pot of boiling potatoes. He filled a glass with water and returned to the table.

She asked, "Why does he want you? Wasn't Harry Rex his lawyer?"

"He was, guess he still is. Maybe it's because Harry Rex is afraid of flying and Mack knew he wouldn't make the trip. There's nothing wrong with going down, I mean, nothing illegal."

"You're not serious."

"Why not? An all-expenses-paid week at a fancy resort in the mountains."

"No."

"Come on, Carla. We haven't had a real vacation in years."

"We've never had a real vacation, like, you know, getting on a plane and flying off somewhere."

"Exactly. This is the chance of a lifetime."

"No."

"Why not? The guy needs help. He wants to come home and, I don't know, maybe make things right with his family. There's no harm in going down and meeting with him. Mack's a nice guy."

"He has two daughters that he left behind."

"He did, and that's terrible. But maybe he wants to make amends. Let's give the guy a break."

"Is he a fugitive?"

"I'm not sure. I'm meeting with Harry Rex at eight and I have some questions. The rumor was that Mack took a bunch of money and left town, but I don't recall hearing about an indictment or anything like that. He filed for bankruptcy and divorce and vanished. Most of the lawyers in town were envious. Not me, of course."

"Of course not. I remember all the gossip. The town talked of nothing else for months."

Jake slid across the brochure and she took it.

(7)

The Riviera was a small 1950s-style motel at the edge of town. It had two wings of tiny rooms, some rumored to be available by the hour, and a dingy bar where lawyers and bankers and businessmen hid to discuss things that could not be overheard.

Jake hadn't been there in years and got a few looks as he walked in. He smiled at the bartender, ordered two draft beers, and took them to a table near the jukebox. He sipped one for fifteen minutes as he waited. Harry Rex was always late, especially for drinks. Getting him to the bar, though, was the easy part. Getting him out of one was usually a challenge. Things were not going well with his third wife and he preferred to stay away from home.

He lumbered in at 8:20 and spoke to three gentlemen at a table as he passed by. At times, it seemed as though he knew everyone.

He fell into a chair across from Jake, grabbed his mug, and drained half of it. Jake knew it wasn't his first beer of the evening. He kept a fridge filled with Bud Light in his office and popped a top each evening after the last client left.

"Poachin' my clients again, huh?" he said.

"Hardly. I doubt if Mack's looking for a new lawyer."

"Tell me what you know."

"He left town, what, three years ago? Any word from him since then?"

"Not a peep. Nothing. The last time I spoke to Mack he was in my office lookin' at the divorce papers. Gave her everything, includin' fifty thousand in cash. That's in the settlement. Nash was her lawyer, told me later that they'd never had fifty thousand in cash, nowhere close to that. He talked to Freda, his old secretary, and she had no idea where the money came from. Said they could barely pay the bills most months."

"So, where did the money come from?"

"Slow down." Another gulp. "This beer's hot. How long's it been sittin' here?"

"Well, I bought it when I arrived promptly at eight, the agreed-upon hour. So, yes, it's not as cold as it was."

Harry Rex unfolded himself, walked to the bar, and

ordered two more drafts. He set them on the table and said, "So, he's contacted you?"

"Yep." Jake told the story about Gene and Kathy Roupp and their surprise visit earlier in the day. He handed over the letter and Harry Rex read it slowly. He paused and said, "You know Lisa's got breast cancer. Nash told me months ago."

"Yes."

Jake rarely bothered to chase gossip. He had Harry Rex to rely on.

He finished reading and took a drink. "Wonder why he didn't offer *me* a nice vacation."

"Could be the airplane thing."

"That, plus I can't imagine goin' anywhere with Millie for a week. You takin' the deal?"

"Carla says no, but she'll come around. There's no harm, right?"

"I don't see a problem. He ain't exactly a fugitive."

"But I recall something about the grand jury poking around."

"That's right. I thought things might get hairy when the DA was askin' questions. Hell, even the FBI stopped by to see me a couple of times."

"You never told me that."

"Jake, my friend, there are a lot of things you don't know."

"So, where'd the money come from?"

"I have no idea, really. Mack was always desperate to make some money because his law practice was a dead end and his wife had bigger dreams."

"And he paid you?"

"Jake, son, I always get paid. Yes, Mack paid me five grand in cash. I didn't ask questions."

"And he's been discharged in bankruptcy?"

"Correct. I handled that too. Not much in the way of assets

and certainly no cash. Hell, the boy didn't have a pot to piss in, at least nothin' above the table. And she got everything. The bank foreclosed on his office. About a month after he left, the FBI came snoopin' around but they were chasin' their tails."

"What did they want?"

"They didn't know. They had nothin', nobody was complainin'. Somehow they'd heard the rumors that Mack had flown the coop with stolen money, but there were no witnesses. Got the impression they were just goin' through the motions."

"So there was no indictment, no outstanding warrants? No one is looking for Mack?"

"Not to my knowledge, which, as we know, is vast. Now, that's not to say he's off the hook. I wouldn't worry about the divorce. Hell, the poor girl is probably dyin', from what I hear. If he hid money, then bankruptcy fraud might be a problem. He could still be investigated for that."

"Who would investigate him?"

"Exactly. Who cares? He's been discharged. I can't believe he wants to come back. Your turn."

Jake walked to the bar and returned with two more drafts. He took a drink and started laughing. "Be honest, Harry Rex, how many times have you thought of Mack and secretly dreamed of chucking it all and heading for the beach?"

"At least a thousand. I thought about him last week."

"I guess we've all had that dream, though I can never see myself leaving Carla and the kids."

"Well, you got yourself a good girl. Me, that's another story."

"So, why does he want to come back?"

"That's where you come in, Jake. You gotta go see him. Take the dream vacation, get the hell out of this place for a week. Go have some fun."

"And you see no risk in doing so?"

"Hell no. Nobody's gonna be watchin' you. Take his cash, buy the round-trip tickets, get Carla off to the mountains of Costa Rica. I wish I could go."

"I'll send you a postcard."

(8)

Postcards could never do justice to the Terra Lodge. It was tucked into the side of a mountain a thousand feet above the Pacific Ocean, and from their poolside lounge chairs Jake and Carla sat mesmerized, drinks in hand, as they tried to absorb the view. Without a single cloud above them, the sun beat down and soothed their frigid bones. It had been sleeting when they took off from Memphis. For the first time, Jake wondered why anyone would want to leave this paradise.

At check-in, they had been escorted to their bungalow, one of only thirty at the lodge. It was a private three-room suite with a thatched roof, outdoor shower, wading pool, plenty of air-conditioning that wasn't needed, all set in the midst of lush tropical gardens. Ricardo, their new best friend, was only seconds away. A rate chart on the door of the bathroom listed the villa at $600 a night.

Jake said, "I don't know how much clout Mack has around here, but it must be substantial."

"This place is unbelievable," Carla replied as she examined a deep tub that could hold three people. Her reluctance in taking the free trip had finally dissipated the moment she saw the ocean.

Ricardo took them to the pool, brought their drinks, and explained that dinner would be served at seven, at a private table, with a view of the sunset they would never forget. After the first drink, Jake jumped into the infinity pool, rested his arms on the ledge, soaked in the warm salt water, and gawked in amazement at the shimmering blue Pacific.

Their honeymoon had been a low-budget trip to the Caribbean eleven years earlier, Jake's first and only trip abroad. Carla's parents were more affluent and she had spent a month in Europe with a group of students. Nothing, though, could ever compare to this.

Late in the day, the other guests, all adults, gathered by the pool and watched a glorious sunset. Dinner was nearby on a patio—fresh-baked lobster with fresh organic vegetables, grown right down the road on the lodge's own little farm. Afterward, they retired to the Sky Lounge, a hideaway flooded with stars, and danced to the beat of a local band.

They slept late the following morning and almost missed the whale boat, a large converted pontoon that also served breakfast, lunch, and drinks. The day was spent in the sun, searching for whales. The captain apologized when they saw nothing but dolphins.

Late that night, as they lay in bed, exhausted, Carla finally broached the obvious subject. "So, no sign of Mack?"

"No. Not yet. But I get the impression he's close by."

Day Three was spent on horses, not Jake's favorite way to travel, but the group was enthusiastic and the guide was a comedian. He talked nonstop as he pointed out exotic birds, spider monkeys, and flowers that could not be found anywhere else in the world. They stopped at hot springs, waterfalls, and enjoyed a full three-course lunch, with wine, at the edge of a volcano. Three thousand feet up, and the views of the Pacific were even more spectacular.

Day Four was a whitewater rafting trip in the morning and a knee-buckling zip line adventure in the afternoon, interrupted by a delicious riverside brunch of tropical fruit and rum punch. Late in the day, as they showered and prepared for the rigors of dinner, the phone rang. Jake limped to it, his crotch still unsettled from six hours in the saddle the day before, and said hello.

It was Mack, finally. They had almost forgotten about him. "Hello, Jake, good to hear your voice."

"And good to hear yours." Jake nodded at Carla who smiled and returned to the bathroom.

"I trust you guys are having fun."

"Indeed we are. Thanks for the hospitality. Not a bad place to spend a week."

"No, not at all. Look, I figure y'all might need some down-time tomorrow, so I've arranged a day at the spa, with all the works. Carla will love it. Could you meet me for lunch?"

"I can probably work you into my schedule."

"Good. How's the food so far?"

"Unbelievable. I haven't eaten this well since I had catfish at Claude's last week."

"I remember Claude. How's he doing these days?"

"The same. Not much has changed, Mack."

"I'm sure. At the front of the lodge you'll see a dirt path next to a sign for the Barillo Trail. You'll walk about half a mile through the rain forest and see another sign for the Kura Grille. All of the tables are outside, nice views and such. I have one reserved for one o'clock."

"I'll be there."

"And let's keep Carla out of our conversations, okay? She won't mind, will she?"

"No, not at all."

"She'll have a busy day at the spa with lunch by the pool."

"I'm sure she'll be fine."

"Good. Can't wait to see you, Jake."

"Same here."

(9)

Mack forgot to mention that the Barillo Trail curved upward, always upward, and after a few minutes Jake felt like he was climbing a mountain, which indeed he was. The half-mile trek seemed more like two miles and he stopped twice to catch his breath. He was winded and frustrated that, at the age of only thirty-eight, he was in such bad shape. Long gone were the endless wind sprints of high school football.

There were no vehicles to be seen at the café—only a few bikes. He was sweating when he walked by the bar and onto the deck. Mack was waiting at a table under a large colorful umbrella. They shook hands and settled in.

"You're looking good," Mack said, his words a bit crisper, the drawl having been flattened out of his speech.

"And so are you." Jake wasn't sure he would have recognized him on the street. Mack was now forty-five and his salt-and-pepper hair was much longer. His neat beard was more gray than dark brown. He wore round tortoiseshell glasses and could have passed for a handsome college professor. He was also leaner than Jake remembered.

Jake said, "Thanks for the trip and the hospitality. This place is incredible."

"First trip to Costa Rica?"

"Yes it is. Hope it's not the last."

"You're welcome back anytime, Jake, as my guest."

"You must know the owner."

"I am the owner. One of three. Eco-tourism has become a big deal down here and I bought in a year ago."

"So you live around here?"

"Here and there." His first evasive answer, the first of many. Jake didn't pursue it.

"How's the family?" Mack asked.

"Couldn't be better. Carla is still teaching, Hanna is in the third grade, growing up fast. Luke's a year old."

"Never heard of Luke."

"We adopted him. A long story."

"I have some of those."

"I'm sure."

"I miss my girls." A waiter appeared and asked about drinks. Jake was open to anything but was relieved when Mack said, "Just water." Jake nodded his agreement.

When the waiter left, Jake asked, "What's your name around here? I'm sure no one calls you Mack."

He smiled and took a sip. "Well, I have several names, but here it's Marco."

Jake took a sip and waited for an explanation. "Okay, Marco, what's your story?"

"Brazilian, of German extraction. That's why I don't look like a native. I'm from southern Brazil, lots of Germans down there. A businessman with several interests in Central America. I move around a lot."

"What's the name on your passport?"

"Which one?"

Jake smiled and took another sip. "Look, I'm not going to dig, and I presume I'm supposed to know only what you're willing to tell me. Right?"

"Right. A lot has happened in the past three years and most of it is irrelevant as far as you're concerned."

"Fair enough."

"You've talked to Harry Rex?"

"Of course. I showed him your letter. He's in the loop."

"How's that fat slob doing?"

"The same. Though I think he's getting meaner."

"Didn't think that was possible. Let's talk about him later."

The waiter was back and Mack ordered shrimp salads. When

he left, Mack leaned on his elbows and said, "I left in the middle of the night, as you know, and fled the country. First stop was Belize, where I lived for about a year. I liked it there, spent the first three months drinking too much, chasing girls, roasting on the beach. But that got old. I did a lot of bone fishing, also permit and tarpon. I got a job as a fishing guide and really liked that. I was always careful, always watching for tourists, guests at the lodge, fishermen, somebody from home. It's amazing what you can hear when you listen hard enough. A Southern drawl, and my radar was up. I checked the books at the lodge to see who was coming in, and steered clear of anybody from Mississippi. They were few and far between. Most of my fishermen were from the Northeast. I assumed nothing, but I figured I was safe. I grew a beard, got a dark tan, lost twenty pounds, always wore a cap or a hat."

"Your accent has changed."

"Yes, and it wasn't easy. I talk to myself a lot, for many reasons, and I'm always practicing. Anyway, I had a scare and decided to leave Belize."

"What happened?"

"One night there was a table of men, older guys, having dinner at the lodge. They were staying next door, fishing, and having a great time. All from the South. I recognized one, a circuit judge from Biloxi. The Honorable Harold Massey. Ever meet him?"

"No, but I've heard the name. It's a small state."

"It is. Too small. I was at the bar, hitting on a girl, not far from the dining patio. We made eye contact and he gave me a look. I've always figured that most of the lawyers and judges in the state knew my story. He eventually left the table for the restroom and walked by me. I thought he stared a bit too long. I kept my cool but I really freaked. So, I eased out of town, left Belize, and made my way to Panama, stayed there a few months. I gotta tell you, Jake, life on the run is not that great."

"How do you know Lisa is sick?"

Mack smiled and shrugged and sat back in his chair. "I have a mole back there, an old friend from high school who married a girl from Clanton. You know how the gossip gets around."

"Harry Rex swears he's had no contact."

"True. I figured the people who wanted to find me might watch my lawyer. There's been no contact with anyone who might make a mistake. No contact until now."

"Who might be looking for you?"

"That's why you're here, Jake. I want to go home, but I can't risk any danger of getting caught."

The salads arrived, large bamboo plates with shrimp salad on beds of leafy greens. They ate for a moment. Jake asked, "So why did you contact me?"

"Because I trust you. Can't say that for most of the old bar. How many lawyers in Clanton now?"

"I don't know. Thirty, forty, maybe more. They come and go. Unlike most towns in the state, Clanton is not dying. Not exactly thriving, but hanging on."

"There were close to fifty when I left, far too many for any of us to make a decent living. And I didn't trust the ones I knew, only you and Harry Rex."

"The cream of the crop, no doubt."

"Is Lucien still alive?"

"Oh yes. I see him all the time."

"I couldn't stand the old bastard."

"You're in the clear majority."

They had a laugh at Lucien's expense as the waiter refilled their glasses. Jake asked, "And what, exactly, is my mission?"

"There is none. I want you and Harry Rex to make sure no one is waiting on me back there. I heard rumors of an indictment of some variety."

"Harry Rex and I have talked at length since I got your letter. He thinks the grand jury met and your case, if you can call it that, was kicked around, but nothing came of it. The FBI showed up a month later and poked around, talked to Harry Rex, but they went away. Not another word in over two years."

Mack frowned and put down his fork. "The FBI?"

"They went through the divorce file and looked at your records, such as they were. The fifty thousand in cash to Lisa raised some eyebrows. No one seemed to know where the money came from. According to the rumors, you took some money and fled town."

Jake paused and took a bite. This was the perfect moment for Mack to fill in the rather substantial gaps in the story, but he chose not to. Instead, he asked, "Harry Rex thinks the FBI is gone?"

"Yes, sure looks like it. I wouldn't say he's worried about anything, but the bankruptcy fraud might be a problem. Apparently, you got some money from somewhere and failed to report it with your other assets."

Mack seemed to have lost his appetite. "And the divorce?"

"It's been final for a long time, and he doubts Lisa has any interest in going back to war. Not in her present condition anyway. But, yes, if you hid assets from her, then that could be a problem. I'm doing all the talking here, Marco."

"And I'm listening real hard, Jake. I'm absorbing and digesting every word. Since I left, I've spent hours every day wondering what I left behind, trying to visualize every scenario in which somebody might be looking for me."

"Harry Rex is convinced there's no one."

"And you? What's your opinion?"

"I got paid to give opinions, Mack, and I'm not your lawyer. I'm not getting involved, but it would be helpful to know the facts. I'll relay them to Harry Rex, in the strictest confidence, of course."

Mack shoved his plate a few inches away and folded his hands on the table in front of him. He glanced around, casually, without a hint of suspicion. In a lower voice, he began, "I had four cases, four clients, all pulpwood cutters who were injured by the same model of chain saw. One guy lost an eye, one his left hand, one some fingers, the fourth guy just had a big scar on his forehead. At first I thought the safety guard was defective. The lawsuits looked promising but they eventually petered out. I tried to bluff the company into a settlement but got nowhere. I lost interest and the files collected dust. You know what it's like. Months and years passed. Then one glorious day I got the magic phone call from New York, big firm, Durban & Lang. Their client, a Swiss outfit, wanted a quick, confidential settlement to get the things off their books. A hundred thousand per case, with that much thrown in for litigation expenses. Half a mil, Jake, just like that. A dream come true. Since I never filed suit, there were no records anywhere except in my office and in New York. The temptation was right there, and it was beautiful. Our marriage was over, had been for a long time, and everything fell into place. It looked like the perfect time for the perfect crime. I could grab the money while getting the divorce and walk out of the law office for the last time. Leave behind a life that was unhappy, to put it mildly."

Jake had finished half his salad and pushed the rest of it away. The waiter appeared and cleared the table. Mack said, "I need a drink. You want a beer?"

"Sure."

"Have you had an Imperial, the national beer?"

"Oh yes. I'll take another."

Mack ordered two drafts and stared at the ocean far below them. Jake waited for the beers to arrive. He took a sip, wiped the foam off his upper lip, and asked, "What about the four clients?"

Mack snapped out of his daydream and addressed his beer. After a drink he said, "One was dead, one was missing. The two I found were more than happy to take twenty-five thousand in cash and not tell anyone. I signed the papers and I handed over the money."

"I'm sure their signatures had to be notarized."

"So I notarized them. Remember Freda, my old secretary?"

"Of course."

"Well, I had fired her, and I forged her name and seal on the documents. For the two clients I couldn't find, I forged their signatures as well. No one knew it. The lawyers in New York didn't care. They were just happy to get the paperwork and close the cases."

"You're not worried about the forgeries?"

"Jake, I've worried about everything. When you've done something wrong and you're on the run, you're always looking over your shoulder, wondering who's back there."

"I'm sure. The haul was around four hundred thousand."

"Yep."

"That's impressive."

"What's the biggest fee you've ever earned, Jake?"

"Well, I got a thousand bucks for Carl Lee Hailey."

"Your finest moment."

"Did you ever know a man named Seth Hubbard?"

"I knew of him. Big timber operator."

"That's him. He died and there was a massive will contest. I represented his estate, billed about a hundred grand over two years."

"In seventeen years on the treadmill my biggest fee was twenty thousand from a nice car wreck. Suddenly, I had twenty times that just lying there before me, like a pot of gold. I couldn't resist the temptation."

"Any regrets?"

"Plenty. Only cowards run away, Jake. It was wrong, all of it. I should've stayed in Clanton, worked through the divorce, and kept some level of presence in the lives of my daughters. And I left my mother, too. I haven't seen her in three years."

"So, what are your plans?"

"Well, I would like to see Lisa and apologize. Probably won't happen, but I'll try. I'd like to at least attempt to reconnect with Margot and Helen. They're seventeen and sixteen now, probably about to be orphaned. My plans include you and Harry Rex. I'm not asking you to get involved, just keep your ears and eyes open. If there's no indictment on the books and none pending, and if there are no warrants for my arrest, then I'll ease back into the country. I'm not going to stay in Clanton, that's an ugly thought. I'll probably hide in Memphis, across the state line. If there's a hint of trouble, I'll vanish again. I'm not going to prison, Jake, I can promise you that."

"You can't keep it quiet, Mack. If you show up anywhere in Ford County, everyone will know it overnight."

"True, but they won't see me. I'll come and go in the night. The two clients who got the twenty-five thousand in cash were Odell Grove and Jerrol Baker. Ask Harry Rex to check on them. Baker was stoned on meth when he signed the settlement agreement, so he could be dead, or in prison again. I don't expect any trouble out of them."

"And the other two?"

"Doug Jumper is in fact dead. Travis Johnson left the area years ago."

Jake finished his beer and sat back in his seat. "What's your schedule?"

"I don't have one. You and Harry Rex poke around for a few weeks. If all is clear, I'll show up eventually. I'll call your office one day."

"And if we get wind of trouble?"

"Send an overnight letter here to the lodge, addressed to Marco Larman."

"That's getting close to aiding and abetting."

"But not close enough. Look, Jake, don't do anything that you're not sure of. I promise you'll never be compromised."

"I believe you."

"How many people know about this little vacation of yours?"

"Harry Rex and my parents. They're keeping Hanna and Luke. We told no one else, said we were just getting out of town for a few days."

"Great. Stick with that story. I really appreciate this, Jake."

"Thanks for the trip. We'll never forget it."

"Anytime, and it's always on me."

(10)

After a day of being massaged and pampered, Carla was ready for the trails. They left the lodge early, on bikes and without a guide, and wound their way through the jungle on well-trodden paths. They stopped for photos at scenic overlooks, usually with the ocean shimmering on the horizon, and they sipped mango juice while sitting in the mouth of a cave. After two hours, they were winded and looking for a place to rest when they happened upon the Swedes. Olga and Luther were staying at the lodge but were rarely around, primarily because they were either hiking or biking up another mountain or off kayaking a raging river. They were at least thirty years older than Jake and Carla, lean and wiry and in superb physical condition. They ate only fruits and vegetables, drank no alcohol, and had slept two nights in a hut at the top of a very tall tree that one had to shinny up with backpacks filled with bedding, food, and water. They claimed to be world-class eco-tourists and had been everywhere. Jake and Carla were quietly envious of people who had seen the world, not to mention the fact that, at the age of seventy, they were fit enough to live thirty more years.

After they sped away, Jake said, "I need a beer. Those people make me want to drink." He was sprawled across a thatched picnic table at the edge of a stream.

"Sip your mango juice. Did we finish the conversation about Mack and his plans?"

"I think so. His plans are vague. He misses home and wants to see his mother and his girls."

"Yes, we covered that."

"You think Lisa will allow it?"

"I can't predict. If she were healthy, she might be tougher to deal with. I can't imagine what he wants to say to Margot and Helen."

"Hey girls, I'm back? Miss me?"

"That might be a tough meeting. Let's go cowboy. How's your crotch?"

"The saddle on this bike is more uncomfortable than the one on the horse."

"Oh, man up."

They reached a peak, or some point up in the clouds where Jake finally quit, and they turned around and coasted down the trails, arriving at the lodge in time for a late lunch. It was followed by a long afternoon, their last, by the pool, with Ricardo keeping their drinks fresh.

Their last dinner was just like the others outdoors on the veranda, with the pool nearby, a magnificent sunset, and the other guests in fine form.

Their week in paradise was over, and they fell asleep to the sounds of wicker ceiling fans and macaws squawking in the distance.

Ricardo woke them at six, the appointed time, and brought them food for the trip. He loaded their luggage onto his cart and they hustled down to the front reception where a van was waiting.

Jake said, "I'll go check out."

Ricardo said, "No, Mr. Jake, it's taken care of."

"But the food and drinks."

"Everything is covered, Mr. Jake."

Which was exactly what Jake was expecting, though he felt obliged to make an effort anyway. He tipped Ricardo generously, and they headed for San José.

(11)

Two months passed without a word. Harry Rex located Odell Grove, and, not surprisingly, found that little had changed in his world. He and his two sons ran a logging business in the western edge of Ford County and stayed to themselves. He owned five acres of scrub forest and lived in a trailer with his wife. His sons had their own trailers just down the road. Jerrol Baker was serving a ten-year sentence for cooking meth. Under the ruse of seeking information in an embezzlement case, Harry Rex contacted the FBI and was told that the agent he'd met after Mack vanished had been transferred to Pittsburgh. He cajoled another agent into checking around the office, and was eventually informed that there was no open file on anybody named J. McKinley Stafford, of Clanton.

Jake had lunch with Sheriff Ozzie Walls, at Claude's, and managed to work Mack Stafford into the conversation. Ozzie said nobody had heard a word and his office had no open file. For some reason, he believed the rumors about Mack stealing a pile of money were not true.

Carla taught third grade at the elementary school, and her

principal was friendly with Lisa Stafford. For the past ten years, Lisa had worked as an assistant principal at the high school. She was now on leave, for health reasons, and her condition was not improving. On the last day of classes in late May, her colleagues threw a small party in her honor in the faculty lounge. She was described as gaunt and pale, and she wore a pretty scarf over her bald head. They did not expect to see her back in the fall.

As the weeks passed, Jake and Harry Rex talked less and less about Mack. They did not correspond with him because there was nothing to report. And they agreed in private that it would be best if he stayed away. His presence back in Mississippi would only complicate their lives, not to mention his. They were convinced no one was looking for Mack, but a return might possibly set in motion events that neither he nor they could control.

The complications began around noon on a Thursday with a phone call to Jake's office. Alicia took it and buzzed Jake upstairs. "It's a Mr. Marco Larman, says you're expecting a call. Never heard of him."

"I'll take it."

Jake swallowed hard and stared at the blinking button on his phone. Then he smiled and said to himself, "What the hell. This might be fun." He punched the button and said, "Jake Brigance."

"Mr. Brigance, I'm Marco Larman," Mack began stiffly, as if someone else might be listening.

"Hello, Marco. What can I do for you?"

"Could you and Mr. Vonner meet me for a drink tomorrow afternoon in Oxford?"

That would be Friday afternoon, and Jake didn't bother to look at his schedule because he knew there was nothing on it. Friday afternoons in warm weather meant the legal business in Clanton would be shut down. Harry Rex would not be in court because there would not be a judge within fifty miles of the courthouse. And, if he had appointments, he would cancel them for the adventure.

"Sure. When and where?"

"Around five p.m. The bar at the Ramada Inn."

"Okay. So you're stateside?"

"Let's talk tomorrow." The line went dead.

(12)

Jake insisted on driving for two reasons. The first was that Harry Rex behind the wheel was as dangerous as Harry Rex in the courtroom. He drove either too fast or too slow, ignored the basic rules of the road, and exploded with rage at the slightest infraction by another driver. The second was that it was Friday afternoon and he was already hitting the Bud Light. Jake declined a beverage and happily drove.

Just past the Clanton city limits, he said, "To be honest, this is kinda fun. Not your everyday client meeting."

Harry Rex chewed on an unlit black cigar in the corner of his mouth. "I think the boy's stupid. He made a clean break, nobody in the world knows where he was, and now he wants to come back to nothin' but trouble. What kinda work's he gonna do? Open up a law office?"

"I don't think he plans to live here. He mentioned Memphis, someplace out of state."

"Brilliant. As if the state line'll stop trouble."

"He's not expecting trouble."

"I get that, but the truth is he doesn't know what to expect. I know things are quiet but her family could cause a ruckus."

"They're good folks. They're more concerned with Lisa's health than any bad memories of Mack Stafford."

"That might be easy to assume, but no one can predict what'll happen."

"What can they do to Mack?"

"I doubt they have any love for the guy, right? They're starin' at the reality of raisin' two teenage girls, something they weren't plannin' on in their golden years. All because their shifty ex-son-in-law took the money and ran away. I'd be pissed all right, wouldn't you?"

"I suppose."

"Stop up there at Skidmore's. I need a cold one."

"You already have one."

"It's not cold."

"How many have you had today?"

"You sound like my wife."

"Just stop, ass."

They bickered for an hour until Oxford came into view. On the west side of town, Jake pulled in to the parking lot of the Ramada Inn at five minutes before five. He knew the bar from his college days but had not seen it in years. The students were gone and it was empty. They got beers and found a table in a corner. Fifteen minutes passed and there was no sign of Mack.

"Must be livin' on island time," Harry Rex mumbled, as if he were a real stickler for punctuality. He lit another cigar and blew smoke at the ceiling. Mack finally appeared, from nowhere, and shook hands with his old buddies. He wanted to sit where he could see the door. Harry Rex rolled his eyes at Jake but said nothing. They huddled over their beers and swapped insults about weight gains and losses, different hairstyles, beards, attire. Harry Rex was impressed with Mack's altered looks—the deep tan, the beard, the longer hair, the funky eyeglasses, which were different from the ones Jake had seen two months earlier. Mack was not surprised at Harry Rex's appearance. Little had changed and nothing had improved. They enjoyed a few laughs and worked on their beers.

Jake got serious with "How'd you enter the country?"

"Legally, with a passport."

Harry Rex said, "Jake tells me you're Brazilian now."

"That's right. Brazilian, and also Panamanian, though my Spanish is not that good. And I still have my American passport, which I assume works. Didn't want to risk it though."

"So you can buy citizenship?" Jake asked with no small measure of disbelief. He had never thought about it. "Is it that easy?"

"Depends on the country, and the cash. It's not that difficult."

They mulled this over for a moment. There were so many questions, so much ground to cover, but only Mack knew where they were going.

Harry Rex asked, "How safe do you feel right now, back in Mississippi?"

"I entered our dear state two days ago, drove to Greenwood to see my mom. Then I left." And went where? He let them hang for a few seconds. They wanted to know where he was staying, or living, but evidently he wasn't saying yet.

"So you feel safe?"

"I'm not worried. Should I be? I mean, there's no active investigation. No one is looking for me, right?"

Harry Rex blew some smoke and said, "Well, we ain't makin' no guarantees, you understand? But it appears as if the bloodhounds are still locked up."

Jake added, "Nothing has changed in the two months since I saw you in the jungle, but nothing is for certain."

"I get it. I know there's some risk involved."

Harry Rex asked, "What, exactly, do you want, Mack?"

"I need to see my girls. I doubt Lisa will have anything to do with me, and that's okay. The feelings are mutual. But she's very close to the girls, and if she dies they'll be in for a rough time. I should never have left them."

"You want custody?" Jake asked with raised eyebrows.

"Not as long as she's alive. Who knows, maybe there'll be a miracle and she'll survive. But, if she doesn't, then what? I'm not sure the girls want to live with their grandparents. God help them."

"What makes you think they want to live with you?" Harry Rex asked.

Jake chuckled and asked, "Or for that matter, what makes you think you want to raise two teenage girls?"

"Let's take it one step at a time, fellas. First, I'll try to meet with Lisa, just to say hello. Then, I'll try to meet with the girls, sort of reintroduce myself. Sure, it'll be painful and awkward and probably just dreadful, but we have to start somewhere. There's a financial angle here that needs to be addressed. College is just around the corner."

They took a break as Harry Rex relit his cigar and blasted another cloud toward the ceiling. Jake sipped his beer, uncertain where the conversation was going. Finally, Mack said, "Jake, I'd like for you to contact the family and tell them that I'm back and would like to see Lisa."

"Why me?"

"Because it's either you or Harry Rex and you have a better understanding of how to handle delicate matters."

Harry Rex nodded his agreement. He had no desire to deal with Lisa and her family.

Jake said, "Go on."

"The best way to do it is to call Dr. Pettigrew, Lisa's brother-in-law. Dean's not my favorite person, never was, a lot of in-law baggage, but maybe that's all water under the bridge now."

"You hope," Harry Rex grunted.

"Yes, I hope. Dean is fairly levelheaded, not a bad guy, really, and I'd like for you to call him to break the news that I'm back in the area and would like to see Lisa."

Harry Rex frowned and asked, "What comes after 'hello'? I'd hate to be in that room."

"Well, you won't be so butt out. Let me worry about it."

Harry Rex gulped his beer and wiped a thick mustache of foam from his upper lip.

Mack continued, "You're not my lawyer, Jake, just a friend, and the Bunning clan will not despise you the way they loathe me and despise Harry Rex."

Harry Rex shrugged it off. He could not care less. It went with the territory.

Jake asked, "And where might this meeting with Lisa take place?"

"I don't know. Her doctors may have some restrictions about where she goes and who she sees. Dean will know all that stuff. Just make the first call and hopefully it will lead to the second and third. Nothing about this will be easy, fellas."

"Got that right."

Jake said, "The family will have some questions. Like, how long are you staying? Is it permanent? Where are you living? Why'd you leave? How much money did you take? Things like that. You can't just drop in from the moon and say, 'Here I am.'"

Mack nodded and took a sip. He watched the door, a habit now, but there was no traffic. "I'm living out of a suitcase, hotels and such. No fixed address for the near future. I will not be staying in Ford County so they can relax, and I will not make an effort to see Lisa and the girls without the family's permission. Promise them that, Jake."

"Whatever you say."

"Word'll leak like crazy and the gossip'll go nuts, you know that, don't you?" Harry Rex said.

"Yes. I know Clanton. There's a ton of gossip when absolutely nothing is happening. I'm sure the place was buzzing when I flew the coop."

Jake and Harry Rex smiled at the memories. Then Jake laughed and said, "We were in chancery court one morning with Judge Atlee, docket call day, a bunch of lawyers going through the usual dog and pony show. Old Stanley Renfrow from down in Smithfield stood up and said, 'Judge, I got this divorce case with Mr. Stafford on the other side but he won't return my phone calls. Rumor is he left town. Anybody seen him?' Several of us looked at each other and smiled. Judge Atlee said, 'Well, Mr. Renfrow, I don't think his telephones work anymore. Seems like Mr. Stafford turned off the lights and walked away. He hasn't been seen in several weeks.'

" 'What about my divorce case?'

" 'I think Mr. Vonner has his old files.'

" 'Okay. Say, Judge, how do you just walk out of your law office?'

" 'I don't know. Never seen it before.'

" 'Well, I wish to hell someone had told me how to do it thirty years ago.'

"We had a big laugh, then we whispered about where you might be. No one had a clue."

"Stuttering Stanley Renfrow," Mack said. "I knew him well and can honestly say I haven't missed him one bit."

"Who have you missed?" Jake asked.

"The two of you. That's it."

Harry Rex said, "Hell, Mack, it took ten lawyers just to pick up the slack after you left."

"Nice try, big guy, but I know better. I may have been missed by a few friends and some family, but I can promise you my clients didn't care."

Jake laughed and said, "The rumors went on and on. They

died down, then there would be a sighting and the whole town would fire up again."

"A sighting?" Mack asked. "Never happened. At least not to my knowledge. I spent the first year in Belize and I'm almost positive I was never sighted. Had a close call one time, but nobody from around here."

"Where'd you go after that?" Harry Rex asked.

Mack smiled and sipped his beer and studied the dark room. After a long pause he said, "A lot of places. I'll tell you guys all about it sometime, but not now."

(13)

Dr. Dean Pettigrew was one of three orthopedic surgeons in Clanton. Twenty years earlier he had married Stephanie Bunning, a pretty coed he met at Ole Miss. She was from a prominent family in town and wanted to live there. He was from Tupelo, an hour away, and that was close enough to his family. He worked hard and prospered, and he and Stephanie and their two sons lived among the upper crust in a fine modern home on the fourteenth fairway of the country club. Virtually all the doctors lived close by, behind gates.

After playing eighteen holes on Saturday morning, Dean returned home in his golf cart and was told by Stephanie that Jake Brigance had called. To their recollection, Jake had never called the house. They knew Jake and Carla but didn't socialize with them. Being a doctor, his first thought was that Jake, a lawyer, wanted to discuss a potential claim for medical malpractice. It was a knee-jerk reaction and he dismissed it quickly. Jake was well liked and didn't sue doctors, or local ones anyway. But with lawyers one could never be certain.

Dean settled into his leather chair in the den and picked up the phone. After a quick round of awkward chitchat, Jake said, "So look, Dean, I'll get right to the point. I met with Mack Stafford yesterday. He's back in the area."

Dean almost dropped the phone and for a second or two could not respond. He finally said, "Okay. We were hoping he was gone for good."

"Yes, it surprised me too. I'm not his lawyer, you understand, just a friend. I wouldn't be making this call if he hadn't asked me to."

"Obviously. What's up?"

"Well, Mack would like to meet with Lisa."

"You gotta be kidding."

"I'm serious. Again, I'm only the messenger."

Stephanie was listening. She eased into the den and sat near her husband, who frowned at her and shook his head. Dean said, "I can't imagine Lisa wanting to ever see him again, Jake."

"I understand."

"Does he know she's sick?"

"Yes. Don't ask me how."

"Where's he been?"

"South of here. That's all I know."

"I don't know what to say." Stephanie was shaking her head in disbelief.

After a long gap, Jake asked, "Is it okay if I ask how she's doing?"

Dean exhaled and said, "Not good, Jake. The last round of chemo didn't work. There's not much else to do. This will not help in any way."

"I'm sure it won't. Look, Dean, I've made the call. The rest is up to Lisa."

"And what might Mack want to talk about?"

"I don't know. He wants to meet with Lisa and then maybe with the girls."

"This is nothing but trouble, Jake."

"I know."

"I can't imagine Lisa wanting to see him and I'm sure she'll keep the girls away."

"I can't blame her for that."

Another pause, then Dean said, "She and the girls are coming over for dinner. I'll have to tell the family about this."

"Sure. I'm sorry to be involved, Dean."

"Thanks, Jake."

Later in the afternoon, Lisa arrived with the two girls, Margot and Helen. She was weak and fragile and had stopped driving. Margot, at seventeen, was more than happy to be the chauffeur. She and Helen quickly changed into bikinis and jumped in the pool. Their two cousins, the Pettigrew boys, were in Oxford at an Ole Miss baseball game.

Lisa preferred to sit on the veranda, in the cool shade, with a heavy ceiling fan rotating slowly above her. Stephanie served lemonade and sat beside her sister. Dean took a seat and they watched the girls bounce off the diving board. Though Margot was only a year older than Helen, the difference was striking. Margot was mature and fully developed and could pass for a young lady of twenty. Her bikini was mostly strings, rather skimpy in Dean's judgment, and it would not be liked by her grandparents, who were due in an hour or so. Dean knew that Margot could not care less what they thought and had spent the last year finding ways to disappoint them. Helen was the quieter of the two, even timid at times, and still had the skinny body of a twelve-year-old. They, along with their mother, had been humiliated by Mack's grand adventure, his sudden disappearance, his abandonment. The whole family had been humiliated.

Over the past year, as one treatment after another failed to stop a very aggressive cancer, the family had whispered about what to do with the girls. There were only two options, neither attractive. They would live with their grandparents, or they would move into the Pettigrews' spacious home. No one really wanted them, especially Margot. Regardless, though, they would land in a warm place, surrounded by loving relatives.

Was there now a third option? Did Mack come back to rescue the girls after their mother died? Dean had serious doubts about this. Mack had abandoned them, and it seemed inconceivable that he would settle down in Clanton and try to be a father.

Dean said, "Let's get this out of the way before your parents get here. Lisa, I got a phone call from Jake Brigance earlier this afternoon. He's in contact with Mack, who's now back in the area."

As frail as she was, Lisa managed a quick and nasty "That son of a bitch."

"Or worse. He wants to meet with you and he wants to see the girls."

Stunned, her mouth fell open and her sad eyes doubled in size. "He what?"

"You heard me."

"When did he get back?"

"I don't know and I don't think he's in town, but he's around. Details are sketchy."

"Can't they arrest him?"

"We didn't talk about that, didn't get that far."

She sat her lemonade on a side table, closed her eyes, and breathed deeply. She was a pitiful sight, and Dean and Stephanie ached for her. She knew she was dying, and now this. The past ten years had been hell. The crumbling marriage to a man who had worked hard but never earned much. His bouts with the bottle. His scandalous disappearance. The endless rumors of him absconding with a pile of money that belonged to his clients. The months and years of no contact. The realization that the scoundrel was really gone and not coming back. She blamed him for her failing health. The stress of the humiliation and the pressure to raise two teenagers as a single mother had taken an ugly toll. She was so tired of crying and tried to control her emotions, but a tear leaked out and she wiped her face. She sniffled, bit her lip, and allowed no more tears.

She opened her eyes and smiled at her sister. She looked at Dean and said, "I take it you're supposed to call Jake back with an answer."

"Yes."

"Well, the answer is no. We have nothing to talk about. The divorce was practically over when he skipped town. Mercifully, it's been final since then. I do not want to see his face or hear his voice. He has nothing to say and we have nothing to discuss. And if he contacts the girls or tries in any way to see them, I'll call the police and take him to court if necessary."

Dean smiled and said, "Clear enough."

(14)

Early Monday morning, at precisely 5:00 a.m., the appointed hour, Jake rolled out of bed, eased from the bedroom, went to the kitchen, and punched BREW on the coffee pot. He went to a spare bedroom downstairs where he showered and dressed. He fetched the Memphis, Tupelo, and Jackson newspapers from the end of his driveway and sat down at the breakfast table with his first cup and the morning's news. At 5:45, he returned to his bedroom, popped Carla on the rump, kissed her on the cheek, told her he loved her, and left. She buried deeper under the covers, convinced, as always, that he was crazy to be up so early. He peeked in on Hanna and Luke, then left the house. He drove seven minutes to the Clanton square, parked in front of his office, and at 6:00 a.m. entered the Coffee Shop where Dell was laughing with a table of farmers and insulting a table of factory workers. No one else was wearing a coat and tie. He found his usual chair at a table where Andy Furr, a mechanic at the Chevrolet place, was waiting. Dell patted his head, bumped him with her ample rear end, and poured coffee. Marshall Prather, a deputy, said, "Say, Jake, you heard that Mack Stafford is back in town?"

The lightning speed of the town's gossip never ceased to amaze him. He decided to play along and see what "they were telling."

"You're kidding, right?"

"No, don't think so. Rumor is he's been seen and wants to hook up with his ex-wife."

A farmer asked, "Weren't you his lawyer, Jake?"

"No sir. Last I heard, Harry Rex handled his affairs. Who saw him?"

Prather said, "Don't know. Heard it made the rounds at the Baptist church yesterday."

"Well, then, it's gotta be true."

"Ain't he wanted by the law?" Andy Furr asked.

"I have no idea."

"Marshall, you know anything about that?"

"I don't, but I'll find out."

"Didn't he take a bunch of money and run?"

Jake said, "That was always the rumor."

From the counter, Dell said, "We don't do rumors around here. All of our gossip is the real stuff."

That got a few laughs. The Coffee Shop was a notorious place for starting rumors, often to see how fast they could race around the square before returning in a greatly altered version. Jake was amused by the fact that no one had actually seen Mack. Evidently, the Bunning clan had spread the word at the First Baptist Church, where they were lifelong stalwarts, that Mack had made contact. This had no doubt electrified the congregation and sent hot rumors like bolts of lightning throughout the Sunday school and worship hour. Jake could only imagine the hundreds of phone calls that were made after church. As the irresistible story gained momentum, someone, a person who would never be identified, added the spicy twist that Mack had actually been seen.

There was no doubt that by noon Monday, after the town had absorbed and embellished the story, someone would have actually chatted with Mack.

One farmer had been sued by Mack years earlier and he still carried a grudge. That took the conversation to the subject of lawsuits, and frivolous ones at that, and the need for more tort reform. Jake ate his breakfast and said nothing.

Before long they were back on the weather and Mack was forgotten, for the moment anyway.

(15)

Promptly at 10:00 a.m., Herman Bunning walked into the law offices of Sullivan & Sullivan and announced to the receptionist that he had an appointment. He was offered a seat but politely said no. He was not planning to wait. He called his lawyer the night before and they had agreed on the hour. If he could be on time, then so could the lawyer. He stepped to the large window and looked at the courthouse. He tried to remember the last time he had sought legal advice from Walter Sullivan. At $200 an hour, he was hoping for a brief visit.

His company, Clanton Redi-Mix, had been in the family for over fifty years. Since the demand for concrete was not that great in such a small town, his company had few serious legal problems. He had never sued anyone, nor had he been sued, other than the occasional accident involving one of his trucks. Walter drafted tight contracts and kept his thumb on the legal matters. Most of the successful businessmen in town relied on Walter, along with the bankers, insurance companies, railroads, big farmers, folks with some money.

That was why Jake and the other lawyers in town loathed the Sullivan firm. It had clients who could pay.

A secretary fetched him and he followed her back to the big office. He said yes to coffee, with one sugar, and sat facing Walter with a massive desk between them.

Walter said, "I can't find anything. Ozzie says there's no outstanding warrant. The grand jury met a couple of times back then but there was no real proof." He lifted a pile of papers and continued, "I have copies of the divorce filings and decree, along with his bankruptcy petition. Not much there."

"Tell me about it," Herman grunted. "The boy never made any money. They lived hand-to-mouth, can't count the number of times I had to bail 'em out."

"How is Lisa?"

"Same as last night when you asked about her."

Walter nodded and remembered Herman's penchant for bluntness.

"I'm sorry."

"Thanks. Look, Walter, isn't it pretty well known among you lawyers that Mack got his hands on some money that wasn't his and then left town? I mean, doesn't that make sense? How could he run away if he didn't have any money? And why would he? Lisa got the house and cars and bank accounts and such, everything was hocked to the max anyway, but he also kicked in fifty grand in cash. The boy never had that kind of money. So you gotta figure that if he suddenly had cash to give her, then he probably had a lot more that he was hiding. You follow?"

"Yes, of course."

"And if he looted his trust accounts or whatever to get the money, he certainly didn't include it with his assets when he filed for divorce."

"Nor bankruptcy. That's the more serious charge. Bankruptcy fraud."

"Great. So how do you prove it?" The secretary eased in and handed both men cups of coffee. She left and closed the door. Herman took a swig and smacked his lips.

"So, let me get this straight, Herman. You want to go after Mack."

"Damned right I do, pardon my language. He abandoned my daughter and granddaughters and ran off with some money. He was a lousy husband, Walter, I've told you about him. Drank too much. Never made a dime. Wasn't lazy but just couldn't figure out the law."

"I knew Mack well, Herman, and I liked him."

"I liked him at first, but you could see the marriage unravel. He's one of those Delta boys, Walter, you know how they are. They're just different."

"I know, I know."

"Anyway, how can we prove he committed fraud?"

"Why bother with it, Herman?"

That irritated the client and he seethed for a moment. He sipped his coffee and let it pass. Then he smiled and said, "Because he's a crook, Walter, and a bad person. Because my daughter probably won't make it to the end of the year, probably the summer, and she'll leave behind two teenage girls that Honey and I will have to raise. And we're up to it, we're ready, but we certainly weren't planning on it. They'll be expensive, and a handful, and, well, we were already thinking about retirement. That can wait. If Mack has some money, then he owes it to Lisa and the girls."

"How much are you willing to spend to find out?"

"How much will it cost?"

"I'll have to pay a private investigator to start digging. I'm not sure about the legal work but there will be some hours involved."

"How much, from soup to nuts?"

"Ten thousand."

Herman grimaced as if stricken by irritable bowels, shifted his weight, gritted his teeth, and said, "I was thinking more like five thousand?"

Walter didn't mind negotiating because he was also thinking about more potential clients. If Mack had shafted others, then they too might have claims. If Walter found the pot of gold, he might well be in charge of it. He scribbled some notes as he frowned and couldn't get the math to work. "Look, Herman, this is not really my cup of tea, you know? I can get this done but it's a pain, right? Let's agree on seventy-five hundred."

"That's still too much but I don't want to bicker."

"Okay, then, write me the check."

"I'll mail it tomorrow." Herman glanced at his watch. So far the meeting had lasted less than fifteen minutes. That was $50, right? He would pounce on Walter's monthly bill when it arrived, to verify the time and the cost.

He thanked him for the coffee and hustled out of the office.

Across the square, Jake was loafing at his desk when the call came. A familiar voice said, "Good morning, Jake, it's Walter Sullivan."

At that moment, there was not a single file in Jake's office that could remotely interest anyone at the Sullivan firm. He was somewhat suspicious, but then calls from nowhere were not unusual. "Good morning, Walter. To what do I owe the honor?"

"We've represented Herman Bunning and his company forever."

Of course you have, Walter. You get all the corporate work in town.

"And he just left the office. As you might guess, the family is pretty rattled right now. What can you tell me about Mack?"

"I'm not his lawyer, Walter. You need to chat with Harry Rex."

"And what might he tell me?"

"Nothing."

"That's what I figured. No idea where Mack is."

"None. Why do you care where Mack is, Walter?"

"I don't. I'm just passing along the warning that he should stay away from Lisa and the girls."

"Well, great. I got that warning from Dr. Pettigrew, loud and clear. I passed it along to Mack. He heard it. I seriously doubt there's anything to worry about, Walter. Mack has no plans to stir up trouble."

"That's hard to believe."

"The message has been delivered, Walter. Relax."

"See you around."

After the call, Jake thought about it for a long time. The notion that Mack Stafford would somehow deliberately harm his daughters was ludicrous. It was a bully call, typical Sullivan. They had the money and power and didn't mind using it.

He remembered when, not too long ago, Harry Rex threw one of his pig roasts at his hunting cabin in the woods south of town. He invited every lawyer and judge, even the ones he despised, and he invited Ozzie and his deputies and the local police from Clanton. Most of the courthouse gang was there, along with an assortment of investigators, runners, process servers, and even tow truck operators. There were kegs of cold beer and plenty of barbecue. A bluegrass band played on the porch. Harry Rex's timing was perfect—there was nothing else happening in the county that day—and the crowd was huge. He wanted a full-blown redneck party and that's what he got. Jake and Carla bumped into Mack and Lisa and tried to have a friendly chat. It was obvious that she was uncomfortable mixing with a lower-class crowd. The country club was far away. Later, Jake saw her sitting alone on the rear porch, sipping a diet soda and looking thoroughly out of place. He later heard the rumor that she left without telling Mack. He hitched a ride home with a friend.

It was common knowledge around town that the marriage was unhappy, primarily because Lisa had dreams bigger than anything Mack could deliver. As Stephanie and Dr. Pettigrew prospered and traded one home for one even larger, they left the Staffords behind in the dust.

His daydreaming was interrupted by the next unexpected phone call. It was Dumas Lee, the nosy and persistent chief reporter for *The Ford County Times*.

"What a surprise, Dumas," Jake said.

"I hear Mack is back," Dumas sang, as if on to something big. "What can you tell me?"

"Mack who?"

"Right. Look, a source tells me you've met with Mack, seen him live and in person."

Dumas always claimed to have a source, whether one existed or not. "No comment."

"Come on, Jake, you can do better than that."

"No comment."

"Okay, I'm going to ask you a simple question, one that requires a yes or no answer, and if you say 'no comment,' then it will be obvious that the answer is yes. Have you seen Mack Stafford in person in the past month?"

"No comment."

"In other words, you have."

"Whatever, Dumas. I'm not playing your game. What's the big deal anyway? Mack is free to come and go. He's not a wanted man."

"Not a wanted man. I like that. Can I use it?"

"Sure."

"Thanks, Jake."

"Anytime."

(16)

Mack's fateful decision to take the money and run, to file for divorce, then for bankruptcy, to close his office, sign everything over to Lisa, say goodbye to her and the girls, and disappear, had been precipitated by a single phone call. A New York lawyer named Marty Rosenberg called during lunch one day and was willing to offer quick cash to settle some dusty old cases Mack had almost forgotten about. Mack answered the phone because Freda, his secretary, was not in. Had she been there, and had she known of the settlement talk, Mack's life would not have taken such a dramatic twist. For five years Freda had handled the phones, typing, clients, books, everything that a secretary does in a small-town office.

Mack fired her that day and she left in a huff. He'd had a few beers and returned to the office nicely buzzed. She snapped at him because he had missed two appointments that afternoon. He didn't care. They argued, said too much, and he fired her on the spot, gave her thirty minutes to clean out her desk and disappear. After dark, he left the office and went to a bar. When he finally went home, Lisa was waiting on the front porch in full combat mode. He slipped on some ice in the driveway, busted his head, and spent two days in the hospital. While he was laid up, Freda returned to the office and went through the books and files. She expected to find little and she was not disappointed. She knew his business better than he did. Mack, like most lawyers in town, often hustled clients in city and county courts for cash, fees that were conveniently kept off the books. One reason for going through his files was to make sure there were no unofficial records of fees paid in cash. That, plus she wanted to know if he had a bank account or two that perhaps Lisa knew nothing about, but there were no records of hidden money. Freda had always kept a ledger of his current files and she made a copy for herself. It was not an impressive lineup of pending cases. When Mack fled, she heard rumors that he had bilked some clients and embezzled funds. At the time, he was representing three guardianships, with a grand total of $22,000 in his trust account. His real estate escrow account had a balance of $350. These monies were untouched when Mack disappeared.

The only possible sources of any substantial fees were four old product liability cases Mack had signed up and then neglected for years. The chain saw cases, once a potential bonanza, at least in his opinion. She had almost forgotten about them, though she did remember typing his blustery letters to the manufacturer a long time ago. When he lost his enthusiasm, the cases got shoved to the bottom of the pile.

While he was in the hospital, Freda obtained his phone records and saw the mysterious calls to and from a law firm in New York City. She made notes and filed them away. About a month after Mack left, two FBI agents paid her a visit and asked some random questions, but it was obvious they were going through the motions. Though she was still angry over the firing, she had no loyalty at all to the FBI and gave them nothing.

She left Clanton and eventually settled in Tupelo where she worked as a real estate paralegal in a prosperous law firm. She was at her desk Tuesday afternoon when a private investigator appeared. Tight sports coat, thickly knotted tie, pointed-toe boots, gun on hip. His line of work was obvious. She had seen a hundred of them in her career as a legal secretary and could spot one on the other side of the street.

He introduced himself as Buddy Hockner and handed her a business card. He said he was doing some investigative work for a lawyer over in Clanton.

"Which one?" she asked. In the recent past she had known all of them.

"Walter Sullivan."

So this was not a messy divorce or a garden-variety car wreck. If the Sullivan firm was involved, the stakes were probably higher. She could not think of any reason Walter Sullivan needed something from her.

"I remember him," she said. "What can I do for you?"

Without asking, Buddy plopped down in the only chair on the other side of her desk.

"Have a seat," she said.

"Have you had any contact with your old boss, Mack Stafford, recently?"

"Why would I tell you if I did?"

"I come in peace."

"That's what they all say."

"Mack is back. Any word from him?"

This amused her and she offered a smile, the first. "No, I've heard nothing from Mack since the day he fired me. Almost three years ago. Look, I'm pretty busy and I'd rather not discuss this on the job."

"Got it. Can I buy you a drink after work?"

"One drink. I'm not much of a talker."

They met two hours later in a downtown bar. They found a dark corner and ordered drinks. Buddy laid everything on the table and promised her he had nothing to hide. From time to time he worked for Mr. Sullivan, who, on behalf of Lisa's family, had been hired to poke through Mack's dirty laundry. They strongly suspected some money had been taken and kept away from the divorce and bankruptcy proceedings.

Freda was saddened to hear about Lisa's health. The two had never been close but they had managed to get along, no small feat in Mack's world.

She said, "Mack never had any money. There was nothing to steal."

Buddy reached into a pocket, pulled out a sheet of paper, and handed it to her. It was a copy of a certified check for $50,000, drawn on a bank in Memphis, and made payable to Lisa. He said, "This was part of the divorce settlement, about the only thing of value she got."

Freda shook her head and said, "Mack never had this kind of money. He kept about five thousand dollars in the law firm checking account, but even that ran low at times. He paid me thirty thousand a year, I never got a raise, and there were a couple of years when I made almost as much as he did."

"Did he have an account with a Memphis bank?"

"Not to my knowledge. He banked in Clanton, though he hated to. Hated the fact that somebody at the bank knew how broke he really was."

"So, where did the money come from?"

Freda had always resented the way Mack had simply vanished, the way he abandoned his wife and two daughters. After he disappeared, she, too, had been implicated by the local gossip. There were rumors that she was involved in his shenanigans and so on. That was one reason she left town. She owed him nothing. Hell, he'd fired her on the spot and watched as she cleaned out her desk.

She took a sip of her vodka soda and said, "I got his phone records, don't ask me how. The day he fired me, he took a call from a New York law firm, came at twelve-ten when I was at lunch, and then he evidently left the office and had a few beers. When he returned around five p.m. we had our fight. He'd missed two appointments, something he never did because he needed the clients. I never saw him again, don't want to see him now."

She reached into her purse and pulled out her own sheet of paper. "This is a copy of his client ledger, all of his open cases. I've highlighted four of them, the chain saw cases. At the top you see the name of Marty Rosenberg, with his phone number. He's the lawyer in New York, the one I assume who called when I wasn't there. Whatever they talked about I don't know, but it was enough to push Mack over the edge. I'm not sure, but I'm guessing Mr. Rosenberg knows the rest of the story."

(17)

It was a slow news week in Clanton. When *The Ford County Times* hit the streets before dawn on Wednesday, there was a front-page story beneath the fold with the headline "Is Mack Stafford Back in Town?" With Dumas Lee reporting, the story said that several "unnamed sources" had confirmed that ex-lawyer Mack Stafford had reappeared. No one had actually seen him, or at least no one who would go on the record. The bulk of the story was Mack's past: his seventeen years in private practice, his divorce and bankruptcy, and his mysterious disappearance. Sheriff Walls was quoted as saying, "I am not aware of any ongoing investigation." When asked if it was true that a grand jury had investigated the bizarre case, Ozzie had no comment. There were two black-and-white photos, one of Mack in a coat and tie, taken from the bar directory. The other was of Jake Brigance, in a dark suit leaving the courthouse. Under Jake's photo was the bold quote: "He is not a wanted man."

Jake read it with his morning coffee and cursed himself for even speaking to Dumas. It was stupid to give the guy anything remotely quotable. The implication was clear: that Jake was involved and was probably Mack's lawyer.

He did not look forward to the Coffee Shop. Skipping it, though, was not an option. As he had learned, skipping out only made the gossip worse.

(18)

Later Wednesday morning, Walter Sullivan called the New York office of Durban & Lang, a mega-firm with thousands of lawyers scattered around the world. He asked for Mr. Marty Rosenberg, and was informed by one of his secretaries that the great man was unavailable, which was exactly what Walter expected. He said that he would fax over a letter that explained his reason for calling and would appreciate a few minutes on the phone. After he hung up, he sent the letter. It read:

> *Dear Mr. Rosenberg:*
> *I am an attorney in Clanton, Mississippi, and I'm seeking information regarding a possible product liability settlement roughly three years ago. I believe your firm represents a Swiss company, Littleman AG, and that this company has a division known as Tinzo Group, out of the Philippines. Tinzo manufactured, among many other products, chain saws that were alleged to be defective. Several plaintiffs down here hired a local lawyer, J. McKinley Stafford, or simply Mack, as we know him, to pursue their claims for injuries. Mack*

closed his practice and left town not long after you spoke to him.

I need a few moments of your time. Please call at your convenience. Your secretary has my number.
Sincerely,
Walter Sullivan

Wednesday passed with no word from New York. At nine the following morning, Walter's secretary buzzed his desk with the call. Marty began with a friendly "Good morning, Mr. Sullivan, how are things down south?"

"Couldn't be better, Mr. Rosenberg. Thanks for the call."

"You betcha. I married a girl from Atlanta and we get down there occasionally."

"Great city," Walter replied. In many ways, Atlanta was closer to New York than to Clanton.

"Anyway, I got your letter and one of my paralegals found the file." Walter could visualize the great lawyer with teams of paralegals lined up outside his door. "What can I do for you?" Marty asked.

"Well, it looks like our pal Mr. Stafford negotiated a settlement of some sort, then skipped town. Is it possible for you to confirm that there was indeed a settlement?"

"Oh boy," he said as he exhaled, as if they were entering a touchy area. "Look, we still represent the Swiss company, Littleman, and yes they gobbled up Tinzo a few years back. At the time there were some of these product claims on Tinzo's books but nothing in the way of litigation had materialized. The Swiss wanted a clean slate. They don't like our tort system, can't blame them for that, and so they told us to get rid of the claims, such as they were. They were dumped on my desk with instructions to make offers. I'm afraid that's about all I can say. The settlements were confidential, as you might guess, and my client admitted no liability at all."

"I see. Is it possible to get copies of the settlement agreements?"

"Oh no. The Swiss are as tight-mouthed as anyone. They would never agree to release any of the details. Not sure why, after so long, and it was a drop in the bucket anyway. Littleman did fourteen billion in sales last year so this was chicken feed. But, that's the way they operate. We're not talking anything criminal, are we?"

"Certainly not on your part. Your client has done nothing wrong."

"Of course not. Who do you represent?"

"Mr. Stafford's ex-wife. They were going through a divorce and, though we certainly don't know for sure, it appears likely that he hid some money."

"Wouldn't be the first time," Marty said with a laugh, and Walter felt compelled to laugh along too. When the humor passed, Walter pressed with "So, there's no way to see the settlement agreements?"

"Only with a subpoena, Mr. Sullivan. Only with a subpoena."

"Got it. We'll get to work on it. I really appreciate your time, sir."

"My pleasure. Good day, sir." And Marty was gone, no doubt engulfed quickly by staff.

(19)

Jake was drafting another simple will, yet another one for an elderly couple with almost nothing to leave behind. They were members of his church and Jake had known the family for years. His secretary buzzed in with "Jake, there's a young woman on the phone with no name, says it's urgent."

His first thought was: *Tell her I'm busy.* Every small-town lawyer was a target for similar calls, and they were always trouble. However, years earlier, when he was fresh from law school, he had declined such a call and found out later that the woman was hiding from an abusive husband. The guy found her and beat her and went to prison. Jake had felt guilty for a long time.

"Okay," he said, and picked up the receiver.

A soft voice said, "Mr. Brigance, my name is Margot Stafford. I'm Mack's oldest daughter."

"Hello, Margot." He had never met her, but a few years back he and Carla had watched a junior high girls' basketball game with some friends whose daughter was on the team. Margot was playing, and playing well, and someone pointed her out as Mack's daughter. "What can I do for you?"

"Is this conversation private?"

"It is, yes."

"Good. I'd like to know if you've seen Mack."

Not "my father" but "Mack."

"Yes, I have."

"So, he's really back in the country?"

"He is."

After a long pause, she said, "Would it be possible for me to meet with him, somewhere in private? My mother has no idea I'm calling you."

"I'm sure Mack would love to see you, Margot. I think I can arrange a meeting, if that's what you want."

"Thank you. Uh, where could we meet?"

Jake racked his brain with this unusual request and could not think of a secret place. "How about my office, here on the square?"

"Don't know about that. Would anybody see us?"

"No. There's a back door." Behind the small kitchen was a rear door that Jake had used many times to avoid troublesome clients. It opened into the alley behind his office, and the alley led to a maze of narrow passages where he sometimes bumped into other lawyers fleeing their work or their ill-tempered secretaries.

He gave instructions to Margot and they agreed on 2:00 p.m. Friday.

(20)

The U.S. Attorney for the Northern District of Mississippi had an entire floor of offices in the federal courthouse in Oxford. His senior prosecutor was Judd Morrissette, the younger brother of Walter Sullivan's best friend from law school. On Thursday morning, Walter rode to Oxford in his fine Cadillac, driven by Harriet, his secretary and chauffeur. Outside of Clanton, and while on the job, Walter preferred to be driven. He said it gave him more time to work—to read thick documents, to make important calls, to ponder legal strategies—but the truth was that as the miles clicked by and the radio played soft country, Walter was usually napping.

He had known Judd Morrissette for years, and they spent the first fifteen minutes catching up with each other and talking about old friends. When they finally got around to Mack, Judd surprised Walter with a story about an old case in which he, Judd, prosecuted a bookie from Greenwood. His defense lawyer was Mack Stafford, who grew up in that town. So, Judd had met Mack years earlier and, along with every other lawyer in the state, had heard the story of his disappearance.

Walter explained that he had been hired by "the family" to explore the mysteries of how and why Mack left town. Mack's ex-father-in-law, Herman Bunning, was a longtime client, and he was convinced Mack hid some money from his daughter in the divorce. And if he did, then he certainly hid the money in his bankruptcy.

In lower voices, they took a moment to divert the conversation to the latest on Lisa's health. She was not doing well and not expected to improve.

Out of courtesy and respect, Judd listened and took some notes, but he initially had little interest in the case. Bankruptcy fraud was just not that exciting. The case, if there was one, was now three years old. The real victim was dying. It was a family mess that Judd preferred to avoid.

Walter was saying, "We found one of the four plaintiffs, a man named Odell Grove. Poor guy lost an eye in the chain saw accident. He wouldn't talk to my investigator, but he might talk to the FBI."

"And your theory is?"

"Stafford settled the cases quickly, kept most of the money, or far more than his share, kept it away from the divorce and bankruptcy, and skipped out."

"How much?"

"Don't know yet. I talked to a lawyer in New York who handled the settlements for the manufacturer, some Swiss outfit, but he wouldn't say much. Send in the FBI and he'll be a regular windbag."

Judd laughed and said, "Yes, they do have a way of loosening tongues, don't they?"

"Once we get the settlement agreements, everything will fall into place. We'll know how much money was on the table and how much Mack kept for himself."

Judd was warming to the idea. "Could be a pretty simple matter, really, you know? Find the plaintiffs and see what kind of deal they had with Mack. At the same time, get the paperwork from New York. Let me have a chat with the FBI."

(21)

The one lunch spot in the county where Jake knew for an absolute certainty that no lawyer, disbarred or otherwise, would ever be recognized was a country store called Sawdust. It was a rustic joint favored by loggers and farmers, all white because blacks had stayed away forever. Jake had been there only once, with Harry Rex who had been looking for a witness in a violent divorce case. Mack Stafford had never been there and could not remember the last time he'd even driven by the place.

They met in the gravel parking lot at 11:30, early to avoid the noon rush, and stopped to look at the two black bears in a cage by the front porch. A confederate battle flag flopped in the breeze from a leaning flagpole.

Jake looked at Mack's car, a boxy Volvo DL with plenty of miles on it, and said, "Nice wheels."

"From Rent-A-Wreck. Six-month lease, all cash, insurance included."

"Under the radar, huh?"

"Completely."

"Tennessee tags."

"I'm staying in Memphis these days, in a very small apartment that no one can find. Another cash deal."

The front door opened into a cramped country store, with creaking planks for flooring, smoked meats hanging above the cash register, low ceilings, half a dozen battered rocking chairs situated around a potbellied stove that was not being used. They nodded to the cashier behind the counter and stepped into the dining room, a large add-on with a linoleum floor that was evidently sinking slowly toward the rear. The walls were covered with football schedules for Ole Miss, Mississippi State, and Southern Miss, as well as junior colleges and high schools.

They took a small table in the corner and a waitress followed them to it.

"Gentlemen, gentlemen, how are we doin' today?" she chirped.

"Just great. We're starving."

"Special is beef stew and jalapeño cornbread. Can't beat it."

Jake nodded. "Ice tea, no sugar."

"Same," Mack said. She left them without writing down a word.

Mack preferred to sit with his back to the wall, face to the door. He wore a cap with the bill pulled low and a different pair of glasses. His chances of being recognized in the dining room of the Sawdust were about the same as being recognized in the rain forests of Costa Rica.

"How long you been back?" Jake asked.

"This is my eleventh day."

"How's the reentry, so far?"

"Pretty rocky, I'd say. It's great seeing my mom. I drive down to Greenwood occasionally and sit with her. She's almost eighty, still in decent shape, still drives. She hasn't seen Helen and Margot since I left, so that's another strike against me. They're adding up. It was a lousy thing to do, Jake. Run away like that. I mean, at the time I was desperate to get out, to get away from Lisa and the practice of law and all that, but you can't run away from people you love. I should've divorced her, closed the office, moved to Memphis or Jackson, got a job selling real estate or new Chevrolets, something, anything to support myself. I would have survived, hell, I would've made more money cutting grass."

Two large plastic glasses of tea hit the table. "Lemon's over there," the waitress nodded.

Jake said, "It's not too late to try again. You're not exactly a geezer."

"We'll see. I'm trying to adjust these days. It's overwhelming at times. Plus, there's still the fear of the knock on the door."

"That doesn't look likely."

Mack took a sip and said, "I can't believe Margot called you like that. I wonder what she wants."

"Maybe she wants to see her father. Her mother is dying. Her world is upside down. Were you guys close?"

"It seemed like a typical father-daughter relationship. Nothing really special. The girls always preferred to spend time with their mother, and that was fine with everyone. To be honest, Jake, I stayed away from home as much as possible. The marriage was crap from day one. To save it, we decided to have a couple of kids, which is not an uncommon mistake. How many times have you heard that with divorce clients?"

"At least a hundred."

"That didn't work. Nothing worked."

"This is a horrible thing to say, Mack, but things might get easier for you after Lisa is gone. Don't you think?"

"They can't get much worse. The girls will be a mess. When I was in the picture the girls were close to their mother, but the teenage years were only beginning. Who knows what's happened since then."

"Will you try to get custody?"

"It's too early. I don't want to cause trouble right now. Besides, the girls are old enough to choose where they want to live. With me, or with their grandparents. I suspect Herman will put up a big fight to keep the girls. I'm not exactly a sympathetic father, you know? If they stay with the Bunnings, I'll be somewhere close by and try to rebuild some trust. It'll be a long process, but I have to start somewhere."

Jake sipped his tea and had no response. Some farmers in overalls made a noisy entrance and assumed a table they seemed to own.

"Recognize anybody?" Mack whispered.

"Not a soul. I'm constantly amazed at the number of people I don't know in this county of thirty thousand people."

It took the same waitress about fifteen seconds to fire up the farmers, and they were soon complaining about the service. She retreated to the kitchen. Someone mentioned last night's Cardinals game and baseball became the topic.

Mack listened and smiled and said, "You know, Jake, at times it's hard to believe I'm back. For the first year or two down there I never thought about coming back. I tried to erase the past, but the longer I was away the more homesick I became. I was in a fishing camp one time, in Belize, and I saw a guy wearing an Auburn cap. It was in October, I suddenly missed the football games at Ole Miss. The tailgating in the Grove. The parties before and after the games. I missed my friends from those days, and I really missed my mother. We began writing letters. I was careful and routed them through Panama. It was so good to hear from home. The more I read her letters, the more I knew I had to come back."

"How'd you find out Lisa was sick?"

"Someone told Mom. There's a family friend from Greenwood with a connection to Clanton. Some of the news filtered through."

The waitress placed two large platters in front of them. Steaming bowls, each with enough stew for a small family, and thick wedges of cornbread slathered with butter. They forgot about any conversation and began eating. The table next to them filled with some locals, one of whom took a long look at Mack, then lost interest.

When they finished lunch, they paid at the front counter. Mack left his Volvo at the Sawdust. Jake drove fifteen minutes to Clanton, and as they approached the square he asked, "So, what are your thoughts right now? Nostalgia? Relief? Any excitement at being back?"

"None of the above. Certainly no fond memories. I was unhappy here, left at the age of forty-two because I couldn't stomach the thought of living the same life until I was sixty or seventy."

"I've had those thoughts."

"Of course you have. Everyone does. And there's no end in sight because you can't retire, can't afford to."

"You want to see your old office?"

"No. What is it now?"

"A yogurt shop. Frozen yogurt. Not bad."

"I'd rather avoid that end of the square."

Jake parked on a side street. They ducked into an alley and within seconds opened the rear door that entered into his kitchen. The front door of the office was locked, per Jake's orders. Alicia stood and smiled but did not introduce herself. Again, at Jake's orders. She was not to mention the name of Mack Stafford. She nodded to the closed door of the small downstairs conference room.

Mack walked to it and took a deep breath.

(22)

Margot was standing at the window, looking through the blinds. She did not turn around when he entered. She seemed not to hear him at all.

Mack closed the door, walked toward her, and stopped a few feet away. He was prepared for an awkward hug, then an hour of even more awkward conversation. He was prepared for tears and apologies and he was hoping for a little forgiveness.

She was much taller and had long dark hair that fell to her shoulders. She was still lean. Lisa had always refused to gain a pound and was a stickler for what the girls ate. The discipline was paying off because Margot, at least from a side view, looked older than seventeen.

He had programmed himself to fight off the emotions, the memories, the cherished photos of little girls in pigtails and pretty Easter dresses and dance costumes. The bedtime stories, the first day of kindergarten, the broken arm, the new family puppy. He had tucked those images away for so long he was convinced he could bury them forever, but when he saw her his knees quivered and his throat closed. He swallowed hard and clenched his jaw and willed himself to get tough, to power through it. A lot depended on her.

She finally turned and looked at him. Her eyes were already moist. "Why are you back?"

"I was hoping for a hug."

She shook her head slightly and without a hint of emotion said, "No hugs, Mack. Not yet anyway."

He was startled to be called "Mack" by his daughter, but then he had tried to prepare himself for a lot of surprises.

She stared at him coldly and her moist eyes seemed to clear. She pointed to a chair at the table, on his side, and said, "Why don't you sit there and I'll sit over here?"

Without a word Mack sat down and she did too, with the table between them. He studied her face and adored what he saw. She studied his and wasn't so sure. She had Lisa's soft brown eyes, full lips, and perfect skin. She had his high cheekbones and rounded chin. Since she had yet to smile he wasn't sure about the teeth, though, as he recalled with horror, the orthodontist had cost a bundle when she was about twelve. The teeth better be perfect.

"What's with the beard?" she asked in a tone that left little doubt she wasn't a fan.

"I got tired of the face."

"Part of the disguise?"

"Sure, along with the glasses."

"You look a lot older than I remember."

"Thanks. So do you. How's your mother?"

"Why do you ask?"

"Because I was once married to her and I am concerned."

She scoffed at this and looked away. "She's very sick, down to eighty pounds. I find it hard to believe you're really interested."

He nodded gamely and admired her pluck. He deserved anything she could hurl across the table. He asked, "And Helen? How's she holding up?"

"Do you really care about us, Mack?"

"You know, I think 'Dad' sounds better than 'Mack,' so can we go with it?"

"Why? Are you trying to be a father again? You gave up the father thing when you abandoned us. You don't have the right to consider yourself my father."

"That's pretty tough. I am still your father, at least biologically. You can argue otherwise."

"Emotionally you're not. You gave that up when you left us. Now you're back, Mack, so what's your game? What are you after?"

"Nothing. I'm back because I got tired of running, because it was wrong to run and I want you to hear me say that I was wrong. I made a mistake, Margot, a terrible mistake, and I apologize. I can't make up for the past three years but at least I can be around for the next three, the next five, the next ten. I'm back because I heard that Lisa is sick and I'm worried about you and

Helen. I don't expect you to welcome me with hugs and open arms, but give me some time and I'll prove myself."

Her stiff lip began to quiver and her cold eyes were moist again. She gave it a moment and it passed. "You're moving back?"

"I don't know what I'm doing right now, but, no, I'm not coming back to Clanton."

"So when Mom dies where do we go? Foster care? Wards of the state? How about a nice orphanage?"

Mack adored this kid. She was quick and tough and had probably been through hell and back because of him. Instead of an emotional reunion, she had Mack pinned to the ropes and was flailing away.

"What about the Bunnings?" he asked.

She rolled her eyes in mock disbelief and shook her head. "Oh, I suppose that's in the grand plan. As you remember, Hermie has the world under his thumb and is the supreme ruler. Since we have no place else to go, it's a given that we'll move into the big house and play by his rules."

"Hermie?"

"That's what I call him, behind his back, of course. Helen won't do it. She's still the perfect one and coos 'Papa' at him."

There was a long pause as Mack savored the nickname "Hermie" and wished he'd had the guts to have been more disrespectful to his ex-father-in-law.

"I asked you about Helen," he said.

"Oh, she's okay. She's sixteen and about as mature as a ten-year-old. She starts each day with a good cry because her mother is sick and then spends most of her time wallowing in the misery. You speak differently."

"I ironed out the accent, part of the disguise."

"Sounds phony."

"Thanks."

She reached for her purse and said, "Mind if I smoke?" It wasn't a question. She deftly flicked out a cigarette, one of those long liberated ones, and lit it with a lighter in a motion so smooth that Mack knew she'd had plenty of practice.

"When did you start smoking?"

"A year or so ago. When did you start smoking?"

"When I was fifteen. Quit after law school."

"I'll quit someday, but right now it's the bomb. Only a pack a day, though."

"Your mother is dying of cancer and you've taken up cigarettes."

"Is that a question? It's breast cancer, not lung. And I like beer, too."

"Anything else?"

"Wanna talk about sex?"

"Let's change the subject."

She smiled and knew perfectly well he was on his heels. She took a long pull, blew a cloud, and asked, "Do you have any idea how awful it is to be a fourteen-year-old girl and abandoned by your father, a man you loved and admired, a man you thought was really somebody because he was a big lawyer in a small town? A man who was a part of your life, usually there, at home, church, school, family, everywhere a father was supposed to be. Everywhere the other fathers still are, except mine. Any idea what that's like, Mack?"

"No. I'm sorry."

"I know you're sorry. You're worse than sorry, Mack. I can think of a lot of colorful descriptions."

"Unload. I'm not arguing. You want me to leave?"

"Go ahead. That's what you do. Flee. Things get sticky, hit the road." She was forceful and strong, but she wiped a tear. She puffed away for a moment as she collected herself.

As the adult, he bit his tongue and kept his voice calm and

low. "I'm not leaving again, Margot, unless I'm forced to. I said I'm sorry, that's all I can do. I'm thrilled to see you now and I'd like to see you again. Helen too."

"Got a question, Mack. When you left here in the middle of the night, did you plan to ever see us again?"

He took a deep breath and gazed at the window. She waited, the slim cigarette delicately resting between two fingers, ready for the next puff. Her eyes were glaring a hole in him.

"I don't know what I was thinking. You remember the night I came home drunk, slipped on the ice in the driveway, busted my head, and ended up in the hospital?"

"How could I forget? We were so proud."

What a little smart-ass, but he let it go. It was actually funny but he didn't smile. "Your mother had you brainwashed into believing that I was some terrible alcoholic and thus a terrible father."

"I don't remember it that way."

"Well thank you. In the Bunning family, two bottles of beer and you're ready for rehab. She was looking for support and she made sure you and Helen knew I was drinking. She told her family and friends, too."

"Yes she did. She was pretty horrible about it."

Thank you, dear. "To answer your question, when I left town my only thought was to just get away. I was sure I would see you again, but that was not in my plans. Not then, anyway. I just wanted to go somewhere far from here and put my life back together. I didn't have a real plan, except to get away from Lisa."

"Did you ever love her?"

It was a question he was not expecting. He gazed at the window again. "I thought I did, at one point, early on, but the romance wore off quickly and there was nothing left. As you know, we were really unhappy."

"Why were you unhappy?"

"There are at least two sides, Margot. I'm sure you've heard the other one, loud and clear. Lisa became discontented with me and my career. I was trying to establish a law practice, which, as I learned, is hard to do in a small town like this. Look around the square, there are so many lawyers. Lisa wanted a lot more. She was raised with money and she was spoiled by her parents. Stephanie married a doctor and before long they were in a bigger house. Lisa watched everything they bought, talked about every trip they took, and so on. Her parents obviously favored Stephanie and Dean and often made comparisons, especially her mother. I never measured up, was never good enough. As you are acutely aware, they're hardcore Baptists and expected me to be in church at least three times a week."

"That hasn't changed."

"I'm sure. It was too much for me. I got sick of their hypocrisy, their materialism, their racism, all in the name of God. I tried to avoid them, and Lisa and I drifted apart. We chose not to fight in front of you and Helen, so we settled into a routine of faking it and trying to ignore one another. We were both pretty miserable. There you have it. My side of the story. The marriage was over and both of us wanted out. I saw an opportunity and ran away."

She cocked her head and took a long drag, much like a beautiful actress in a crime movie, a sexy move she had down pat. She extended her bottom lip and exhaled a stream of smoke that rose to the ceiling. She had yet to offer anything close to a smile. She said, "Helen, of course, was oblivious, but I knew from the age of ten that things weren't right. You can only hide so much from kids."

"I'm sure I've caused you a lot of embarrassment."

She rolled her eyes as if to say, *If you only knew,* then placed the cigarette in the ashtray and said, "Yes, you have, but it's not all bad, Mack. It has really opened my eyes and it has taught me a lot about people. The rich kids, my old gang, have enjoyed the gossip behind my back, the put-downs, the snide comments, the stuff they've heard at home. The middle-class kids want to hang with the rich ones so they've piled on too. The poor kids have enough of their own problems. The black kids actually think it's cool that my father beat the system and got away. They know what it's like to be judged, so they don't judge. They're a lot more fun. I've learned a lot about people and most of it's not good. In some weird way, I should say thanks, Mack."

"Don't mention it."

"Always the smart-ass, right?"

"Sorry."

"Don't apologize. I get that from you. Mom has always said that I'm a natural smart-ass, just like my father."

"That's the nicest thing she's said about me in years."

"See." And she finally smiled. The expensive teeth were dazzling.

Neither spoke for a long time. There was so much to say, but then they had already covered a lot of ground.

She took her purse and said, "I need to be going. I told Mom I was running some errands. She wants us to stay close."

"And she has no idea we're meeting?"

"No, no way. She would be furious if she knew. We've been lectured by her, and by Hermie too, that we are to report any effort by you to contact us."

"I'm not surprised." Mack had worried that the meeting was a ruse by the family to confirm the rumors that he was indeed back in the area. Now that he had been spotted, they could make their next move, whatever it might be. But those concerns were over. His beautiful daughter was blunt and honest, and could be trusted.

He said, "I'll be thinking of you and Helen, and Lisa too. The next few weeks will be difficult."

"Thanks, I guess. I gotta tell you, Mack, I'm tired of crying. I love my mother and I'll die when she dies, but at some point I'll wake up and get on with life. And it won't be around here."

"Got someplace in mind?"

She shook her head as if she'd had enough. "Not really. Look, let's talk about it next time."

"So we can meet again?"

"Sure." She stood and walked to the door, where she stopped and looked at him. "Maybe next time, Mack, I'll be ready for a hug."

"I love you, Margot."

Without a reply, she opened the door and left.

(23)

Of the four Special Agents assigned to the Oxford office of the FBI, the one with the least seniority was a rookie named Nick Lenzini. He was a cocky sort from Long Island, and when he left training at Quantico the last place he wanted to go was Mississippi. But, as he knew well, that was the way the Bureau operated. He would do his five years and transfer to a bigger assignment as soon as possible. The file landed on his desk when the other three agents quickly passed on it. They were too busy fighting terror, hate groups, cybercrime, and drug cartels. Bankruptcy fraud was not a priority.

Lenzini reviewed the Stafford bankruptcy case, and he slipped into Clanton and got a copy of the divorce file in the chancery clerk's office. At the city library, he went through the archives of *The Ford County Times* and found three articles about Stafford's disappearance. He was careful, dressed casually, and told no one he was with the FBI. He assumed, correctly, that any word of his presence would stir up the rumors and send the wrong signal to Mack, wherever he happened to be hiding.

Lenzini was delighted when his boss okayed a trip to New York. He could see his family, but, more important, he could rub elbows with veteran agents from the Manhattan office.

Two of them accompanied him as they entered a tall building in the financial district in downtown Manhattan. They rode an elevator to the seventy-first floor and stepped into the gilded world of Durban & Lang, at that moment the third-largest law firm in the entire world. A paralegal was waiting for them in the plush reception suite, and they followed him to a conference room with a stunning view of New York Harbor. Marty Rosenberg greeted them warmly and a secretary offered them coffee.

When they were seated, Marty took charge and was all charm. He began with "Sorry to be a pain about this, fellas, but I have my orders from my client, Littleman AG. A fine company with nothing to hide, you know. This is a simple matter involving the settlement of some rather dubious product liability cases from years back. I've reviewed the subpoena and all the paperwork is right here."

He waved to a pile in the center of the table.

"We've made copies for you. I'm sure you have questions."

Lenzini cleared his throat and said, "Thank you, Mr. Rosenberg. Perhaps you could hit the high points before we plow through the paperwork."

"Certainly. We paid one hundred thousand dollars per claim, four of them, and we threw in another hundred thousand for litigation expenses. Total of half a mil. I handled it directly with Mr. Stafford and it was quite easy. He seemed eager to get the money."

"And you wired it to him?"

"Yes, to a bank in Memphis. I sent down these settlement agreements and he got them signed, ostensibly by his four clients. Signatures are right there on the agreements, notarized and all, and he sent them back, quite promptly I might add. I reviewed them and released the money. Not a peep about anything until now."

"And there's a copy of the wire transfer?"

"Yes. You now have copies of everything in our files, including the initial demand letters sent from Mr. Stafford way back when. It's all there."

"Thank you, Mr. Rosenberg. We'll take these and have a look."

"My pleasure, gentlemen. Always happy to assist the FBI."

The coffee arrived and they chatted for a few moments. Marty said, "Off the record, it looks like Mr. Stafford left town in a hurry not long after the settlements, right?"

All three agents stiffened at the question. Mr. Rosenberg was not in a position to know much about the investigation.

Lenzini cautiously said, "That appears to be the case. Did you have any reason to be suspicious?"

"None whatsoever. These settlements were mere formalities for my client, just a rather generous way of closing some old files. Littleman didn't have to offer a dime to these plaintiffs, and Mr. Stafford certainly showed no interest in pursuing the claims."

"Were there other complaints about the product?" Lenzini asked, biding time. It seemed a shame to leave such splendid surroundings so quickly.

Marty tapped his fingertips together and tried to recall. "Yes, seems like there were a few dozen around the country. Look, it's a chain saw, right? A dangerous product when handled by experts. Come to think of it, we did go to trial in someplace like Indiana. Poor guy lost a hand, wanted a couple mil. The jury was sympathetic but found in favor of Littleman anyway. When you use a chain saw you assume the risk."

It seemed odd to be sitting high above Wall Street, sipping coffee from designer china, and talking about . . . chain saws!

Marty glanced at his watch and was suddenly needed elsewhere. The agents took the hint, thanked him, gathered the paperwork, and were led back to the elevators.

(24)

Out of boredom, Mack found a job tending bar for cash wages, no paperwork, five bucks an hour plus tips. It was a college dive called the Varsity Bar & Grill, near Memphis State, and, typically, the students were not big tippers. Nor were they curious about who might be mixing their drinks. They were at least twenty-five years younger than Mack, couldn't care less about where he was from or who he was, and none of them had ever been to Clanton, Mississippi.

He figured his chances of being recognized were nil. He used the name Marco with the owner and the other bartenders.

Within days, Marco was quietly taking over the bar, primarily because he would actually show up on time, work hard when things were busy, stay late if needed, and didn't steal from the cash register. He worked circles around the other bartenders, mostly students, and enjoyed the friendly banter with the customers. Marco had learned to mix everything working in a beach bar in Costa Rica. With the owner's permission, he added some colorful tropical drinks laced with cheap rum and the coeds went crazy over them. He expanded happy hours, found calypso and reggae bands for the weekends, jazzed up the menu with spicy finger foods, and the Varsity became an even more popular hangout.

Mack moved into a two-room apartment above a garage that was attached to an old house in central Memphis. The owner of the Varsity knew of the place and referred Mack there. It was a dump, but at $200 a month, with utilities, he expected little. It was temporary and there were no records anywhere.

His routine was to rise early, in spite of the late nights, and most mornings drive south ninety minutes through the Delta to Greenwood and have breakfast with his mother. They still had ground to cover but they were catching up nicely. After an hour or so with her, he enjoyed little excursions deeper into the state as he dropped in on old pals from his law school and lawyering days. He never called ahead. If they were busy, he left without leaving a name. If he caught them at the right time, then he drank their coffee and answered their questions. All were delighted to see him and all confessed they at times had found themselves jealous of his getaway. After a few laughs and as much conversation as their schedules allowed, he left with promises to keep in touch.

By noon, he was back at the Varsity, ordering beer and booze, restocking the coolers, premixing the fruit juices, prepping the bar, and taking inventory of mugs, glasses, and stemware. Several were broken every night. After two weeks on the job, the owner gave Marco the green light to overhaul the menu.

The current chef was on his way out the door, though he didn't know it yet. Marco had him in his sights. The chef was stealing food out the back door, and when Marco had enough proof he would have a chat with the owner.

(25)

Freda was not too keen on having another drink with Buddy Hockner. She had not really enjoyed the first one, and besides, she had told him everything she could remember about Mack's final days.

But on the phone Buddy was persistent, and the deal was closed when he informed her that the FBI wanted to have a chat. Most citizens, especially law-abiding ones, are startled to hear such ominous news and immediately resist. Buddy went on to explain that either the FBI could barge into the law firm where she worked and disrupt things, or they could meet secretly someplace where no one would know.

Nick Lenzini had wisely decided to use Buddy Hockner to facilitate the meeting. He spoke the local language and he had met Freda. If Nick had gone in flashing his badge and talking the way they do on Long Island, Freda would have reacted badly.

And so they met at a hotel bar on the outskirts of Tupelo. Buddy and Freda ordered drinks with alcohol. Lenzini abstained because he was on duty. He was all charm as he thanked her and assured her the FBI had no interest in her as a suspect.

Buddy listened wide-eyed, enthralled to be working with an FBI agent and in the middle of the case.

Nick was saying, "So I went to New York last week and met with the lawyers, big firm, and pressed them with a subpoena. They came around and gave us copies of all the paperwork." He tapped a neat stack of documents about an inch thick. "Care to take a look?"

Freda shrugged, took a drink. Buddy smiled at her.

Nick lifted the first settlement agreement and said, "This is for Odell Grove, plaintiff number one. He was supposed to receive sixty thousand dollars. Back here on the last page is his signature and your notarization. Please take a look."

Before she looked at anything, Freda said, "Well, I can assure you I never notarized a signature for Odell Grove. Never met the man."

They went through all four settlement agreements. Freda admitted that whoever signed her name, and they were assuming it was Mack Stafford simply because there was no other suspect even remotely connected to the matter, had done a passable job of forgery. All four notarizations were done with an outdated stamp and seal, and certified with Freda's forged signature.

She said, "When I left I took my current stamp and seal, still have it. I had a couple of old ones in a drawer in the file room. Looks like Mack just used one of them and nobody in New York caught it."

Nick said, "I had to use a magnifying glass to read the seal."

"No one ever looks that close. As you know, when you get something notarized, you're standing in front of the notary herself. It's all very routine."

Buddy asked, "What's the penalty for forging a notarization?"

"Up to five years," Nick said. "Times four, plus he may have forged the plaintiffs' signatures as well. We don't know yet."

"Who'll prosecute him?" Freda asked, suddenly concerned.

Nick put the settlement agreement away and said, "Don't know. We'll have to wait and see where the investigation leads. I'll ask you to sign a statement that covers everything we just discussed."

She hesitated and said, "Okay, but I really don't want to go to court, you know? I don't want to testify against Mack. Will they really put him in jail?"

Nick frowned and looked around. She was asking questions he couldn't answer. "Don't know. Again, we'll have to finish the investigation first. I'll ask you to keep this conversation private, okay? If Mack is back in the country, he might skip out again if he catches wind of our involvement."

Freda nodded grimly and was tempted to explain to this young man from Long Island how fast the gossip flew around Clanton, but she let it pass.

He asked, "And you never met any of the four plaintiffs?"

"No. I don't think these guys came to town very often. I remember typing the original letters to the manufacturer years ago."

"I have the letters right here. All four are dated April 17, 1984."

"Seven years ago," she replied. "Seems longer than that."

"Nothing much happened after the first letters. Do you remember why Mack lost his enthusiasm for the cases?"

"Not really. Mack didn't handle product cases like this. I seem to recall that he tried to shop them around to bigger law firms, but nothing happened. He forgot about them. So did I."

"And you knew nothing of the settlements?"

"No, nothing at all. As I said, he fired me and I left the office immediately."

Nick zipped his briefcase and held it in his lap. The meeting was over.

(26)

The FBI had little business in Ford County and rarely ventured there. The call from Special Agent Lenzini was taken by a secretary and routed to Sheriff Ozzie Walls. It was a call Lenzini made with great hesitation since it was his first official contact with anyone in Clanton. He explained to the sheriff that he was pursuing a routine investigation, but one that was nonetheless quite sensitive. Discretion was needed, and so on.

Ozzie was intrigued and eager to help. Any involvement with the Feds was an exciting change of pace. When he asked the nature of the investigation, Lenzini deflected him with "Might be some drug activity. I'll explain it all tomorrow."

The following day, Ozzie and Marshall Prather, his chief

deputy, drove to the small town of Karaway, the only other incorporated municipality in the county. They met Lenzini at a coffee shop on Main Street midmorning and huddled in a booth, as far away from prying ears as possible. Most of the old gentlemen drinking coffee and talking politics had hearing problems anyway.

Lenzini briefed them on his investigation into Mack Stafford and asked for their help. He had verified the fact that Jerrol Baker, one of the four plaintiffs, was in prison. There was no sign of Travis Johnson, nor of Doug Jumper.

"He's dead," Prather said. "Boy got killed in a truck wreck a few years back, over near Tupelo. My cousin knows his family."

Lenzini made a note of this and said, "That leaves Odell Grove. Any idea where he might be?"

"Yep, he lives not far from here," Prather said. "Still cuttin' pulpwood with his sons."

They decided the wisest course would be for Prather to pay a visit to Odell late in the afternoon when he was probably at home. An FBI agent in a dark suit might not be as welcome. In his two elections for sheriff, Ozzie had done well in the precincts around Karaway, but still he was black and always cautious when knocking on doors deep in the woods.

In the car driving back to Clanton, Ozzie said, "You know, Jake was asking about Mack Stafford. Wanted to know if the case was still open. I told him no. He asked me to let him know if I heard anything."

"You gonna tell him?" Prather asked.

"Hell no. It's a criminal investigation. He has no business knowing about it. Plus, he ain't even Mack's lawyer."

"Has anybody seen Mack?"

"Not that I know of. Lots of gossip and such, but you can't believe everything you hear."

"Well, he's up shit creek now, what with the FBI on his trail."

"You got that right," Ozzie said. "I guess the rumors were true about Mack. He took some money that wasn't his and disappeared. I never believed it."

"I always thought the guy was shifty, like most lawyers around here."

"That, and he hired Harry Rex. That's always a bad sign."

"Someone needs to indict that big ass."

They enjoyed a good laugh at Harry Rex's expense.

Late in the afternoon, Deputy Prather parked at the edge of a gravel road and walked the dirt driveway to a mobile home that had seen better days. From a chain-link pen beside it, four or five beagles yelped and warned everyone for miles, though the nearest house could not be seen. Years ago, a rickety porch had been attached to the trailer, and by the time Prather approached the front door, Odell was waiting for him. Like most men who spent their days cutting down trees and wrestling logs, he was thick in the shoulders and chest, with huge hairy arms that bulged from under a clean white T-shirt. He wore a patch over his left eye, courtesy of Tinzo. He stepped onto the porch and said, "Afternoon."

"Odell, I'm Marshall Prather, deputy sheriff."

"I know who you are, Prather." He whistled sharply at the dogs and they stopped barking.

Odell stepped down and they shook hands. Marshall held some papers in his left hand.

"What brings you out here?" Odell asked, unconcerned.

"Mack Stafford. Remember him? The lawyer."

"Rings a bell. What's he done now?"

"Not sure. Did he settle a case for you a few years back?"

Odell pointed to the patch over his left eye and smiled. "He was my lawyer, said he was gonna sue the chain saw company for big bucks. Nothin' much happened."

"Was there a settlement? Did he get you any money?"

"A few bucks, said it was all confidential. How do you know about it?"

Marshall held up the papers, four sheets stapled together. He flipped to the back page and pointed at a signature. "Did you sign this?"

Odell took it carefully and studied the signature. "That's mine all right."

"Did you sign in front of a notary public?"

"A what?"

"Down there under your signature is a stamp and a seal, and under them is the signature of a notary public. A woman. Was she around when you signed it?"

"No sir. Just me and Mack. Met him outside the truck stop. Nobody was with him."

"How much money did you get?"

"I ain't done nothin' wrong, have I?"

"Nope, but there's a chance Mack did."

"So, I don't have to talk about this, do I?"

"Nope, not now. But if you don't, then the FBI will be here in a few days to ask questions. They may want you to go to Clanton for an interrogation."

Odell stuck a toothpick in his mouth and began working on it as he studied the situation. Prather took the papers back, flipped to the second page, and said, "This is your settlement agreement. Did you read it?"

He shook his head, chewed on the toothpick.

"Says you agreed to settle the case for a hundred thousand dollars. How much did Mack give you?"

"You swear I ain't done nothin' wrong?"

"I swear. The FBI figures Mack gave you some cash and kept most of the money for himself."

"That thievin' son of a bitch."

"Sure looks that way. He had four of these cases."

"I sent him another. Boy named Jerrol Baker lost a hand."

"That's right. Jerrol is at Parchman. Drugs."

"So I heard." Odell shook his head and mumbled, "That son of a bitch."

"How much did you get?"

Odell took a deep breath and said, "Twenty-five thousand, all cash. Said nobody would ever know. Said it was a quick settlement, had to be done right then, no chance of any more money. Told me to keep everythang quiet. Son of a bitch."

Prather handed back the papers and said, "This is your copy. In paragraph four, second page, you'll see the amount of one hundred thousand."

"Where's the rest of it?"

"Only Mack knows. You may want to hire a lawyer to check on it."

"I don't need a lawyer. I keep a baseball bat under the seat."

"I wouldn't advise that, Odell. That would only lead to a lot of trouble you don't need."

"Where is he?"

"Don't know right now, but there's a rumor he's back in town."

"Y'all gonna put him in jail?"

"Don't know yet. Right now it's just the FBI."

"All right, Prather. Let me know what's goin' on."

"Will do."

They shook hands and Marshall walked back to his car.

(27)

The second meeting also took place in Jake's small conference room downstairs, and it, too, began without hugs. Mack was waiting when she entered the room, ten minutes late. They gave each other a smile and not much else. This time her dark hair was pulled tight into a ponytail and she wore stylish designer frames that made her look even prettier. They sat on opposite sides of the table, and she broke the ice with "Mind if I smoke?"

"What if I said yes?"

She considered this for a second or two before saying, "Well, I'd probably smoke anyway."

"That's what I figured. Go ahead. They're your lungs."

She whipped out a pack of skinny cigarettes and lit one.

"May I ask how your mother is doing?"

"Sure, you can ask anything, and so can I. Deal?"

"Deal."

"Well, she's certainly not improving. She's not telling us everything the doctors are saying, but I hear a lot. They've decided against another round of chemo. She's too weak."

"How are you holding up?"

She took a puff and wiped an eye. Her voice quivered as she said, "I'm okay, Mack. I have to be the strong one because Helen is not. She sits with Mom all day in her room, reading to her, praying, crying. Me, I have to get out. I'm so tired of that house."

"So was I."

"Ha, ha. But I don't have the option of running away from my problems. That was really a shitty thing to do, Mack."

"I agree and I thought I apologized."

"You did and I accept your apology, but a few sincere words here and there can't erase what you did."

"What do you want me to do?"

"I want you to sit there and take it while I pound away. Makes me feel better."

"Fair enough."

She blew a cloud at the ceiling. He noticed her hands trembling, her eyes watering. He felt so sorry for her and so lousy for himself. She sniffed and suddenly her voice was stronger. "Did you ever get along with Hermie?"

"Hermie. I had no idea that was his nickname. We got along okay, but only because we had to. Early in my career I was driven by the desire to make more money than Herman. You know how much status means to them."

"Tell me about it. They still talk about people with bigger houses. Last week Honey got bothered because a friend's husband bought her a new Mercedes. Wanna know a secret, Mack?"

He chuckled and said, "Forgive me, but it's kinda funny to hear my daughter call me Mack. Sure, tell me a secret."

"The money isn't there."

Mack couldn't suppress a smile and said, "Oh really. What's the dirt?"

"Two years ago a company out of Tupelo tried to buy out Hermie, and for a good price. Of course he said no, said he would buy them. You know how arrogant he is. But he couldn't swing it. The company from Tupelo put in a ready-mix plant on the south side of town, the first competition Hermie has ever faced."

"They had a monopoly for decades."

"Well, no longer. The new company came in with lower concrete prices and the two companies have been cutting each other's throats ever since. Hermie thinks they're trying to run him out of business so they can pick up the pieces when he's gone. It might be happening. There are signs that they're tightening their belts. Hermie sold his hunting lodge on the lake and they're talking about selling their beach house in Destin. He seems a lot more stressed these days. Poor guy's about to lose his daughter, and his business empire is on the rocks."

"You do hear a lot."

"You know what Sunday lunch is like around there. They talk a lot, and they think us kids are too stupid to listen and understand. Plus, with Mom sick I spend more time over there than I'd like. I love Honey and we get along well, but Hermie's around a lot more and when he talks on the phone he forgets anyone in the house is listening."

"Heard anything else?"

"Aren't we the gossip? We had a big fight a couple of days ago. I'm sure you'd like to hear about it."

"Do tell."

"We were having another one of those horrible conversations about life after Lisa. Mom was there, in the den, and she said she wanted them to sell the house and put the money in trust for our college. I said I wanted to stay in the house. Helen and I can manage on our own, I think, and, anyway, I really don't want to live with Hermie. Of course the adults freaked out at the idea of two teenage girls living alone, in Clanton. What would the rest of the town think? Got nowhere. As usual, everybody got beat up and nothing good happened. But it was firmly established that the house will be sold."

"I can't really fault the decision. If I had a vote, I wouldn't want you two living alone."

"Why not? I'll be off to college next year, on my own, and I'm damned sure not coming back here."

"Where are you going?"

"I don't know. I'll find a summer internship somewhere so I can avoid this place. Not sure about college. Hermie has let it be known that he'll pay for State or Ole Miss, but nothing more. Gotta be in-state. We won't know how much the house will net until it's sold, but it won't be a bonanza. There's a mortgage and the place needs some work. Any recollection here, Mack?"

"I remember it well. It was always too small for Lisa and I didn't want to spend money on it. Didn't have the money. And I wasn't much of a handyman."

"I want to get away, Mack. Away from here. Away from Mississippi. Away from the South."

She stubbed out what was left of the cigarette in the ashtray.

"Got a place in mind?" he asked.

"Out west. California, maybe Colorado. I want to go to a little art school somewhere out there, far away. After Mom dies and after I'm forced to live with Hermie and Honey for a while, I'll be ready to sprint out of Ford County and never come back. Poor Helen will get left behind, but then she's not ready to run. I am."

"Art school?"

"Yeah, art school. Something different, Mack, something really crazy. All the girls I know, and I don't call them friends anymore, can't wait to join the sororities and look for husbands. Then they can move back to Clanton or Tupelo, have some kids, hang out at the country club and live like their mothers. Not me, Mack. I'm outta here."

Mack was moved by her rebellious attitude and couldn't hide a smile. "I'll make a deal. You pick an art school out west, get yourself admitted, and I'll help with the tuition."

She put her hands to her mouth and closed her eyes, as if she couldn't believe that a dream might come true. When she opened them she spoke softly, "You would do that?"

"It's the least I can do, Margot."

She seemed to agree with this. "I've never seen the mountains."

Another sad reminder, but how true. When the girls were little the family vacation was always a week in the family condo in Florida. Lisa dreamed of seeing the world like her sister, but the credit cards would never stretch that far.

At that moment, Mack vowed to show his girls the world.

He said, "Here's a plan. Squeeze as much as you can out of Hermie. Take what you can from the sale of the house, and I'll cover the gap to make it happen."

"What if Hermie puts his foot down and says not a dime?"

"Margot, I said I'll make it happen."

The chip on her shoulder lifted a bit as she relaxed and smiled. It was beginning to dawn on her that ole Mack here might just be her ticket out of Clanton.

"I don't know what to say," she said.

"You don't have to say anything. You're my daughter and I owe you big-time."

She flicked out another cigarette and looked at him as she lit it.

Mack said, "I have an idea. It's summer and you're supposed to be looking at colleges, right?"

"Yes."

"So next Saturday, tell Lisa that you're taking a day trip to Memphis to visit Rhodes College. It's a beautiful little private school in the city. I'm staying not too far away. We'll hang out and have lunch."

"They'll freak at the idea of me driving to Memphis alone."

"You're seventeen years old, Margot, almost a senior in high school. I was driving to Memphis when I was fifteen. Put your foot down and don't take no for an answer."

"I like it, but Hermie'll go nuts at the mention of private tuition."

"It's just a ploy to get out of town. Who knows? You might like Rhodes."

"It's too close. I'm talking serious distance, Mack."

"So it's a lunch date?"

"I'll try." She glanced at her watch and reached for her purse. "Need to go. I'm running errands for Mom."

"Is she suspicious?"

"I don't think so. For a few days you were breaking news as they panicked, but things have died down. No one has seen you around here, Mack."

"That's good. And I'm tired of meeting here. This town gives me the creeps."

"Makes two of us."

(28)

The new district attorney for the Twenty-Second Judicial District was Lowell Dyer, of the small town of Gretna, in Tyler County. If the FBI had little interest in Ford County, it had even less in Tyler, and Dyer was rather excited to welcome the Feds into his office in the county courthouse. On the phone, Special Agent Nick Lenzini gave no clue as to the reason for his visit. He came alone and was welcomed in the conference room with pastries and coffee. Dyer and his assistant, D. R. Musgrove, were at his complete disposal.

Lenzini began by announcing that he was investigating the disappearance of Mack Stafford, and wanted to know how much Dyer knew about the case. They were surprised to learn that someone was looking for Mack. They had known him back in the day and assumed that he was gone for good. As far as they knew, there had never been an investigation. So, they had nothing.

Lenzini accepted this with an exaggerated smugness, as if they had sat idly by and missed obvious criminal wrongdoing. Now it was up to the FBI to ride in and get to the bottom of things. He began his narrative about the Tinzo chain saws, the four cases signed up by Mack, his pitiful neglect of them, and so on. He made much of the fact that he had flown to New York City and met with the FBI there, and together they had tracked down the source of the settlements and the paperwork. He began pulling files from his briefcase.

The first was the settlement agreement signed by Odell Grove. The signature was legit, the notarization was forged. The contract for legal services signed by Odell gave Mack 40 percent of any recovery. Instead of receiving $25,000, Odell was due $60,000.

The second was Jerrol Baker, now serving time in prison. Lenzini had visited him there and taken his statement. The signature was his—such as it was, because he was missing most of his left hand and couldn't write that well, thanks to the chain saw—but, again, the notarization by Freda Wilson was forged. Jerrol got $25,000 in cash, not $60,000.

The third was Travis Johnson, whereabouts unknown. Forged signature, forged notarization. The fourth was Doug Jumper, deceased. An FBI handwriting analyst studied the signatures and was certain that Mack Stafford had forged all the signatures on the Johnson and Jumper settlement agreements. There was little doubt he had kept the entire $200,000.

All in all, it appeared as though Mack's haul from his fraudulent scheme totaled $400,000, not the $200,000 he was entitled to—40 percent of the half a million dollars wired down by Mr. Marty Rosenberg.

Lenzini said, "Call it what you want—embezzlement, larceny, or grand theft, not to mention the forgeries. It's a two-hundred-thousand-dollar crime. And it's state, not federal. In other words, guys, it's all yours."

"What's your game?" Dyer asked.

"Bankruptcy fraud is federal. The documents speak for themselves, gentlemen. The cases are open-and-shut, no way he can wiggle out. He forged the sigs, paid off Odell Grove and Jerrol Baker, and kept the rest for himself."

Dyer studied some papers and Musgrove asked, "And you think he's back in the country?"

"Well, we haven't seen him. You got any sources around town?"

"Not really, just the local gossip. I know Jake Brigance pretty well, bumped into him in court last week, but he's not talking."

Lenzini lifted another sheet of paper and frowned at it. "We've checked with the airlines, and no one of that name has entered the country in the past month. I'm sure he's using another name." He laid down the papers, took a sip of coffee, and said, gravely, "Gentlemen, I don't have to tell you how delicate this is. When you convene your grand jury—"

"You mean 'if' we convene," Dyer interrupted.

"Well, surely—"

"I'm in charge of our grand jury, Mr. Lenzini. I decide if and when it's called, without direction from the FBI. I'm sure the U.S. Attorney in Oxford would not want me meddling with his grand jury."

"Of course not, Mr. Dyer, but these crimes are serious and they're open-and-shut."

"Sure looks that way, doesn't it? However, we'll do our investigation and decide. I'm sure we'll indict, but we'll do it our way."

"Very well. As I was saying, this is a touchy situation because we're dealing with a man who knows how to disappear."

"Got it," Dyer snapped.

"We have to be very careful who we talk to about Stafford."

"Got it," Dyer snapped, even quicker.

After he left, Dyer and Musgrove reviewed the paperwork for half an hour, and what was obvious became even more so. Both had known Mack for years, though they were not close friends, and they were reluctant to get involved in a case that would send a fellow lawyer to jail. It was apparent that the victims, the clients who were bilked, had no knowledge of Mack's wrongdoing until the FBI told them about it.

But the more they talked, the more they liked the case. It was a nice change of pace from their daily docket of meth cookers, drug dealers, car thieves, and wife beaters. Rarely were they presented a case involving white-collar crime, and never had they seen one so blatant. Mack had chosen to steal from his clients, and it was their duty as representatives of the State to solve the crime and bring about justice.

Keeping it quiet would be the challenge.

(29)

On a sweltering Saturday, Mack was busy at the Varsity Bar & Grill, and as he puttered around and served the handful of customers, he kept one eye on the parking lot. At precisely 1:00 p.m., he saw a familiar car turn off Highland and park in the front.

It was a 1983 Mercury Cougar he had purchased used about two years before he left town. Lisa, of course, got the car in the divorce, along with everything else, and evidently it had now been handed down to his daughter. Margot bounced out of it and looked almost giddy at the thought of entering a college bar. She was dressed for college, in skin-tight jeans, sandals, and a plunging blouse that was almost indecent. He told himself not to say a word about her appearance.

He met her at the door and they retreated to the back of the restaurant. Mack flagged over a waiter, one he didn't like and who leered a bit too long at his daughter, and they ordered cheeseburgers and ice tea.

"I can't get a beer?" she asked, her first attempt to provoke him.

"You're seventeen years old, young lady. The law says twenty-one, plus you're driving today."

"I have an ID, says I'm twenty-four. Wanna see it?"

"No. I spend half my time checking fake IDs. Where'd you get it?"

"I'll never tell."

"Figures."

"Everybody has one, Mack."

"I'm still Mack."

"I like Mack better. You were never much for the Dad thing."

"May I ask the latest on your mother?"

The smile vanished and her eyes watered. The tea arrived in tall glasses and she took a sip. She gazed out a window and said, "Nothing has really changed, except that she's not eating much. She's weak and frail and, well, just pitiful, really." Her lip quivered and she closed her eyes and put a hand over her mouth. Mack patted her arm and whispered, "I'm so sorry."

The moment passed, and Margot stiffened her spine, smiled, and gritted her teeth. A tough kid, whom Mack was proud of.

She said, "Of course, I'm not making it any easier for her. Yesterday I asked if I could make this trip to Memphis by myself, told her I had an appointment with an admissions dude at Rhodes, and so on. Which is true. She didn't like the idea, said no, I couldn't come alone. We had dinner last night in the big house and she told Hermie and Honey about me coming to Memphis alone. They freaked, as usual. You'd have thought I wanted to walk naked through a ghetto. It turned into a pretty good fight. I reminded them that I've had my license for two years and have driven to Tupelo, with friends, several times. Hermie was growling and hissing and said I didn't know how to find Rhodes College. So I asked him where in the big city it's located. He guessed, got it wrong, then I laid it out perfectly: take Highway 78 into Memphis, fifty-four miles from here, stay on 78 after it becomes Lamar Avenue, then turn right on South Parkway, follow it north past Union, past Poplar, turn left and go west on Summer Avenue for about a block, the zoo's on the left and Rhodes is on the right. I nailed it. Helen even laughed. Mom smiled. Needless to say, I didn't mention the little detour here to the Varsity—left on Park, north on Highland, two blocks east on Southern—where I planned to meet you. That would've really upset them."

"So my name is still mud?"

"Worse than that. Anyway, Hermie was not impressed with my navigational skills. He said no, I couldn't go to Memphis alone. I decided to fight him because he's got to respect me. Before long, Helen and I will be living under his thumb and I can't stand the thought. He is not my father and he is not going to be my boss."

Mack had to smile. *Atta girl.*

"So we had a brawl."

"Who won?"

"Nobody wins a family brawl, you should know that. Everybody loses. I got up this morning and left the house. I stopped at the square, called Mom, told her I was on the way to Memphis. She told me to be careful and we swapped *I love yous.*"

"So your grandparents don't know?"

"Well, I'm sure they know by now. Don't get me wrong, Mack. I love my grandparents but I cannot imagine living with them. I pray every day that Mom can hang on for just a few more months. I know it's a selfish prayer, but then most of them are, don't you think?"

"I suppose."

Two large platters of cheeseburgers and fries landed in front of them and they spent a few moments fiddling with the condiments. The waiter was quite attentive and eager to flirt with Margot. Mack glared at him and was ready to bark.

After the waiter disappeared, Mack asked, "You're certain no one knows we're meeting, right?"

"Well, I've told no one. Can't speak for you."

"No suspicions?"

"None. I mean, a month ago you were hot news, but that sort of blew over. I heard Hermie tell Honey the other night that as far as he knew no one in Clanton has laid eyes on you." She ate half a fry, chewed like a teenager. "So you're living in Memphis, huh?"

"For the moment."

"What are your plans, Mack?"

"Don't know that I have any. I'll hang around for a while, make sure things are safe."

"Safe? How so?"

"I want to make sure no one is looking for me. There are some skeletons in the closet and I'd like to keep them there."

"That's what I figured. You stole a bunch of money and disappeared, right?"

"That's fairly accurate. I'm not proud of it."

"But you've kept the money, right? Why don't you just give the money back to the people you stole it from?"

"It's not that easy."

"Nothing is easy with you, Mack. Everything is so complicated."

To avoid a response, Mack took a large bite of his burger and looked around the restaurant. Two college boys at the bar were gawking at his daughter. After he swallowed, he said, "Yes, Margot, I've done a fine job of making my life extremely complicated. I'd rather skip the past and talk about your life, college, stuff like that. It's far more exciting."

"When will you ever tell me the truth?"

"Yes, when you turn twenty-one, I'll visit you in college and we'll have a long dinner, with drinks, and I'll tell you all the bad stuff I've done. Fair enough?"

"I suppose. I probably won't care by then."

"Let's hope not. Have you picked a college?"

"I'm looking. Rhodes might be fun, but it's too close to home. When Hermie was snarling last night he made it clear that 'the family,' as he likes to call it now, like he's in charge and making all the big decisions for us since Mom is on her deathbed—anyway, he said 'the family' will not pay private school tuition. He says it's ridiculous when there are so many good publics in Mississippi. I think the real reason is that he can't afford private tuition."

"That's hard to believe."

"I'm telling you, Mack, money is tight and getting tighter. Things are tense around there. And I get it. Their daughter is dying. They're about to inherit two teenage girls nobody really wants. Hermie's got competition with his business. Instead of planning a nice retirement, they're looking at the next few years and don't like what they see."

"Wasn't there talk about living with the Pettigrews?"

She rolled her eyes and said, "Oh give me a break. I'd rather stay in a homeless shelter. Those people are impossible." She bit into another fry and Mack noticed her eyes were wet again. The poor child was an emotional mess.

"Are you okay?" he asked.

"Just swell, Mack. It's such a great feeling to know that you're not wanted. When Mom dies we'll be forced to leave the only home we've ever known and go stay in someone else's house where we don't belong. And you share some of the blame, Mack."

"Yes, I do, and we've addressed that."

She took a deep breath, gritted her teeth, wiped her cheek, and said, "Yes, we have. Sorry."

"Don't apologize."

"I don't suppose you could move back and rescue us, could you?"

"No, not now anyway. I can't live in Clanton and I'm not completely sure things are safe around there. Plus, Hermie would hire every lawyer in town to keep me away."

"Did you ever like Hermie?"

"Not really."

She had only nibbled around the edges of her burger and chewed on some fries, but she was finished. She shoved her platter a few inches toward the center of the table and glanced around. In a lower voice, she said, "I need to tell you something, Mack. Mom likes to go over there and sit on the patio under the fans. It's not nearly as depressing as sitting around our house, so we've been over there a lot. I drive her over, she and Helen sit on the porch with Honey, and everybody whittles away the hours as the clock ticks. Hermie is hanging around too, and twice in the past week I've overheard him mention the FBI. I have no idea why."

Mack swallowed hard and glanced around. "Who was he talking to?"

"Don't know. He was on the phone and didn't know I was in the house. Kinda weird, right?"

"Something to ponder, I guess."

"I'll keep my ears open."

Any mention of the FBI bothered Mack. He appeared indifferent, but his appetite had vanished too.

Margot glanced at her watch and said, "I guess I should be going. I have a one p.m. appointment."

"Do you want me to go?"

"You mean like a real dad. Father and daughter, off to visit college campuses?"

"Something like that."

She smiled and said, "Sure, Pop, I'd be honored."

"You drive. I want to see you in city traffic."

"I can handle it better than you."

"We'll see."

(30)

Seven hours after she left home, Margot returned, and it seemed like days. She could not believe a simple, unhurried drive to Memphis and back could be so exhilarating, so liberating. When she crossed into Ford County, she actually slowed to fifty miles an hour and ignored the traffic behind her. In town, she circled through a fast-food hangout looking for a friend, but saw no one.

She had been locked down on death duty for months and the ordeal was not over. The last thing she wanted that Saturday afternoon was to sit in their gloomy little house and wait for the inevitable. The family had finally accepted the reality that Lisa was not going to improve, that the doctors had done everything and were finally giving up. The waiting was brutal; the uncertainty of when it would be over; the watching as she grew thinner and paler each day; the horror of seeing your mother inch closer and closer to the grave; the utter fear of life without her. Measurements came in strange ways: just last month she was still driving; just last week she was puttering around the kitchen baking cookies; yesterday she could barely get out of bed. Soon they would send for the nurse, an old babysitter who would care for her in the last days. It had all been arranged by the Bunnings. Margot and Helen were supposed to make the call and inform their grandparents when the moment was at hand.

Helen was in the den watching a movie. In a hushed tone she said, "She's resting. It's been a quiet day."

Margot sat on the sofa next to her sister and asked, "Is she upset with me?"

"No. She's had a good day. We spent most of it at Honey's, on the patio, but that exhausted her."

"Are they pissed?"

"They were at first, but Mom settled them down, told them to knock it off, said you can take care of yourself. How was Rhodes?"

"Beautiful, a really lovely place. Nice people. Very small, though."

"I can't believe you're going to college next year."

"I can't either."

"Can I go with you?"

They chuckled, then froze when they heard Lisa's voice. They went to her room and found her sitting up in bed with a big smile. Margot hugged her gently. She patted the pillows on both sides and the girls joined her in bed. She wanted to know all about Rhodes College and the trip to Memphis, and Margot spared no details, except, of course, the rather significant detour to the Varsity and lunch with Mack. She pulled out colorful brochures from the college and went on about a conversation she had with a real professor. Rhodes was definitely on her short list. Lisa said they would worry about the money later.

On the one hand it was a relief to see her so excited about her oldest going off to college, but on the other hand it was heartbreaking to know that she would not be around to share in the experience. Margot mentioned a few other colleges she might visit in the coming weeks, schools that were further away from home. Lisa encouraged this. She was certain her parents would step up and make sure the girls were properly educated, whatever the cost. Margot had Mack's promise, the ace up her sleeve she could not discuss.

Lisa dozed off again and the girls eased out of the room.

Helen began crying and said, "She's hardly eaten a bite in the past five days."

They debated whether to call their grandparents and decided to wait. It was a long night as Lisa grew irritable and complained of pain. The girls rarely left her side and napped fitfully whenever she was awake. At dawn, Margot called Honey with an update. The nurse arrived two hours later and cranked up the morphine. The Bunnings stopped by on the way to church and had a chat with Lisa, who happened to be awake and lucid. They never missed church and wouldn't think of it now, even as their daughter drifted away.

Of course, they asked for prayer during the service and passed along the grim news that Lisa's condition was deteriorating. Few things aroused a bunch of Baptists like the rituals of a final passing, and by 3:00 p.m. Sunday afternoon the caravan of casseroles was underway. Most of the friends were thoughtful enough to stop at the porch and hand over the dishes and settle for tearful hugs, but some of the pushier ones breached the perimeter and got inside where they loitered in the cramped kitchen and balanced paper plates while straining for a look down the hall at the bedrooms. Several of the older gossips, true veterans of the glories of funerals, even asked Honey if they could have a word with Lisa. Honey knew damned well that all they wanted was the visual so they could hurry off and talk about how gaunt Lisa looked. Honey declined and even posted herself in the passageway to ward off any trespassers.

Helen retreated to the bedroom and kept a vigil at her mother's side. Margot, weary of that room, took charge of the front and welcomed each visitor with a big, sad smile that was completely phony, but only she knew it. She became quite the lady of the house, and Hermie, who only the day before wanted to reprimand her for her trip to Memphis, beamed with pride as his often wayward granddaughter charmed the crowd. The day dragged on as the food piled up in the kitchen, but the crowd began to thin as 6:00 p.m. approached and their friends headed back to church.

The nurse moved into Helen's room for the duration. The girls slept in Margot's bed and took turns throughout the night checking on Lisa and whispering to the nurse. By Monday morning, she was not responsive and her breathing was even slower.

(31)

Nick Lenzini was leaving the FBI office in Oxford Tuesday morning for a quick trip to Clanton when he got word that Lisa Stafford had passed. Two hours later, he parked near the courthouse and slipped into the law offices of the Sullivan firm. His meeting with Walter was at eleven thirty.

Once coffee was served, Nick began solemnly, "Very sorry about Mrs. Stafford. I know she was a friend."

"Thank you," Walter said gravely. "A lovely girl. I've known her all her life. This firm has represented her family for thirty years. Great people."

"What will happen to the girls?"

"Oh, the family will circle the wagons, make the best of it."

"No sign of Mack?"

Walter grunted and took a sip. "I was planning to ask you the same thing. What's the latest?"

"Have you talked to Judd Morrissette?"

"Not in the past two weeks."

"Well, he's ready to go to the grand jury. Our investigation is basically done. Looks like an open-and-shut case. Problem is, we can't seem to find Mack. That's one reason I'm here. I don't suppose you have any ideas where he might be?"

"That's your job, isn't it?"

"It is, of course. And we're looking, though we haven't sent in the bloodhounds yet. Given his penchant for disappearing, the U.S. Attorney would like to have him in our sights before there is an indictment."

"That's smart. But no, I don't know of anyone who has actually seen Mack since he supposedly resurfaced. It's safe to assume he's living somewhere else. His mother still lives in Greenwood, right?"

"Yes, and we're keeping an eye there. Have funeral arrangements been completed?"

"Yes, Saturday at two p.m."

"Don't suppose Mack would make an appearance, would he?"

Walter laughed and said, "I assure you, Mr. Lenzini, that the last place you'll find Mack Stafford is the First Baptist Church this Saturday."

"I suppose you're right. It'll be okay if we stop by, take a seat in the balcony?"

"Sinners are always welcome. It's open to the public."

(32)

Sunday morning, the day after Lisa's funeral, Lucien Wilbanks entered Jake's suite of offices through the rear door. He used the same key he had been using for decades. It was Jake's office, but then it wasn't. The law firm of Wilbanks & Wilbanks had been founded there in the 1940s by Lucien's grandfather. Lucien had run the place until he was disbarred in 1979, a year after he had hired young Jake Brigance right out of law school.

Lucien still owned the spacious suite and leased it to Jake for a modest rent. Part of the deal was the understanding that he could come and go as he pleased. He kept a small windowless office on the first floor, far away from Jake's domain upstairs, and he kept to himself as he read the Sunday papers and smoked his pipe and drank his coffee and bourbon. Sunday mornings were his favorites because the square was deserted, the stores were closed, there was no traffic, and everyone was in church. Lucien had given up on organized religion when he was fourteen years old.

He was in the same conference room Mack and Margot had used, at exactly 9:14, when he heard the first sounds. He glanced at his watch, knowing full well that Jake was in church and no one else would come near the office that morning. Since he had practically grown up in the place, he knew every window, hallway, hiding place. He stepped into the copy room and peeked through the blinds into the alley that ran behind the row of buildings facing the courthouse. Surprisingly, there were two men fiddling with the rear door that opened into the kitchen. They were dressed in matching navy shirts with the words CUSTOM ELECTRIC in bold letters across their backs. They wore black rubber gloves and black foot covers.

Several things were wrong with it. First, Lucien had lived in Clanton his entire life and never heard of such a company. Second, no one worked on Sunday morning. Third, if they had been hired by Jake, why were they trying to sneak in the rear door? Fourth, they kept glancing around as if guilty as hell. Fifth, rubber gloves and foot covers were never used by repairmen in Clanton.

They managed to open the door and enter the kitchen. Lucien retreated to the shadows and listened carefully. The two men whispered to each other as they quickly moved through the downstairs. They missed Lucien as he slid between some bookshelves. They hurried upstairs, quietly opening and closing every door, then they were back by the receptionist's desk, where they opened their tool kits and made their preparations. Next to the copy room was a large closet packed with wires running to everything—thermostats, AC units, phones, fuse boxes, electric meters.

Lucien stayed in the dark and listened. The men were whispering about phone lines, receivers, transmitters, with some slang that was indecipherable. They were quick and efficient, obviously skilled, and at 9:31 they simply disappeared. Lucien caught a glimpse of them as they left through the same rear door, locking it behind. He waited a few minutes, then moved slowly into the kitchen and checked the door. A pot of fresh black coffee was sitting on the counter, partially obscured by a roll of paper towels. If the men had seen the coffee, they would have known someone had just brewed it. They should have smelled the aroma.

He poured another cup and returned to his desk. Who was behind Custom Electric? The local cops wouldn't have the capability. The state police did, but there was nothing in Jake's office at the moment that would interest them. Lucien knew virtually every case, because he and Jake talked weekly and enjoyed discussing his clients. Was Jake cheating on Carla? Or was she cheating on him? Either scenario seemed highly unlikely. They adored each other and Lucien would never believe that they were fooling around. Could it be another lawyer crooked enough to tap Jake's phones? Highly unlikely. Such outrageous behavior would lead to a disbarment, something Lucien knew a lot about. In all of his years as a lawyer and now as an observer, he had never known of a case where one law firm illegally cavesdropped on another.

It had to be the FBI. They were on to Mack Stafford and figured Jake knew where he was.

Lucien was startled, then amused. What fun Jake could have knowing the FBI was listening.

He finished his newspapers and dug through some old law-books. He smoked his pipe, sat on the balcony outside Jake's big office and watched the courthouse, and at noon had a reasonable serving of Jack Daniel's. He napped for an hour, and at 2:00 p.m. headed for Jake's house, assuming lunch would be over. Carla invited him in but he preferred to sit on the back terrace, in the shade. Jake joined him and she brought them ice tea, and when she closed the door Lucien described what had happened that morning.

Jake was stunned and could think of no reason the FBI, or anyone else, would be listening to his phone calls. Indeed, things were so slow around the office that he was contemplating another painful trip to the bank to beg for more credit.

"So it has to be Mack, right?" Lucien asked.

Jake was flabbergasted, and also angry at the intrusion. When his thoughts cleared, his first impulse was to hire a private detective to inspect his phones, to confirm things. Lucien didn't like the idea because he had no doubt about what had happened. And, why include anyone else? Someone might say too much. It was best to play along and be careful about what he said on the phone. His office had not been bugged, only the phones.

He said, "It's safe to assume they're listening here, too. You'd better tell Carla."

"Of course," Jake said, dreading that conversation.

"And you gotta tell Harry Rex."

"They can't bug his lawyer's phones, can they?"

"They can and they will. You can't trust the FBI. Hell, you can't trust anyone."

"Do I tell Mack?"

Lucien sipped his tea and considered this. "I'd be careful. I'd whisper this to Harry Rex and let him deal with it."

"You whisper it. I'm afraid to use the phones. Tell him to meet me on your front porch at five this afternoon."

As soon as Lucien left, Carla was on the patio and asking, "What was that all about?"

"You are not going to believe it." He told her everything, and she did not believe it. His words of caution were not well received. Assume someone is listening to every phone, including those in our house. Use them as always, keep things normal, but stay away from sensitive matters. And whatever you do, don't mention Mack Stafford or anyone in his family.

Carla was furious at the violation and wanted to hire someone to confirm the wiretaps. They had to be illegal and she wanted something done. Jake promised her he would get to the bottom of it, he just needed some time. He was stunned too and trying to clear his thoughts. He and Harry Rex would meet at Lucien's and decide what to do.

But that afternoon they met at Lucien's and couldn't agree on what to do. They assumed that Harry Rex's phones were tapped too, and he was ready for war. The surveillance was illegal, in his opinion, and he wanted to sue the government. Lucien kept things calm and thought they could use the knowledge to their advantage, or at least have some fun with it.

(33)

Monday morning, Jake's first phone call, and the first with a potential audience, was to the circuit clerk's office across the street, routine business. He made three more and tried to grow accustomed to the possibility that someone else was listening. He was careful with his language and tried to sound natural. It was still difficult to believe. He went downstairs to the kitchen, poured some more coffee, walked to the closet, stared at the phone lines and wires running everywhere, and kicked himself because he didn't know beans about his own systems. Somewhere hidden in one of those boxes was a wiretap. Touching nothing, he retreated and returned to his office. At precisely 11:00 a.m., as rehearsed, he called Harry Rex and they discussed a zoning dispute they had been arguing about for three months. As usual, Harry Rex showed no signs of controlling his tongue, regardless of who might be listening.

Then Jake said, "Look, something's come up. You're alone, right?"

"Of course I'm alone. I'm locked in my office. It's Monday morning and half of my idiot clients out there have either guns or knives. What do you want?"

"I heard from Mack."

A long pause, in which both Jake and Harry Rex smiled at the visual of some half-asleep FBI flunky with a headset getting jolted in the ass with the reference to Mack.

Quietly, suspiciously, Harry Rex asked, "Where is he?"

"Says he's living in a cheap apartment on the south end of Tupelo. Wants us to drive over this afternoon for a drink."

"Where's he been all this time?"

"He's not too generous with the facts, but he did mention a trip to Florida. Now he's back and says he's found a job."

"A job? What's he want with a job? I thought he stole enough."

Harry Rex thought this was clever, sort of a left-handed admission that his client had indeed stolen something. Jake smiled too. Both were almost snickering at the fun and games.

"We didn't talk about that, but he said he's bored and needs to get busy. Said he's going to work as a paralegal in Jimmy Fuller's law office."

"Fuller? Why's he working for a crook like that?"

"I like Jimmy. Anyway, he wants to meet us at the Merigold at six."

"I got four piles of shit on my desk and a nasty divorce trial first thing in the morning."

"Since when do you prepare for trial?"

"And I got a room full of blubbering women out there all wanting me to hold their hands."

"What else is new? We really can't say no. I'll be there at four thirty."

"All right, all right."

With his ever-expanding girth and natural lack of coordination, Harry Rex did not enter the passenger side as much as he crashed onto the seat and rocked the car from side to side. As soon as he slammed the door he asked, "You think your car is bugged too?"

"I doubt it," Jake said.

"Kinda weird talkin' on the phone with the FBI in the background."

"Tell me about it."

"I need a beer."

"It's four thirty."

"You sound like my wife."

"Which one?"

"You gonna chirp all the way to Tupelo?"

"Probably. Any thoughts about the penalties for impeding a federal investigation?"

"Sure. You?"

"Yep. I did some research this afternoon and I think we're okay. We're not touching the investigation, if in fact there is one. We're just playing cat-and-mouse with the FBI."

"Sounds harmless to me, unless of course we get caught."

"We're driving to Tupelo to have a drink with Mack, who, as far as we know, is not under investigation. We have not met with the FBI and do not know what they're up to. So, we're fine. So far."

"Okay, so why are we doing this?" Harry Rex pointed to a gas station. "Pull in there. You want a beer?"

"No, I'm driving."

"So. Can't drive with a beer in one hand?"

"I prefer not to. We're doing this to see if the FBI shows up at the bar so we can confirm it's the FBI."

"Brilliant. And how are you supposed to know if and when the FBI shows up in the bar? Ask them to whip out their badges?"

"Haven't got that far yet. I'll take a Diet Coke."

Harry Rex rolled himself out of the car and went inside.

(34)

The Merigold Lounge was one of three well-known bars on the west side of Tupelo, in Lee County, which happened to be wet. For fifty miles in all directions the counties were dry as a bone. The drinkers who lived in those small towns and rural places had little choice but to drive to the big city for refreshments. Back home, most of them continued to support bans on the sale of all alcoholic beverages.

At 6:00 p.m. there were thirteen vehicles parked in the paved lot to the side of the lounge. The main entrance did not face the highway, giving more cover to those who slipped in and out. Of the thirteen, six were sedans, six were pickup trucks, and one was a white van. A quick scan of the license plates revealed that the patrons came from four different counties. Inside the van, two FBI technicians worked the cameras, a Minolta XL with a long-range lens, and a Sony high-def video recorder. Through one-way glass, they shot and filmed every person who entered and left the Merigold.

The problem with the van was that someone had painted CUSTOM ELECTRIC on the outside panels, along with phone numbers. Jake and Harry Rex chuckled at this and couldn't believe their good luck, nor could they believe the FBI's sloppiness.

"Well, well," Jake said as he parked. "They're already here."

"Don't smile for the cameras," Harry Rex said as they got out and went inside. They found a table with four chairs in a corner and sat with their backs to the wall. A waitress arrived and they ordered beers and a platter of fries. A jukebox near a dance floor played country tunes. The Merigold was a higher-end lounge and not known for bad behavior. Jake had been there a few times over the years. Harry Rex dropped in at every chance. They ignored the others and engaged in what appeared to be serious conversation. At 6:15, Jake glanced at his watch and looked around. There were no obvious electricians. Several of the men even wore ties.

Nick Lenzini sat alone sipping a soft drink and pretending to read a newspaper. Though he had never seen Jake or Harry Rex, the boys in the van had radioed him when they were entering. He was excited at the possibility of finally laying eyes on Mack Stafford, but managed to appear bored. He was quite smug with his success in convincing a federal magistrate to allow wiretaps.

Jake and Harry Rex sipped beers from frosted mugs and nibbled on fries and seemed to grow irritated as the minutes passed. No sign of Mack.

More drinkers arrived and the lounge was almost full. At 6:30, Jake went to the men's room and walked beside Nick's table. The two made eye contact for a second, and Jake thought the guy could pass for an agent—clean-cut, dark suit, no tie, a bit out of place. When he returned he fetched two more beers from the bar and sat them in front of Harry Rex. Both looked at their watches and frowned. Whoever they were supposed to meet was running late. Even later, at 7:00, they paid their tab and left the lounge, showing as much frustration as possible. The van was still there. Jake started his engine as Harry Rex grabbed the car phone and punched in the phone number of Custom Electric. Whatever it had once been, it was now disconnected.

They had a good laugh as they sped away, certain they had outfoxed the FBI while doing nothing wrong. When the laughter died, they debated what to do next. The Feds were after Mack, which could only mean an indictment was in the works.

(35)

The following day, Jake drove to the Stafford home to deliver a chocolate cake Carla had baked, along with an arrangement of flowers from their favorite florist. Margot answered the door and invited him into the den. Honey, her grandmother, was there, and Jake solemnly passed along his condolences. The house was as gloomy as a funeral parlor. They were gracious and thankful and invited him to stay for coffee and cake. He had no desire to, but he needed to have a word with Margot. They sat at the kitchen table and managed a laugh at all the food that lined the counters.

"Would you like a pound or two of fried chicken?" Honey asked with a smile.

"Or half a dozen casseroles?" Margot chimed in.

Helen stepped in to say hello and Jake again told her how sorry he and Carla were. All three looked as though they had been crying for a week, which was probably true. Helen soon disappeared and Honey whispered, "She is really struggling. I guess we all are."

Jake could not respond and took another bite. The phone rang and Honey went to answer it. Jake quickly handed Margot a small envelope and whispered, "Read this later. It's confidential."

She nodded as if she knew, and stuffed it in her jeans.

He finished his cake and coffee and said he had to get back to the office. Honey thanked him again, and Margot showed him to the front door and onto the porch.

He waved to her there as he drove away.

The note instructed her to avoid his telephones. If she wanted to talk, stop by the office or call his secretary at her home. And, he passed along Mack's number.

(36)

The federal grand jury met in the U.S. Courthouse in Oxford for its regular monthly session. Eighteen registered voters from eleven counties were currently serving a six-month term, and most were eager to be done with it.

The docket began with the usual string of drug cases—selling, manufacturing, distributing—and within an hour fourteen indictments had been approved. It was depressing work and the grand jurors were bored with drug felonies. Next was a slightly more interesting case involving a gang of car thieves that had been rampaging for the past year. Five more indictments.

J. McKinley Stafford was next. Judd Morrissette, the assistant U.S. Attorney, handled the presentation and recited the facts as he now understood them. Lawyer Stafford diverted some settlement funds away from his clients and into his own bank accounts, which in itself was a state crime, not federal, but he then filed for bankruptcy and hid the money.

Special Agent Nick Lenzini took over and presented copies of the settlement agreements, the bankruptcy petition, affidavits from the jilted clients Odell Grove and Jerrol Baker, an affidavit from Freda Wilson, and the wire transfers.

Morrissette presented evidence from the IRS that Mr. Stafford had not bothered to file tax returns for the past four years.

One grand juror asked, "Is he that lawyer over in Clanton who stole the money and disappeared?"

"That's correct," Morrissette answered.

"Have y'all found him?"

"Not yet, but we're getting close."

In less than an hour, Mack was indicted for one count of bankruptcy fraud, with a maximum sentence of five years in prison and a fine of $250,000. For good measure, the grand jury also hit him with four counts of tax evasion, with similar penalties. At Morrissette's insistence, the grand jury voted to seal the indictments until further notice. Mr. Stafford was a significant flight risk.

(37)

Jake was in chancery court, along with at least a dozen other lawyers, waiting for Judge Reuben Atlee to assume the bench and begin signing routine orders. Harry Rex was resting his ample backside on a table and regaling the crowd with the story of a divorce client who had just fired him for the third time. Jake listened to the story for the third time. As order was called by the bailiff, Harry Rex whispered, "Meet me upstairs in the law library, as soon as possible."

The law library was on the third floor of the courthouse and was seldom used. In fact, it saw so little traffic that the county supervisors were toying with the idea of getting rid of the outdated and dusty collection of ancient tomes and using the space for storage. The lawyers and judges were fighting back, thus creating another rancorous turf battle small towns are famous for. In years past, Harry Rex had been known to eavesdrop on jury deliberations through a heating vent, but a renovation tightened up the walls.

When they were alone, he said, "Lowell Dyer is calling a special meeting of his grand jury for tomorrow, and they're meeting down in Smithfield. Believe that?"

Jake was thoroughly baffled. "Say what?"

"You heard me. The Ford County grand jury will convene itself in the courthouse in Smithfield."

"In another county?"

"That's right. Ain't never heard of it before. I checked the statute and it's pretty vague, but it does not prevent him from doing so."

"Any idea why?"

"Sure. It's all a big secret. He has informed his grand jury that the meetin' is extremely confidential and they are to tell no one about it."

"Mack?"

"I'd bet on it. Can you think of another crime in this county in the past year that anyone gives a shit about? There's been nothin'. Break-ins, burglaries, honky-tonk fights, the usual run-of-the-mill crap, but nothin' even remotely interesting."

Jake was shaking his head. "No, folks are behaving. I'm in the middle of a long dry run in my office. We need some more crime."

"It's gotta be Mack. Dyer's afraid Mack'll pull another vanishin' act and disappear. So, he gets an indictment out of town, sits on it until somebody finds Mack, then arrests him. And, I'll bet he's doin' what the Feds tell him."

Other than the startling news, the obvious question was: How did Harry Rex know about a secret meeting of the grand jury? Jake wanted to ask, but he knew there would be no answer. His close friend moved in mysterious circles and had a wide net of informants. Sometimes he shared the inside dirt, often he did not, but he never revealed a source.

Jake asked, "So you think the Feds are a step ahead?"

"I'll bet they have an indictment and are sittin' on it. They gave Dyer the green light. It makes sense and it's a smart move. You got federal charges and you got state charges, multiple indictments, and suddenly everyone is lookin' for Mack."

"You're his lawyer. What's your advice?"

"Get the hell out of town. Again."

(38)

Two weeks after her mother's funeral, and ten days after moving into the home of her grandparents, Margot woke up on a Saturday at 8:00 a.m., an early hour for her, and quickly showered and dressed in jeans and sneakers. At the breakfast table she was polite to Hermie and Honey because they were trying to be polite to her, but the tension was palpable. They had some rules they wanted to impose, and Margot seemed determined to ignore them. One rule was about respect—respect for elders, for grandparents, for her guardians now. She accepted this and asked that they respect her as a seventeen-year-old young woman who had a mind of her own. She had an appointment at 1:00 p.m. that day with an admissions counselor at Millsaps College in Jackson, and she was certainly capable of driving herself down there and back. The trip to Rhodes in Memphis had been a breeze. Hermie and Honey didn't like the idea at all and had made the mistake of saying no. A disagreement followed, and though all sides managed to keep their cool and not say anything they would regret later, two things became apparent: (1) the Bunnings were not quick enough to verbally spar with Margot, and (2) she had no plans to spend the next year taking orders from them.

She left at ten and thoroughly enjoyed the open road, all alone with her choice of music and the entire day to spend as she wanted.

She had never visited Millsaps, knew no one there, and was certain she wouldn't fit. Like Rhodes, it was too close to home. But she would visit and collect the brochures to leave on the kitchen table. And she would apply there in the fall, as she would Rhodes and Ole Miss and maybe some others not too far away. She would lean toward Ole Miss because the in-state tuition chatter would ease Hermie's concerns. She would make the usual fuss over the application process, feign the usual angst and anxiety, and include her grandparents from time to time to make them feel better, but she would not tell them about the two art schools out west. Nor would she tell Helen, at least not anytime soon. She was waiting for Helen to grow up and leave behind the adolescent routine, but there was little sign of progress.

Their father's disappearance, coupled with their parents' divorce, had forced Margot to mature and distrust the motives of almost everyone. She guarded her emotions and feelings and rarely offered friendship. She had made the decision to leave home and return only when necessary, and she would soon lose contact with the girls she had grown up with. The sooner the better. A big world was waiting. She wanted her sister to grow up and get away too, after high school, but Helen seemed trapped in an almost pre-teen state of silly emotions and perpetual gloom. Since Lisa's death she had gravitated more toward Honey. They were still sharing tears, something Margot had grown weary of.

She found Millsaps in central Jackson and stopped by a cafeteria for a quick sandwich. At one o'clock, she met an admissions counselor who went through the standard spiel—small school, one thousand students, serious about liberal arts, plenty of extracurricular activities, sports, intramurals, every club you could think of. It was all covered in the brochures. She joined a group of five high-schoolers and walked the campus with a third-year student who just loved the place and never wanted to leave. They sat on benches under an old oak and sipped sodas while their guide answered questions.

After two hours on a campus she would never see again, Margot was ready to leave. Her group broke up, and as she was walking away, her father suddenly materialized from between two buildings. They walked stride for stride until they were far away from anyone else.

"So how do you like Millsaps?" he asked.

"It's nice. I'm sure I'll apply here. Where have you been?"

"Here and there." He pointed and said, "The football field is over there and it's not locked."

"How long have you been here?" she asked.

"Long enough to scope out the campus."

"You act like you're being followed."

"These days you never know."

They walked through an open gate, climbed ten rows of bleachers, and sat next to each other, but not that close. In a far end zone a maintenance man puttered along on a riding mower and trimmed the immaculate turf.

After an awkward pause, Mack asked, "So how's home life?"

She didn't answer for a long time and finally said, "It's okay, I guess. Everybody's trying real hard."

"I'm sorry about your mom, Margot."

"That sounds weird, coming from you."

"Okay, but what am I supposed to say? No, I don't miss Lisa, but I'm saddened by her death. She was far too young. I'm trying to be polite and offer my condolences."

"So offered. We'll survive, somehow."

Another awkward gap. "How's Helen?"

"Still crying a lot. Pretty pathetic, really."

"Have you told her about our meetings?"

"No. She can't handle it. She's overwhelmed as it is. If I told her you're back and trying to weasel into the picture she'd probably have a total breakdown."

"Weasel?"

"What do you call it?"

"I'm trying to reestablish some type of relationship with my daughters, beginning with you. I've said my apologies and all that, and if you want to flog me some more for being a coward and a deadbeat and a crook, then go right ahead."

"I'm tired of it too."

"Good to hear. I'd like to be your father."

"I think we're getting there."

"That's nice, because I have some bad news."

She shrugged as if it couldn't matter. "Hit me."

"I have to leave again."

"No surprise there. That's what you do, Mack. Things get rough, then slither out of town again. What's up this time?"

"Well, I'm not sure, but I think the cops are closing in. I need to disappear for a while and let things cool down."

She shrugged again and went silent.

"I'm sorry, Margot. My quiet little homecoming has not gone exactly as I planned."

"Since I have no idea what you're talking about, how am I supposed to respond?"

"No, just try to understand. I don't want to leave again. I'd rather hang around here, stay close to you and Helen, and live a normal life. I'm tired of running, Margot. It's not a good life, and I really missed my girls."

Slowly, she lifted a hand and wiped her eyes. For a long time they gazed down at the field and listened to the lawn mower. Finally, she asked, "How long will you be gone?"

"I don't know. It's likely that I'll face some criminal charges and you'll probably see something in the newspaper. I apologize again. I'm not going to jail, Margot, and that's why I'm leaving. My lawyers will handle everything, and with time, they'll work out a deal."

"What kind of deal?"

"Money. Fines. Restitution."

"You can buy your way out of trouble?"

"Something like that. It's not always fair but that's the way things work."

"Whatever. I don't understand any of this and don't really want to."

"I don't blame you. Just understand that I have no choice but to 'slither out of town,' as you say."

"Whatever."

"I want to keep in touch. Mr. Brigance has a secretary, Alicia."

"I've met her."

"Stop by the office and she'll give you some envelopes addressed to me at a building in Panama. When I write to you, I'll send the letters to Alicia. Call her at home if you need something, but do not use the office line."

"Is this illegal or something?"

"No, I would never ask you to do something illegal. Please trust me."

"I was just beginning to, and now you're disappearing again."

"I'm sorry, Margot, but I have no choice."

"And what about the tuition thing?"

"I made you a promise and I intend to keep it. Found a school?"

"Yep. Rocky Mountain College of Art and Design, in Denver."

"Sounds pretty exotic."

"I plan to study fashion design. I've already talked to an admissions person."

"Good for you. I can tell you're excited."

"I can't wait, Mack. Just don't screw up the tuition."

"Got it covered. Can I come visit?"

"Are you serious?"

"Yes, I'm serious. Look, Margot, I'm determined to be a part of your life."

"Are you sure that's a good thing?"

"What a smart-ass." Mack couldn't help but chuckle. She smiled too and soon both were laughing.

They walked to her car without a word.

When it was time for the goodbyes, Mack said, "I gotta go. Please keep in touch."

Her eyes were moist as she looked at him. "Be careful, Mack."

"Always." He took a step closer and said, "I'll always be your father and I'll always love you."

She reached up for an embrace, and Mack finally got the hug.

She sniffled and said, "I love you, Dad."

(39)

Mack drove an hour west on Interstate 20 to the river town of Vicksburg and took an exit. He entered the grounds of the national military park commemorating the crucial Battle of Vicksburg, another one lost by the South. He parked near the visitors center, walked through the cemetery, and followed a pathway to the top of a small hill where some picnic tables were arranged in an opening, with batteries of cannons nearby standing guard. In the distance, the Mississippi River curled for miles. The tables were empty but for one. A couple of Bubbas sat with a shoebox filled with roasted peanuts between them. Empty shells covered the ground. Harry Rex was drinking a beer from a tall can. Jake had a bottle of water. Both wore jeans, golf shirts, and caps.

It was six forty-five. Harry Rex looked at his watch and said, "You're fifteen minutes late."

"Good afternoon, fellas," Mack said, as he scooped up a handful of peanuts.

"How was Millsaps?" Jake asked.

"Nice, but too close to home. She wants some distance."

"Not a bad idea," Harry Rex said, chomping.

"What do you know?" Mack asked.

"Indictments, Ford County grand jury. Don't know how many counts, but one's enough. I suspect the Feds are doing the same."

"I'll bet Herman's behind this," Mack said. "Someone's pushing hard."

"He's the type," Harry Rex said.

"Yes, he is. He's wounded because his daughter is dead and now he has two teenagers to raise. I guess I underestimated the danger."

Jake said, "All of us did."

Mack asked, "What are the chances of cutting a deal?"

Harry Rex cracked another peanut, flung the shell on the ground, added to the pile, and looked at Jake. "You're the criminal guy."

Mack said, "What's your opinion, Jake?"

"As a friend, and not as a lawyer, I'd say it'll run its course. It'll hit the newspapers and be the news for a month, and if you're arrested—"

"There won't be an arrest."

"Okay, if they don't find you, then pretty soon they'll lose interest. Let a few months go by, maybe a year, then test the waters. See if they'll take some fines and restitution and forget about it."

"That's what I'm thinking."

Harry Rex said, "As your lawyer, I advise you to turn yourself in and face the music. I cannot advise you to flee the country."

"Jake, as a friend?"

"Flee the country. Nothing good will happen if you stay here. Go back to Costa Rica and live the good life."

Mack smiled and ate another peanut. He faced them both and said, "Thanks, guys, for everything. I'll be in touch." And with that, he abruptly turned and walked away and disappeared down the path.

He drove six hours and stopped at an interstate motel near Waco, where he slept late Sunday morning. He had biscuits and eggs at a truck stop, then drove seven hours to Laredo. He left the Volvo DL in the lot of a cheap motel, unlocked and with keys in the ignition, and caught a taxi. He carried a small backpack with some clothes, $40,000 in U.S. cash, and four passports.

At dusk, he walked across the bridge over the Rio Grande and left the country.

STRAWBERRY MOON

(1)

It took a federal lawsuit to get the shelving for Cody's collection of paperbacks, almost two thousand of them. They covered three walls of his eight-by-ten cell and were arranged in near perfect order by the author's last name. He had read and reread every one of them and could find any book in an instant. Almost all were fiction. He had little interest in science or history or religion, boring subjects, in his opinion. The fiction took him to other worlds, other places, and he spent most of his twenty-three hours a day in solitary with his nose stuck in a novel.

The books were everywhere—paperback only because the wise men who ran the prison had decreed long ago that a hardback could be used as a weapon, at least by inmates. United States crime data had yet to record a single incident of a victim being slaughtered by a hardback book, but such was life on the outside. On death row almost everything was deemed potentially dangerous. And besides, the well-used books were gifts from a lady who lived on a pension and certainly couldn't afford to buy and ship heavier novels. Plus, there was always the question of shelf space. The collection was now twelve years old, and from all indications was about to come to an end. If Cody dodged the latest bullet, and it appeared as though he would not, his cell would soon be overrun with books. Transferring to a larger one was out of the question—they were all eight-by-ten.

In one corner there was a stainless-steel sink and toilet, and above it a small color television was mounted to the wall. Books were stacked next to the toilet and on top of the television. It was a Motorola, a gift from a charity in Belgium, and when it arrived almost ten years ago Cody burst into tears and cried for hours, overwhelmed at his good fortune. He and the other inmates lucky enough to have televisions were allowed to watch anything on the networks from 8:00 a.m. to 10:00 p.m., an arbitrary schedule imposed by the wise men with no explanation.

His bed was a concrete slab with a foam-rubber mattress, and for the last fourteen years he had struggled to get comfortable enough to sleep. Above it, there was once a top bunk with a metal frame, back when each cell on The Row housed two men. Then the rules changed, the bunks were replaced by concrete, and Cody filled the wall above him with rows of books.

The spines of the paperbacks were a lively mix of all colors and brightened his sad little world. When he took a break from reading, he would often sit on his bunk and stare at the walls, covered from floor to ceiling, as high as he could reach, with a dizzying assemblage of stories that had taken him around the world and back many times. Most of the men on The Row were insane. Solitary confinement does that to any human. But Cody's mind was hyper, active, sharp, and all because of his books.

On occasion he would loan one to a guy down The Row, but only to those he liked. A short list. Failure to return them promptly would cause a ruckus, with the guards intervening. Once a week a trustee would arrive pushing his cart from the main prison library and offer two titles, never more than two. As usual, they saved the worst for death row and the paperbacks were all well worn, dog-eared, smudged, and often missing covers and even pages. What kind of creep carefully removes a page or two just to screw with the next reader? Prison was full of them.

Though Cody had never seen the prison library, he suspected his was in far better shape and had more titles.

His fourth wall was nothing but thick bars, with a door in the center and a slit for food trays. Directly across the hall was Johnny Lane, a black guy who had killed his wife and two stepchildren in a drug-fueled rage. When he arrived nine years earlier he was basically illiterate. Cody had patiently taught him to read and shared many of his books. Then Johnny got religion and read only the Bible. Years ago he decided that God was calling him to preach and he delivered long sermons at full throttle up and down The Row until the complaints finally silenced him. When it became apparent that God was not going to rescue him, he withdrew even further into his cell and covered the bars with bedsheets and old cardboard so that his isolation was complete. He refused the twice-weekly showers and the one hour of daily exercise in the yard. He declined most of the food and had not shaved in years. Cody could not remember the last time he had seen or spoken to Johnny, who slept on a slab twenty feet away.

The prison had strict rules about what could be kept in a death row cell. Ten books was the max until Cody had filed suit. The warden at the time had been furious when he lost in federal court. In fourteen years, Cody had filed, on his own and with no lawyer, a total of five lawsuits. Books, television, food, exercise, and he'd won them all but air-conditioning and proper heat.

But his litigating days were over. Indeed, all of his days were over. He had three hours to live. His last meal had been ordered—pepperoni pizza and a strawberry milkshake.

(2)

The boss of death row was Marvin, a burly African American guard who had been keeping things in order for over a decade. He liked his turf because the men were isolated and caused little trouble. As a general rule, he treated them well and expected the same from the other guards, and most complied. Some, though, were hard-asses, a few could even be cruel. Marvin wasn't there twenty-four hours a day and couldn't watch everything.

A buzzer rattles at the far end of the hall and a heavy door opens with a thud. Marvin soon appears at the cell. He looks through the bars and asks, "How you doin', Cody?"

The Row is quiet for a change, the only noise the muted sounds from a few televisions. The usual bantering between the bars isn't there. It's a big night, time for an execution, and the inmates are withdrawn into their own worlds, their own thoughts, and the reality that they are all sentenced to death and this moment is inevitable.

Cody is sitting on his bed, staring at the television. He nods at Marvin as he stands and points his remote at the screen. The voice of a news anchor grows louder:

"The execution of Cody Wallace is still on schedule. Despite the usual last-minute appeals by the lawyers, the execution should take place in about three hours, at ten p.m. to be exact. A petition for clemency is still pending in the governor's office but there is no word."

Cody takes a step closer to the television.

"It has been fourteen years since Wallace, now age twenty-nine, was convicted of killing Dorothy and Earl Baker in their rural home during a botched break-in and robbery."

On the screen, the news anchor disappears and is replaced by the two faces of the victims.

"Wallace's brother, Brian, died at the scene. Wallace was only fifteen when he was convicted of capital murder, and if things go as planned he will be the youngest man ever executed in this state. Experts are expecting no further delays in the execution."

Cody presses a button, turns off the television, and takes a step toward the bars. "Well, there you have it, Marvin. If Channel 5 says it's gonna happen, then I'm as good as dead."

"I'm sorry," Marvin says in a soft voice. Others might be trying to listen.

"Don't be sorry, Marvin. We knew this day was coming. Let's get it over with."

"Anything I can do for you?"

"Not now. You could've helped me escape years ago. We missed our chance."

"I guess it's too late. Look, your lawyer is here to see you. Can I send him back?"

"Sure. And thanks, Marvin, for everything."

Marvin backs away and disappears. The buzzer rattles again and Jack Garber appears, holding thick files. He has long hair pulled back in a ponytail, a rumpled suit, the perfect picture of a frantic death penalty lawyer about to lose another one.

"How you doing, man?" he asks, almost in a whisper.

"Great. Tell me something good."

"The Supreme Court can't make up its mind, got those clowns chasing their tails. And the governor won't say yes or no but then he likes to wait until the courts have slammed all the doors so he can come out of his cave for a dramatic announcement."

"Has he ever granted clemency at the last minute?"

"No, of course not."

"And didn't he campaign on the promise of more and quicker executions?"

"I believe so."

"Then why are we wasting time with the governor?"

"You got a better idea? We're running out of options here, Cody. Things are getting rather dicey."

Cody laughs and says, "Dicey?" Then he catches himself, lowers his voice, and says, "I'm three hours away from getting my ass strapped to a gurney and a needle stuck in my arm, so, yes, Jack, I'd say things are pretty dicey. For some reason I do feel, should I say, rather vulnerable."

Cody walks closer to the bars and looks at Garber. For a long moment they stare at each other. "It's over, isn't it?"

Jack shakes his head and in a low voice says, "No, but it's almost over. I'm still tossing Hail Marys."

"My odds?"

Jack shrugs and says, "I don't know. One in a hundred. It's getting late."

Cody moves even closer and their noses are inches apart. "It's over and I'm cool with that. I'm tired of the drama, tired of the waiting, tired of the food, tired of a lot of things, Jack. I'm ready to go."

"Don't say that. I never give up."

"I've been here for fourteen years, Jack. I'm tired of this place."

"The Supreme Court will one day declare that it is not right to put minors on trial for capital murder, but it won't happen tonight, I'm afraid."

"I was fifteen years old, in that courtroom, with a terrible lawyer. The jury hated me and hated him. I never had a chance, Jack. I wish you'd been my lawyer at the trial."

"So do I."

"Come to think of it, Jack, I've never had much of a chance anywhere."

"I'm sorry, Cody."

Cody takes a step back and manages a smile. "Sorry for the self-pity."

"It's okay. You're entitled to it right now."

"How many executions have you witnessed, Jack?"

"Three."

"Is that enough?"

"More than."

"Good, because I don't want you to watch me die. No witnesses on my side of the room. Got that? Let the Baker family pray and cry and cheer when I stop breathing. I guess they deserve it. Maybe it'll make 'em feel better. But I don't want anybody crying for me."

"Are you sure? I'll be there if you need me."

"Nope, I've made up my mind, Jack. You've fought like hell to keep me alive and you're not going to watch me die."

"As you wish. It's your party."

"It is indeed."

Jack looks somewhat relieved and glances at his watch. "I need to go, gotta call the court. I'll be back in an hour."

"Go get 'em, tiger."

Jack leaves and a door clangs somewhere down the hall. Cody sits on the edge of his bed, deep in thought. The buzzer sounds again and Marvin is back. Cody returns to the bars and says, "What now?"

"Say, look, Cody, the warden is here to go over the last-minute stuff."

"I thought we did that yesterday."

"Well, he wants to do it again." Marvin leans in closer to the bars. "You see, Cody, he's pretty nervous because this is his first execution."

"Mine too."

"Right, well he needs to go over some things, rules and procedures, stuff like that. Be nice to him because he's my boss."

"Why should I worry about being nice to the warden? I'll be dead in three hours."

"Come on, Cody. He's got a doctor with him so don't make trouble."

"A doctor?"

"Right. One of the rules. They need to make sure you're healthy enough to take the needle."

Cody laughs and says, "You're kidding, right?"

"Dead serious, Cody. Nobody's kidding around tonight."

Cody backs away and laughs hysterically. As he does, the warden and a doctor in a white coat appear at the door as Marvin eases into the background. The warden holds a legal pad with his checklist and is visibly nervous. Cody eventually steps back to the bars. The doctor cautiously keeps his distance.

The warden says, "Okay, Wallace, as I said yesterday, we have procedures to follow. If you don't like them, don't blame me. They were on the books before I got here. This is Dr. Paxton, the head physician here at the prison."

"A real pleasure," Cody says.

Paxton nods but only because he has to.

The warden says, "A physical exam is required before an execution, so that's why Dr. Paxton is here."

"Makes perfect sense to me, Warden. Same as all your other rules."

"I didn't make them, as I said."

"This is your first execution, right. You seem a little nervous."

"I know what I'm doing."

"Just relax, Warden. We'll get through this together."

"Would you please step over here and cooperate?"

Cody steps to the bars and thrusts his right arm through them. Paxton quickly pulls on a pair of plastic gloves and wraps the blood pressure cuff around Cody's right bicep. Using his stethoscope, he checks here and there, a cursory exam.

The warden holds his legal pad and says, "You still have no approved witnesses, right? No one?"

"Warden, I've been here for fourteen years, two months, twenty-four days, and I've not had a single visitor, other than my lawyer. I have no mother, father, siblings, cousins, no family whatsoever. No friends, neither here nor out there. So who in hell would I invite to my execution?"

"Okay, moving right along. What about your arrangements?"

"Arrangements? You mean my dead body? Burn it. Cremate it. Flush the ashes down the toilet because I don't want a trace of me left on this earth. Got that?"

"Clear enough."

Paxton lowers his stethoscope and removes the cuff. "Blood pressure is one-fifty over one hundred, a little elevated."

Cody pulls back his arm and says, "Elevated? Gee I wonder why."

"Pulse is ninety-five, above normal."

"Normal? What's normal when you're three hours away from getting killed? Don't I get a sedative or something to knock off the edge?"

Paxton says officially, "You're entitled to two Valium."

"Valium? That's nothing. Hell, I'm about to be murdered. Why can't I have some crack or at least a beer?"

The warden is quick to say, "Sorry, we have rules."

"Yeah, yeah, and one of your rules is that I gotta be healthy enough to execute."

"It's right here in black and white."

Cody laughs again and shakes his head in disbelief and disgust. They might be in a hurry but he is not. "Ten years ago, long before you guys got here, there was a bad dude named Hacksaw Henderson. Everybody called him Hack, for short. He killed a bunch of people and let's just say a hacksaw was involved. Anyway, Hack finally got his date with the needle, and the day before the big event he overdosed on a bunch of painkillers and Valium he'd been stockpiling. They found him on the floor of his cell, out of it. I'm sure there's a rule, probably right there in black and white, says you can't kill yourself on death row, and certainly not right before all the fun and excitement of a big execution, so they freaked out, rushed Hack to the hospital, pumped his stomach, barely saved his life, then raced him back over here in the nick of time for his execution."

The warden says, "That's nice. Are you finished?"

"Frankly, I couldn't stand the son of a bitch and I was happy when he was gone."

"Are you finished?"

"Almost, got about two hours and forty minutes."

Dr. Paxton clears his throat and says, "If we could wrap things up here."

Cody glares at him and asks, "Are you the same doctor who'll pronounce me dead?"

"I am. It's part of my job."

"Job? Is this the kind of job you were thinking about when you went to med school?"

"Come on, Wallace," the warden says.

"You must've finished dead last in your class to end up with a dipshit job like this."

"Knock it off, Wallace."

"How many men have you pronounced dead after a lethal injection?"

"Three."

"And does that bother you?"

"Not really."

Cody suddenly grabs the bars in front of Paxton and says, "I hereby declare myself healthy enough to be murdered by the state. This little exam is over. Now, get out of here."

Paxton offers a small plastic tube and says, "You got it, pal.

Here's your Valium." He disappears quickly and the door clangs in the distance.

The warden studies his legal pad and says, "Moving right along. Your last meal will be served at nine p.m. Do you really want a frozen pizza?"

"That's what I said. Got a problem with it?"

"No, but you could do much better. I mean, how about a big thick steak with fries and chocolate cake. Something like that?"

"Is everything going to be difficult tonight? Why do you care what I eat?"

"Okay, okay. What about the chaplain? Would you like to see him?"

"Why?"

"I don't know. Maybe have a chat."

"What would we talk about?"

"I don't know, but he's been through this a few times and I'm sure he'll think of something."

"I doubt we have much in common. Never been to church in my life, Warden, at least not to worship. Me and Brian robbed a few out in the country when we were hungry. Some really crappy food. Peanut butter, cheap cookies, stuff like that. The food was so bad we stopped robbing churches and went back to doing houses."

"I see. Most people, when they come this far and the end is near, want to make sure things are right with God, maybe confess their sins, things like that."

"Why would I confess my sins? Hell, I can't even remember them."

"So, no to the chaplain?"

"Oh, I don't care. If it makes him feel like he's doing his job, run him through. Anybody else on your checklist there? Reporters, politicians, anybody else want a piece of me before I go under?"

The warden ignores the question and checks off something on his legal pad. "What about your estate?"

"My what?"

"Your estate. Your assets. Your things."

Cody laughs and waves his arms. "This is it, boss. Look around. Eight-by-ten, my world for the past fourteen years. All I own is right here."

"What about all the books?"

"What about 'em?" Cody steps to the center of his cell and admires his collection. "My library. One thousand, nine hundred and forty books. All sent to me by a sweet little lady in North Platte, Nebraska. They're worth everything to me and nothing to anyone else. I'd say ship 'em back to her but I can't afford the freight."

"We're not paying for the shipping."

"I didn't ask you to. Give 'em to the prison library. Hell, I got more books than they do."

"The library can't accept books from inmates."

"Another brilliant rule! Please give me the rationale behind that one."

"I really don't know."

"There is none, same as most of your rules. Burn the damned things. Throw them in the fire with me and we'll have the first literary cremation in the history of this wonderful state."

"And your clothing, court files, television, letters, radio, fan?"

"Burn, burn, burn. I don't care."

The warden scribbles on his list, lowers his pad, clears his voice, but keeps it low. "Now, Wallace, have you given any thought to your last statement, your final words?"

"Yes, but I haven't decided. I'll think of something."

"Some guys go down swinging, claiming they're not guilty

to the bitter end. Others ask for forgiveness. Some cry, some curse, some quote Scripture."

"I thought this was your first execution."

"It is, but I've done my homework. I've listened to some of the last statements. They're recorded, you know? And kept on file."

"And why do you record them?"

"I have no idea. Just one of our little procedures."

"Of course. How long can I talk when I give my last words?"

"There's no limit."

"So, under your rules, I could do one of those filibuster things and talk for days while you guys wait, right?"

"Technically, yes, I suppose, but I'd probably get bored and eventually give the executioner the high sign."

"But that's against the rules."

"What are you going to do, sue me?"

"I'd love to, believe me I would. I'm four out of five, you know? But I never got the chance to pop you for one."

"Too late now."

"And who's the executioner?"

"His identity is always protected."

"Is it true that he sits in his little dark room not far from my gurney and looks out through one-way glass and waits for you to give him the thumbs? Is that the way it happens, Warden?"

"That's close enough."

"He sneaks in, sneaks out, gets paid a thousand bucks in cash, and no one knows his name?"

"No one but me."

"I have a question for you, Warden. Why all this secrecy? If Americans love the death penalty so much, why not do the killings in public? They used to, you know. I've read about plenty of executions in the old days. Folks loved them, would come from miles around for an official hanging or a firing squad. Great entertainment. Justice was done. Everybody rode their wagons home and felt good about themselves. An eye for an eye. Why don't we do that now, Warden?"

"I don't make the laws."

"Is it because we're ashamed of what we're doing?"

"Maybe."

"Are you ashamed, Warden?"

"No, I don't feel shame, but I don't like this part of my job."

"That's hard to believe, Warden. I think you like this. You chose a career in corrections because you believe in punishment. And this is the ultimate, the big moment. Your first execution and you are the man. How many reporters have you talked to today, Warden? How many interviews?"

"I need to go check on your pizza." The warden backs away, his checklist complete.

"Thank you. And it's pepperoni, not sausage."

When the warden and Marvin are gone and the door bangs shut, Cody looks around his cell and mumbles, "My estate." He sits on the edge of his bunk and shakes out two tablets from the small plastic pill bottle Paxton gave him.

He tosses them through the bars.

(3)

The minutes drag by as The Row grows even quieter. Cody tries to read a paperback but has trouble concentrating. He sits on the floor, breathes heavy and slow, and tries to meditate.

The buzzer sounds again and he wonders who's next.

Like a ghost, and without the slightest noise or footfalls, Padre appears from nowhere and stands at the bars. As always, he wears pointed-toe boots that add an inch or two to his slight frame, and old jeans so faded that college kids wouldn't wear them. But from the waist up he's all business, with a black shirt, white collar. It's June, the first day of summer, but the air is cool so he's wearing a crisp black blazer.

Padre is a retired priest who's been counseling the convicts for a decade. His rounds bring him to The Row and he stands outside the cells and whispers through the bars to the few who wish to talk to him. Most do not. Most condemned men have lost faith in everything, with God getting more than his share of blame.

The rules allow the chaplain to sit with the condemned man in the final hour before he's strapped down, so, in theory, he's the last confidant available. About half the men choose to confess and ask forgiveness at the last moment. Others just want someone to talk to. A few avoid the ritual.

"How are you, Cody?" he asks softly.

Cody stands and smiles and walks to the door. "Hello, Padre. Thanks for stopping by."

Father, Pastor, Reverend, Preacher—all the usual names had been used, but Padre stuck when Freddie Gomez was around. He was a devout Catholic, his murders notwithstanding, and he wanted the priest at his cell at every opportunity for a quiet little Mass. He and Padre became extremely close. Everybody loved Freddie and his execution hit The Row hard.

"How are you, my friend?"

"I'm all right, under the circumstances. My lawyer just left and says we've run out of bullets."

"I'm so sorry, Cody. No one deserves this."

"I'm at peace, Padre. I really am. If given the choice of living in this hole for another forty years or taking the needle, then I'd happily check out. I guess somebody else chose for me."

"I understand, Cody. Would you like me to sit with you in the holding room?"

"Not really, Padre. I'd rather be alone."

"As you wish."

Both men study the floor for a moment. Cody says, "Just curious, Padre. How many men want you to pray with them at the last minute?"

"Most have given up on prayer."

"Any dramatic last-minute come-to-Jesus conversions?"

"No, never. Men on death row have plenty of time to either grow with the faith or reject it altogether. By the time they get to the end, they are well grounded and secure in whatever they believe. So, no. No last-minute conversions, at least not on my watch."

"Not going to happen tonight."

"As you wish, Cody. We once talked all the time, remember those days?"

"I do. We had some pretty serious conversations about God and all his mysteries, and we didn't agree on much, as I recall."

"That's my recollection. You stuck to a rather strong opinion that God does not exist."

"Yes, I did, and I don't really want to go back there, Padre. I haven't changed."

"I'm sorry to hear that, Cody. Are you still reading the Bible?"

"Not really. I mean, I've read it cover to cover, from Genesis to Revelation, at least three times, and I always enjoy it, especially the Old Testament. But I don't rely on it for inspiration, if that's what you mean."

"You know it better than most ministers."

"I doubt that."

"What do you think will happen to you, Cody, after you die?"

"They'll burn me, along with my estate here, and take the

ashes and flush everything down the toilet. Those are my wishes. I don't want a trace of me left on this earth."

"No afterlife, no heaven or hell or anyplace in between for your spirit to rest?"

"No. We're animals, Padre, live-born mammals, and when we die that's the end of us. All that nonsense about spirits rising from our dead bodies and floating up to glory or plunging into fire is a load of crap. When we die we're dead. Nothing about us keeps living."

"You aren't planning to see Brian?"

"Brian died fifteen years ago. I was there. It was awful. There was no funeral, just a pauper's burial on the back side of the city cemetery. I've never been allowed to go there, to see his grave. Probably doesn't even have a tombstone or a marker. I doubt a single person has ever stood above his grave and wiped a tear. We were outcasts, Padre, orphans, pathetic kids who were not supposed to be born. And when we die, we're dead, buried or cremated or whatever, and that's the end. No, I won't see Brian or anyone else for that matter, and that doesn't bother me at all."

Padre smiles and nods as he accepts this with love and compassion. There was nothing Cody or anyone else could say that would fluster or provoke him. He'd heard it all and had an endless repertoire of responses, all well grounded in Holy Scripture, but timing was everything. And this wasn't the time to argue faith or theology with Cody.

"I see you haven't changed your beliefs."

"No sir. You once said God doesn't make mistakes. That's not true, Padre. I'm the perfect example of one. My mother got paid for sex. My father left behind a little cash and some semen. He never knew I was born and my mother couldn't wait to get rid of me. I'm a mistake."

"God still loves you, Cody."

"Well, he sure has a strange way of proving it. What did I do to deserve this?"

"He works in mysterious ways and we'll never have all the answers."

"Why does it have to be so damned complicated and mysterious? You know why, Padre? Because he's not there. He was created by man for man's own benefit. What the hell are we doing? Arguing again?"

"I'm sorry, Cody. I just stopped by to say hello and goodbye and see if you needed me."

Cody takes a deep breath and calms himself. "Thanks, Padre. You were always one of the good guys."

"I'll miss you, Cody. I'm praying for you."

"If it makes you feel better, then keep praying."

(4)

At eight o'clock, Cody turns on the television, checks the three networks, sees nothing of interest, and turns it off. He stretches out on his foam mattress and tries to close his eyes.

He once threatened to sue the prison because it didn't allow access to cable channels, but a similar lawsuit had been thrown out in another state, according to Jack.

Back in the day, he and Brian had stolen several small TVs, but found that they were generally more trouble than they were worth. The fences hated to fool with them because the cops checked the pawn shops frequently and looked for serial numbers. Storage was another problem. After hitting a house, he and Brian always waited days, even weeks, before fencing their loot. Let things cool off, Brian always said. Let the cops make their rounds. Give the homeowners time to file their insurance claims and buy new guns, televisions, radios, stereos, jewelry. Even toasters, mixers, hell, they'd steal anything if they could get a buck from the fences.

As they waited patiently in the woods, they hid their inventories in old barns and abandoned houses and constantly moved them at night to other sites. Televisions were the most difficult to haul around and hide.

Guns made the market and were instant cash. When they got lucky and cleaned out a gun cabinet, they forgot about anything else and laughed all the way to their hideout deep in the woods. The Beretta 686 Silver Pigeon over-and-under was their finest hour. The homeowner had a dozen shotguns in his cabinet, which, for some reason, was unlocked in the den. Not that a locked door would have slowed them down. There were Brownings and Remingtons, but when Brian saw the Beretta he let out a whistle. They grabbed four shotguns and rifles each, plus two Smith & Wesson revolvers, and made a quick exit. They watched the house for the next three days and saw no movement. No one was checking on it as the newspapers piled up in the driveway. The house had no alarm system. People could be so careless.

Since their break-in had yet to be discovered, they went back and stole the rest of the guns. The homeowners were obviously away on a long trip. It was July, vacation time. Brian decided they should move quickly before anyone returned home. They rode their (stolen) bikes into the city and stopped at a favorite pawn shop. They knew the owner well and considered him trustworthy, or as honorable as one might be in the shady business of stolen merchandise. His front-room pawn shop was always crowded with customers, its shelves stocked with everything from saxophones to vacuum cleaners. His back room was where he made his money dealing in hot weapons. He gave them $50 each for the revolvers. When Brian asked if he had any interest in a Beretta 686 Silver Pigeon, he was floored.

"Holy crap, man!" he'd gushed. "Where in hell?" But then he'd caught himself and stopped talking. Never ask a thief where he found his inventory.

Brian laughed and assured him they indeed had one in stock, and it was in mint condition.

"I'll check around," the dealer had said, obviously excited.

A week later they returned with the shotgun and left the pawn shop with $200 in cash, a record for them. They went to an old motel on the edge of town and paid $30 a night. They showered, washed their clothes, ate cheeseburgers at a joint across the street, and for two days lived like kings.

When it was time, they retreated to the woods and moved their campsite miles away. They had hit enough homes in the area and the police were patrolling more.

(5)

It's eight thirty and Cody walks back and forth, pacing zombie-like with his eyes closed, touching a bookshelf, then touching the bars. Back and forth. He is anxious and wishes he hadn't thrown away those pills. He suspects his lawyer will soon return for the last time and deliver the news that everyone expects.

There was usually a flurry of last-minute pleas and appeals, with lawyers running frantically from one court to another, but not always. A year earlier, Lemoyne Rubley went all the way with little fanfare. He was two doors down and he and Cody were friendly. They chatted for hours as the clock ticked away, though they couldn't see one another. The day before the execution, the courts pulled all the plugs and his lawyers gave up. It was the most peaceful execution Cody had lived through in his fourteen years on The Row.

Frankly, now that it's his turn, he's thankful he has someone out there still firing away, though with very little ammo. He's not looking forward to his last visit with Jack Garber.

He's paid the guy nothing. For the past ten years Jack has represented him with a loyalty that has been amazing. On several occasions, Jack came within one vote of convincing an appellate court that Cody should get a new trial. He once asked Jack why he had chosen to be a death penalty lawyer. The answer was vague and brief and touched on some lofty ideas about capital punishment. He asked Jack who was paying him, and he explained that he worked for a nonprofit foundation that represents people like Cody, death row inmates.

The buzzer rattles again in the distance and Cody jolts back to reality. He walks to the bars, waits, and Marvin appears again. He smiles and says, "Cody, I have some good news."

"I doubt that. Right now the only good news can come from my lawyer."

"No, not that kind of good news. It's something else. You have a visitor. It ain't your lawyer or the chaplain or some reporter. It's a real visitor."

"I've never had a real visitor."

"I know."

"Who is it?"

"It's a nice little lady from Nebraska."

"Miss Iris?"

"Miss Iris Vanderkamp."

"No way!"

"I swear."

"But she's eighty years old and in a wheelchair."

"Well, she made it. Warden says you can see her for fifteen minutes."

"What a great guy. I don't believe this, Marvin. Miss Iris finally made it."

"She's right here." Marvin disappears for a second, then

returns pushing Miss Iris in a wheelchair. He parks her at Cody's door and fades into the darkness of the hallway.

Cody is awestruck, speechless. He inches closer to the bars and studies her smiling face. "I can't believe this," he finally says softly. "I don't know what to say."

"Well, how about something like, 'Hello and nice to meet you after all these years'? That work?"

"Hello and nice to meet you after all these years."

"Same on this end. I got here as fast as I could. Sorry it took me twelve years."

"I'm so glad you're here, Miss Iris. I can't believe this."

Cody slowly eases his right hand through the bars. She takes it with both of hers and gives a good squeeze. "I can't believe it either, Cody. Is this really happening?"

He nods as he slowly pulls his hand back and looks at her. She's in a wheelchair because, as she explained in one of her many letters, she suffers from bouts of severe bursitis in her knees and other joints. Her lower legs and feet are covered with a thin blanket. Above that she wears a pretty green floral dress and plenty of jewelry—long necklaces and bulky bracelets. Cody notices the jewelry because he certainly stole enough of it in his heyday. She has a round face with a big smile, a long nose with red-framed glasses perched on the tip, and sparkling blue eyes. Her white hair is thick and wavy and has not thinned at all.

She sees a skinny boy with bushy hair who could convince no one that he is twenty-nine years old.

In their twelve-year correspondence they have divulged most of their secrets.

"Yes, Miss Iris, this is really happening. My lawyer, Jack, says we're down to the lick log, as they say. Got that from one of those cliché books you sent."

"You use too many of those clichés and metaphors."

"I know, I know. So you say. But I love a good cliché, one that isn't used too often."

"Well, you need to avoid them, most of the time."

"I don't believe this. Here I am at the end and you're still grading my papers."

"I am not, Cody. I'm here because I care about you."

This hits him hard and his knees almost buckle. He's never heard this before. He walks to the bars, grabs two of them and sticks his face between them, as close as he can get. He whispers, "I care about you too, Miss Iris. I can't believe you're here."

"Well, I am, and evidently I don't have much time."

"Neither do I."

"So, what can we talk about?"

"How'd you get here?"

"I convinced Charles to drive me. He's my new boyfriend."

"What happened to Frank?"

"He died. I thought I told you that."

"I don't think so, but in all honesty, it's not easy keeping up with all of your romances. You were quite fond of Frank, as I recall."

"Oh, I'm fond of all of them, at least at the beginning."

"There have been quite a few."

"I suppose. To be honest, Cody, I was kind of tired of Frank. So far I'd say that Charles has far more potential. You know what they say. If you really want to know someone, just take a trip with them. Well, we're in the middle of this trip, and so far so good."

"Thank you, Miss Iris. I can't believe you've come here. It's a thousand miles, right?"

"Nine hundred and twenty-seven, according to Charles, who has this odd habit of counting everything. It's sort of annoying but I haven't said anything yet."

"When did you leave Nebraska?"

"Around noon yesterday. Stayed in a motel last night, separate rooms of course, then drove all day today. I've done it before, if you'll recall."

"How could I forget? Eight, ten years ago. You showed up here and they wouldn't let you in."

"It was awful. My son Bobby drove me all the way down, our last road trip together I can promise you that, and they made us wait in this small, smelly room with no air-conditioning, it was August if I remember correctly, and then they told us to leave, rather abruptly. Said you had done something wrong and got put on probation and couldn't have visitors. It was just awful."

"And it was a lie. I've never been on probation. They didn't like me because I kept suing them in federal court and kicking their butts. We had a terrible warden back then and he hated every one of us on death row. He somehow managed to make our miserable lives even worse."

She takes a deep breath and looks around, trying to absorb the place. "So this is death row?"

"Smack in the middle of it. Twenty cells on this wing, twenty on the other, no vacancies anywhere. No room at the inn. Around the corner, behind the East Wing, known here affectionately by the guards as the 'Beast Wing' because that's where they tend to put the nastier boys, there's a small square addition known as the Gas House. That's where they do the dirty work of killing us in private so the good Christian folks who love the death penalty don't have to actually see it in action. I'll be going there in less than two hours."

As she listens she keeps looking around. "Well, I must say, first impressions are not very good."

Cody takes a step back, releases the bars, and enjoys a good laugh. "It's designed to be an awful place, Miss Iris."

"And how long have you been here in this cell?"

"Fourteen years. I was fifteen when I was convicted, fourteen when I was arrested. Dead at twenty-nine, the youngest to be executed in this country since the Wild West days when they would string up anybody."

"It's a pretty depressing place. Could you ask to be moved?"

"Why? Where would I go? All the cells are the same. Eight feet by ten. Same rules, same food, same guards, same unbearable heat in the summer, same freezing cold in the winter. We're just a bunch of rats trying to survive in the sewer and dying slowly every day."

"You were just a baby."

"No, I wasn't a baby. I was a tough kid who'd been living in the woods for four years. I had no other place to live, except for the orphanage or another foster home. Brian found me and we escaped and lived the way we wanted for a few years. I wasn't a baby, Miss Iris, but I was too young for this."

"Do you feel safe here?"

"Sure. Death row is a very safe place, even though it's full of murderers. We're all locked down in solitary so there's no one to fight, no one to hurt."

"You said that in one of your letters."

"What have I not said in my letters, Miss Iris? I've told you everything. And you've been pretty honest with me."

"I have, yes."

"So, if we assume we've already talked about everything, in our letters, what can we talk about now? We only have a few more minutes."

"Did you save my letters?"

"Of course." Cody quickly falls to his knees, reaches under his bunk, and pulls out a long, flat cardboard box filled with colorful envelopes. "Every one of them, Miss Iris, and I've read them all a dozen times. One letter each week for the past twelve years, plus cards for my birthday, Christmas, Easter, and Thanksgiving. All in all, six hundred and seventy-four letters and cards. You're pretty amazing, Miss Iris. Has anyone ever told you that?"

"All the time."

Cody carefully chooses an envelope and removes the letter. "The very first. April twenty-second, 1978. 'Dear Cody. My name is Iris Vanderkamp and I live in North Platte, Nebraska. I am a member of St. Timothy's Lutheran Church, and our ladies' Bible class is starting a new project. We are reaching out to young men on death row. We are opposed to the death penalty and want to see it abolished. This may sound a bit odd—but is there anything I can do for you? Please write back and let me know. Sincerely, Iris.'"

"I remember it like it was yesterday. We were having a Bible study at my house one night and Geraldine Fisher said she'd read a story about a lady in Omaha who'd been pen pals with a death row inmate for over twenty years, some poor man down south. They were about to put him in the gas chamber. That's how it all got started. We searched for some names. Yours jumped out because you were only seventeen at the time, so young. So I wrote that letter, and I waited and waited."

"I read your letter and I couldn't believe it. Somebody out there knew my name, knew that I was on death row, and wanted to do something nice for me. Keep in mind, Miss Iris, and I know I've told you this a hundred times, but I have no family anywhere. And no friends. Not a single friend until you came along. Jack's my friend, I guess, but he doesn't really count because he's my lawyer."

"And you wrote me back."

"I was so intimidated. I had never written a letter before and I'd never received one, other than stuff from the courts. But I was determined. I borrowed a dictionary from the library and studied every word. I wrote in block letters, like they tried to teach me in the first grade, I guess."

"It was a beautiful letter. Not a single word was misspelled. I got the impression it took a long time to write it."

"Hours and hours, but, hey, I have plenty of time. It kept me busy, gave me a purpose. I wanted to impress you."

"You made me cry, and not for the last time."

"You know, Miss Iris, when I came here as a boy I couldn't read much. I dropped out of school when I was ten. I had bounced around so many schools, had so many teachers, that I didn't care about learning. Brian escaped from a juvenile home and found me in foster care, again, and we ran away. That was the end of my schooling. I could read a little, but not very well. When I got this letter, I knew I had to answer it. I borrowed some paper and a pencil, got the dictionary, and I wanted every word to be perfect."

"It was amazing to watch your handwriting improve over the years, Cody. At first you printed like a child."

"I was a child."

"But before long you were switching to cursive."

"You asked me to, remember? Or I should say that you strongly suggested that I learn cursive and write like an adult."

"I did. And I sent you a book on penmanship."

Cody tosses the letter on the bunk, studies a wall of books for a second, then removes one from the shelf. "Here it is— Abbott's *Art of Cursive Penmanship*. I spent hours with this book, Miss Iris. You sent me some money and I bought paper and pencils and practiced for hours and hours."

Cody puts the book back and pulls out another one. He shows it to her and says, "And here's the first dictionary, Miss Iris. *Random House Webster's College Dictionary*. Paperback, of course, so we can't be murdering one another with dictionaries. I've read the whole thing, Miss Iris, cover to cover, and more than once."

"I know, I know. If you'll recall, I've had to caution you about using big words. At times, you like to show off."

Cody laughs and tosses the dictionary on the bunk. "Of course I'm showing off, but there's no one else in the audience. What was the word that really ticked you off?"

"There have been so many, but 'obstreperous' comes to mind."

"That's it. Love that word. Noisy or unruly. There were other adjectives that you cautioned me about. Obsequious, lugubrious, pernicious, ubiquitous."

"That's enough. My point was that big words do not always convey big emotions, and a fancy vocabulary can get in the way of good writing."

"I fell in love with words, the bigger the better." Cody stares at the walls of books.

Miss Iris says, "You know, Cody, this place gives me the creeps, but all those books do add a bit of color to your little room."

"These books saved my life, until now. You sent every one of them, Miss Iris, and you have no idea what they mean to me."

"What was the first one?"

Cody smiles, points, then removes a paperback. "*Mustang Man,* by Louis L'Amour," he says proudly as he opens the book. "The first time I read it, or I should say finished it, was June the tenth, 1978. It took me two months, Miss Iris, because I didn't know so many of the words. When I saw a word I didn't know, I would stop and write it down, then get the dictionary and look it up. When I finished a paragraph and knew every word, then I would stand up and pace back and forth and read it all the way through. It took forever, hours and hours, but I loved every minute of it. I loved the words, loved learning them, the long ones, the short ones. I kept a list of words I knew but wasn't sure how to pronounce, so I would save it for Jack or the chaplain, or maybe even Marvin. I practiced and practiced until I knew all of them, Miss Iris. The entire dictionary."

"I know, I know. I had to use a dictionary just to read some of your letters."

"I loved the words, but I craved the stories. They took me away from here, took me all over the world, in this century, last century, the next century. They set my imagination on fire and I realized I was not going crazy, like everybody else around here."

He puts the book back in its place, then turns slowly and admires his collection. "And you kept sending them, Miss Iris. Every week another book, sometimes two or three, and I read them all. Read them over and over. I usually read ten to twelve hours a day, and all because of you."

"Who's your favorite writer?"

Cody laughs at the question and shakes his head. "Too many favorites, I guess. But if I had to name one it would be Louis L'Amour." He points at the shelf and continues, "I've read forty-one of his books. I love Mickey Spillane, Ed McBain, Elmore Leonard, Raymond Chandler, John D. MacDonald."

"You always said you loved mysteries and crime."

"Hey, I'm a criminal. Got papers to prove it."

"You're not a criminal."

"Oh really? Then why am I in here?"

"That's a very good question, Cody. I wish someone could give me a good answer."

Cody stares at the books, mesmerized. He finally asks, "Where did you get all these books, Miss Iris?"

"Oh, I'm sure I've told you before in a letter."

"Well humor me, dammit. I'm running out of time."

"Don't swear."

"I'm sorry. Should've taken the Valium."

"The what?"

"Never mind."

"I got 'em here and there. Garage sales, flea markets, library fundraisers, used-book shops. Never paid more than a dollar for one."

"And you read all of them before you sent them to me?"

"Well, almost all of them. I really don't like the dirty stuff, writers like Harold Robbins, you know? Pure filth. But I sent them to you anyway."

"And I'm so grateful you did, Miss Iris. I love the dirty ones too."

"Pure filth."

"Are you sure you didn't read a few chapters here and there?"

"Well, maybe a little. I had to take a look to see what was there."

"How about *Valley of the Dolls*? I've read it five times and it still gets me excited."

"Let's talk about something else, okay?"

"What? You don't want to talk about sex?"

"Not really."

"Miss Iris, I've never had sex. Can you believe that? They threw me in jail when I was fourteen and I came here when I was fifteen. Brian always said he had sex when he was thirteen in an orphanage, but he was four years older than me and he lied a lot too. Me, I never got the chance. That's why dirty books are so much fun."

"Please, can we talk about something else?"

"No, Miss Iris. I have less than two hours to live so I'll talk about anything I want."

"Name your favorite three books."

This knocks him off his stride and for a moment he doesn't respond. He stares at the shelves, rubs his hands together in deep thought, and finally pulls out a book. He shows her the cover and says, "*The Grapes of Wrath*, by John Steinbeck. The story of the Joads and the Okies and their desperate trip to California during the Dust Bowl. Heartbreaking but also uplifting." He opens it and looks at the inside cover. "You sent it to me in November of 1984, and I've read it seven times."

He carefully replaces the book on the shelf and finds another. "*In Cold Blood,* by Truman Capote. A true crime masterpiece." He shows her the cover. "Have you read it, Miss Iris?"

"Of course. I remember when the Clutter family was murdered in 1959. All four of them. It happened down in Kansas, the western part, not too far from where I live."

"They hung those boys, Dick Hickock and Perry Smith. And you know what, Miss Iris? I was glad when they hung them. Weren't you?"

"Well, I really wasn't that sad about it."

"How weird is that, Miss Iris? Here I am sitting on death row reading a true story about a home invasion where innocent people were sound asleep and some bad guys broke in and killed them. Sound familiar? And I'm actually happy they got caught and put to death."

"Yes, that's pretty weird."

"That's the strange thing about the death penalty, Miss Iris. Sometimes you hate it because it's so unfair, and sometimes you catch yourself secretly applauding it because the son of a bitch deserved to die. I mean, I've been here for fourteen years and eight men have gone down. Four in the gas chamber, four by the needle. One was probably innocent. The other seven, guilty as hell. I felt sorry for six of them, but the other two got what they deserved."

"I'm opposed to capital punishment in all cases."

"Well, you should meet some of my colleagues here on The Row. You'd change your mind."

"Are these guys going to feel sorry for you?"

"Who knows? I don't care. I can't worry about their feelings."

He puts the book back in its place and admires his collection.

"And your third favorite book?"

He takes his time and finally pulls out another one. "I guess this is the last book I'll ever read. Finished it yesterday, for the fifth time. It's all about death and dying young."

"*Sophie's Choice?*"

"How'd you know?"

"You've mentioned it more than once in your letters."

"I've gone through hell here, Miss Iris, but it's nothing compared to what those people went through. Everything is relative, isn't it? Even suffering."

"I suppose."

"Plus it's full of sex."

"I couldn't finish it."

"It's brilliant. Such a powerful story, and it's a novel, a great work of fiction, but so realistic. Styron won the Pulitzer for it, you know?"

"No, he won the National Book Award. His Pulitzer was for *The Confessions of Nat Turner.*"

"That's right. You know all these books, don't you? A high school English teacher for over forty years."

"And I loved every minute of it."

He puts the book back on the shelf and touches the spines of other books. "My favorites. *Lonesome Dove, A Confederacy of Dunces, Catcher in the Rye, Catch-22.* And here, one of my true favorites, the Travis McGee series by John D. MacDonald. I couldn't get enough of ole Travis."

"I know, I know. You went on and on."

"Twenty-one books in the series, and you, Miss Iris, found every one of them. You're pretty awesome, you know that."

"So I've been told."

"Truth is, Miss Iris, I've enjoyed every one of them. Just look at them. How beautiful. Look at all the colors. Look at how they've brightened up this awful place. I have the prettiest cell on death row."

"What will happen to them?"

Cody shakes his head, then freezes, smiles, and says, "Wait a minute. I have a great idea. I want you to have them. I want you to inherit my complete estate—my library, my letters and cards and legal files. All of my assets, Miss Iris. They're all yours."

"Oh no. I'm not sure what I would do—"

"You have to, Miss Iris. If you don't they'll just burn all this stuff. There's no one else to take it."

"They can't do that."

"Oh hell yeah they can, and they will. They'll throw this stuff in the fire with me and have a good laugh. They gotta clear out this place for the next guy."

"But I can't take it with me."

"No, of course not. Look, I have seventeen dollars in my account, money you've sent me for paper and stamps and stuff. Take it, and maybe add a little to it, and then maybe you can afford to ship it all to Nebraska. Please, Miss Iris. It would mean so much to me for you to keep my library and papers. All these beautiful books, plus the cards and letters and files. You gotta do it, Miss Iris."

"Well, I suppose—"

"Sure you can, Miss Iris. These clowns would love for you to take all my stuff so they won't have to fool with it. Please."

"Well, okay, I guess."

"Great, Miss Iris. This is wonderful."

"I'll make it happen, Cody. I promise."

"Thank you, Miss Iris. And you'll put all of our letters together, right?"

"Of course. I'm thinking, and I know just the right spot.

There's a wall in my study that I can clear out, and I'll keep your books there forever, Cody. What a lovely idea."

"This is incredible, Miss Iris. I was planning to check out of here and leave nothing behind, but now I love the idea of leaving something behind, something to remember me."

"I'll always remember you, Cody."

He walks to the bars and sticks an arm through again. She clutches his hand and they share a quiet moment.

Marvin emerges from the darkness and says softly, "Warden says time is up. I'm sorry."

Cody doesn't acknowledge him. He looks at her face and says, "Thank you, Miss Iris. Thank you for coming here and saying goodbye."

With one hand she wipes tears from her face. "This is so awful, Cody, and so wrong. You shouldn't even be here."

"Thank you for coming, and for caring all these years, and for being my friend, and for all the books and cards and money, money that you couldn't really afford to send."

"I consider it an honor, Cody. I just wish I could've done more."

"You did more than anybody else."

"I'm so sorry."

"Please remember me."

She reaches up and touches his face. "I can never forget you, Cody. Never."

Marvin gently takes the handles of her wheelchair and pulls her away and they leave. Cody strains to watch her as she disappears down the darkened hall. He tries to pull himself together. When the door clangs in the distance, he walks to his bunk, takes a seat, and buries his face in his hands.

(6)

8:50 p.m. The buzzer sounds in the distance and Cody stands to see who's coming. It's Jack Garber, moving slowly, hands stuck in pants pockets, absent his usual stack of files and papers. He stops at the bars and Cody walks over.

In a low, dispirited voice, Jack says, "The Supreme Court said no. The governor's office just called with more bad news."

"No more Hail Marys?" Try as he might, Cody can't quite keep his shoulders up. They sag and his chin drops.

"Nothing, Cody. I got nothing left. I've unloaded everything, tried every trick in the book."

"So it's over?"

"I'm sorry, Cody. I should've done something different."

"Come on, Jack. You can't beat yourself up. You've been fighting for me for ten years. Fighting like hell."

"Yeah, fighting and losing. You should have won, Cody. You don't deserve to die. You were just a kid who didn't kill anyone, never pulled a trigger. I let you down, Cody."

"You did not. You're a warrior until the bitter end."

"I'm so sorry."

"Let it go, Jack. I'm at peace and I'm ready to go."

"You've always been brave, Cody. I've never had a client so brave."

"I'll be all right, Jack. And if there happens to be something in the next act, then I'll see you on the other side."

Cody steps closer, reaches through the bars, and puts a hand on Jack's shoulder. The two men embrace as best they can with the bars between them. They have a long hug and then let go. Finally, Jack steps back and wipes his face. He turns and walks away, and Cody watches him disappear.

He closes his eyes and takes a deep breath, then walks over

to the television, picks up the remote and turns it on. The governor has the screen. Outside an elaborate office, and with a wall of grim-faced flunkies behind him, he steps to a bank of microphones and, as solemnly as possible, says, "I have just been informed that the Supreme Court has refused to hear the final appeal of Cody Wallace. I have carefully reviewed his request for clemency. The issue of his age is indeed troubling. However, I am much more sympathetic to the victims of this horrible crime, the Baker family, and their great loss. They need our prayers at this hour. They are opposed to clemency. The people of this state have repeatedly said they believe in capital punishment, and it is my solemn duty to uphold the law. Therefore, I am denying the request for clemency. The execution will proceed as scheduled, at ten p.m. this evening."

He bows his head as if he might start praying himself as he backs away. Reporters instantly start yelling questions, but he is much too burdened to deal with them.

Cody mutes the television and stares at it. Suddenly the screen changes and there's Jack again, standing somewhere on the prison grounds with a guard on each side. Cody quickly hits the volume.

Jack says to the camera, "Cody was fourteen years old, a child, an orphan, a homeless kid living in the woods, a kid no one wanted. He never pulled a trigger and he didn't kill anyone. It's barbaric for this state to treat him like an adult, and it's immoral to execute him. The system failed Cody at every turn, and now the system will kill him. Congratulations to the God-fearing, gun-loving, law and order die-hards of this miserable state."

When the news anchor appears, Cody hits the remote and the screen goes blank.

(7)

Marvin pushes a food cart down the darkened hallway. Dinner is usually served at five p.m., lunch at eleven, breakfast at five in the morning. The courts had long ago declared that every man in prison is entitled to 2,200 calories a day, 1,800 for women. It might have been edible in other camps around the prison, but on death row it was an unbearably dreadful menu of powdered food and old vegetables and canned slop served long after the shelf life. The meals often included five or six slices of stale white bread to run the tally up to the magical 2,200 calories and stave off another lawsuit. Cody's had slightly improved things ten years earlier. Some of the men ignored the food and ate only enough to remain alive. Others got fat off extra white bread tossed up and down the hall. A handful were lucky enough to receive a little cash from home to buy tastier items from the canteen.

"Your last meal, Cody," Marvin says as he slides a medium-sized frozen pepperoni pizza through the food slot in the door. Cody steps over and takes it. Marvin hands him a tall paper cup with a straw and says, "Your strawberry milkshake."

Cody smiles and sits on his bunk. He removes a wedge of pizza and takes a bite. "It's over, Marvin. It's really gonna happen, isn't it?"

"Sure looks that way, Cody. I'm real sorry."

He takes another bite, then a pull on the straw. He looks at Marvin and says, "This is a pretty lousy frozen pizza."

"What did you expect?"

"I don't know. I've had much better."

"You specifically ordered a frozen pizza. Ain't never seen that before for no last meal."

"I guess it really doesn't matter, you know? I don't have much of an appetite. You want some pizza?"

"No thanks."

Cody hits the straw again, then starts laughing. "You remember when they killed Skunk Miller, what, two years ago?"

"Sure. I remember it well. I liked Skunk."

"And what was his last meal?"

Marvin chuckles at the memory. "Oh, that was something. Skunk wanted everything, a sirloin steak, fries, two cheeseburgers, a dozen raw oysters, baked potato, eggs and bacon, chocolate cake. And he ate every bite of it."

"And you served it to him, right?"

"Yeah, and watched him eat it. He kept trying to offer me some of his last meal, but it just didn't seem right."

"And he ordered a bottle of wine, too."

"Yeah, but he didn't get it. No alcohol, of course."

Cody takes a small bite but it's obvious he's losing interest. "You know that a few minutes after you die your bowels and bladder relax and release everything, a real mess. I guess Skunk got the last laugh."

"I don't think he was laughing."

"Do you get the cleanup duty?"

"Nope. That's somebody else's job, thank goodness."

"What happens to me after they cut off my clothes and hose me down?"

"I don't know, Cody. I ain't never been that curious."

"You ever watch an execution, Marvin?"

"Nope. This is as close as I want to get."

"I wish you'd eat some of this pizza. It's not that good but it's sort of filling."

"No thanks."

"Let me guess. You don't like frozen pizza?"

"You got that right."

Cody chuckles and hits the straw. "That's hard to believe,

Marvin. When me and Brian broke in a house, we'd always go for the guns first, guns and jewelry, valuable stuff that's easy to carry and even easier to fence. After we looked around real fast, it was my job to go to the refrigerator and freezer and find some food. We were usually hungry by the time we broke in a place. If we got lucky, there'd be frozen pizza in the freezer. We had this little charcoal grill that we'd stolen, hell, everything we had was stolen down to the shoes on our feet, and, anyway, we'd grill a frozen pizza at midnight and watch the stars." He stands and faces Marvin and closes his eyes for a long pause. Then he smiles and says, "Those were happy days, Marvin. Me and Brian, free as birds, living off the land, so to speak, sleeping in pup tents, always moving around so no one could find us. Think about that, Marvin. Nobody in the world knew where we were and no one cared. And we damned sure didn't care about anybody else. Total freedom out there, hiding in the woods. Those were the best days, and I was just a kid."

Marvin has nothing to say. A long minute passes as Cody seems to be in a trance. Down the hall, the door clangs again, but no one joins them. Finally, Marvin says, "Look, Cody, I'm not being a hard-ass here, but you need to finish eating. We gotta move you to the holding room in a few minutes."

"Why can't I just stay here until the big moment?"

"I don't know. I don't make the rules."

"I know, I know."

"Sorry."

"Say, Marvin, I was kinda hard on the Padre earlier. Is he still around?"

"Yeah, he's up front with the warden."

"Could you ask him to sit with me in the holding room?"

"Sure. He'd like that."

"You wanna watch my execution? I got plenty of tickets."

"No thanks."

Cody breaks into a big smile and starts chuckling. "Say, Marvin, how about a favor?"

This is funny and Marvin laughs. "A favor on death row?"

"Sure. You can do it. A simple favor and it would mean a lot."

"What is it?"

Cody walks to the bars and lowers his voice. "Marvin, I haven't seen the moon in fourteen years, and I would love to see it just one more time."

"Come on, Cody."

"No, you come on, Marvin. I'll be dead in less than an hour, so who gives a damn if I sneak outside for a bit of fresh air. What's the harm?"

"It's against the rules."

"You make most of the rules around here, Marvin. Nobody will question you. Hell, nobody will ever know. We ease down the hall, take the side door to the yard, and there it is. A big moon, nice and full, the first summer moon. Right up there in the eastern sky."

"It's too risky."

Cody laughs and says, "Oh, get real. What am I gonna do, Marvin? Beat you over the head, jump half a dozen fences, dodge a thousand bullets, outrun the bloodhounds, and then, exactly where would I go, Marvin? Hell, they got half the state police out there just waiting to celebrate because we damned sure love our executions. Come on, Marvin, do something nice. I'm so dead here, okay?"

Marvin glances around, uncertain. "I'll go ask the warden."

"No! Don't waste your time with that fool. You know he'll say no. Just ease me out the side here and nobody will see us. Just five minutes, Marvin. Please."

"Can't do it."

"Sure you can. Who are you afraid of?"
"No way. I'll get fired."
"No you won't. Nobody'll know."
"Sorry, Cody."
"Just five minutes."
"Two minutes. Then right back in here."

(8)

The yard is a small outdoor space, with a picnic table on a slab of concrete surrounded by a few sprigs of grass. Twenty-four feet by twenty, to be exact, and the death row inmates know its precise dimensions because they walk the fence lines daily. Dirt paths had been worn between the concrete and the chain-link and below the shiny razor wire. They were allowed one hour each day, alone and unsupervised, to inhale the fresh air, to gaze into the distance and dream, and to shuffle along the paths. Seven or eight long steps, then a ninety-degree turn and more of the same. In the old days, the yard was much larger and had a set of old weights and a basketball hoop. Four men were allowed at each break, and rowdy games of two-on-two were the norm. Then there was a fight and one was bludgeoned by a dumbbell.

There are no lights around the yard. It's never used after dark. The squat, flat-roof building that is death row is attached to it and runs forty yards east and west. At the far end is the Gas House, another tumor-like appendage added on decades earlier.

The thick metal door opens and Cody walks out, without cuffs and chains. Marvin, unarmed, follows and watches him closely. In the distance, searchlights sweep the sky and a heli-copter is heard somewhere. It's time for a killing and the air is filled with excitement.

Cody stands in the center of the yard and stares at the full moon, so large it's almost within reach. "Well, it hasn't changed, has it? Same old moon."

Marvin leans on the picnic table, says, "You were expecting something different?"

"It seems closer, don't you think?"

"I doubt it. How'd you know it was a full moon?"

"Because it's June twenty-second, the first day of summer. That's called a strawberry moon."

"Never heard of that."

"Come on, Marvin. You serious?"

"Never heard of it. Why's it called a strawberry moon?"

"Because in late spring and early summer the strawberries and other fruits finally ripen. The Indians gave it the name of strawberry moon."

"What does that mean?"

"It means the full moon looks closer for a few days."

"How do you know that?"

"Oh, I used to know all the stars and constellations, Marvin. Me and Brian lived in the wild, slept during the day, roamed at night. You wanna hear a story, one of my favorites?"

"Sure, but you'd better talk fast. If the warden catches us out here there'll be hell to pay."

"I'm not worried about the warden."

"Well, I am. I'm not sure this is a good idea."

"Me and Brian broke in a house one time and we couldn't find any guns or jewelry or anything we could sell. Hell, they didn't even have any frozen pizza. But the dude who owned the house had this really nice telescope set up in his den, in front of a big window so he could watch the stars. We were pissed off at him so we took his telescope, figured we might be able to fence it for a few bucks. That night we set it up in a field and started playing around with it. I'll never forget the thrill of looking at the surface of the moon, the craters and ridges and valleys. 'Magnificent desolation,' as one astronaut described it. We looked at it for hours, completely mesmerized. A week or so later we broke into another house and it was a gold mine. Guns, jewelry, radios, a small television. Quite a haul. Even pizza. We fenced the stuff and had a pocketful of cash. We found a cheap motel, paid for a room, took showers, slept under the air-conditioning. Lived the big life. We did this from time to time when we had the money. Not far away was a library, a branch of the main one downtown. We went there—my first time in a library, I can promise you that—and we were surprised to learn that anybody could walk in off the street, for free, and read newspapers and magazines. We browsed around, and upstairs we found this beautiful picture book on the solar system and constellations, the various phases of the moon. So we stole it and took it back to our campsite. We studied it from cover to cover, I couldn't read that well but Brian had finished the eighth grade, and we learned all about the stars. We spent hours every clear night with the telescope. We could look at the moon, without the telescope, and tell what day of the month it was. When there was no moon and the sky was thick with stars, we could spot, with the naked eye, all the constellations. Orion, Scorpius, Gemini, the Northern Cross, Taurus the bull, Ursa Major, more commonly known as the Big Dipper. And with the telescope we found stars and solar systems that they never teach you in school. We got in a big fight one time because Brian swore he found Pluto. Can you believe that?"

"I'm not sure what to believe."

"We kept that telescope, never fenced it, not even when we were hungry."

"That's a nice story, except for the part about breaking and entering and stealing."

"What were we supposed to do, Marvin? Starve to death?"

"That don't make it right."

"Whatever." Cody points to the moon. "Brian liked the dark nights, the Milky Way, thousands of stars, but me, I loved the moon. And when it was full, like tonight, it was almost impossible to see the constellations. Didn't bother me. I spent hours exploring its surface, convinced there was somebody living up there. You see that dark area just to the right of dead center? That's the Sea of Tranquility, where Apollo 11 landed in July of 1969. Remember that, Marvin?"

"Everybody remembers that. You were just a kid."

"I was eight years old, living with a foster family, the Conways. One of many, back then. They were okay, I guess, but one of the bad things about being a foster kid is that you always know that you really don't belong. Anyway, it was a Sunday night and Mr. Conway made us all gather in front of the TV and watch the moon landing. It didn't mean much to me. You?"

"I don't know, Cody. It was a long time ago. Back then little black boys didn't dream of growing up to be astronauts."

"Well, I was a little white boy and I damned sure didn't dream of being one either. All I remember dreaming about was having a mother and a father and living in a nice little house."

Cody backs away and leans on the picnic table next to Marvin. They watch the searchlights sweep the sky in the distance.

"What were your dreams, Marvin?"

"I don't know. Playing baseball. I had good parents, still do, with lots of brothers and sisters, aunts and uncles, one big family, happy most of the time. In that respect, I'm a lucky man."

"You sure are."

"Willie Mays was my hero and I dreamed of playing in the big leagues. My dad was a player, did three years in the minors, but that was before Jackie Robinson. He couldn't make any money so he quit and came home. He taught me the game and I loved it."

"How far did you go?"

Marvin finds this amusing. "Not far. In 1965 the White Sox drafted me in the forty-fifth round, which happened to be the last round, and they offered me two hundred dollars to sign."

"Did you?"

"No. My dad said don't do it. He knew I couldn't make it in the bigs, too slow, and he didn't want me to waste the next five years bouncing around the minors. He wanted me to go to college, but we couldn't quite swing it."

"He must have been a smart man."

"Still is. I listen to him, off and on, and he still likes to give advice."

"And your mom?"

"Oh, she's still around. They've been married for fifty-something years. She likes to give advice too."

Cody is too nervous to stay in one place. He walks to the fence and stares at the moon. "One time, I guess I was about twelve, me and Brian were in the woods and we were hungry, cold, it was wintertime, and we were scoping out houses to break into. It was night, just after dark, and we sneaked up behind this house at the edge of the woods, a new subdivision. We shinnied up a tree for a better look. We were like cats in the night, moved so quick. We looked down into the house. There was a big window near the kitchen, and there was this perfect little family all gathered around the table having dinner. Father, mother, three kids, one boy about my age. Eating, talking, laughing, behind them was a fire in the fireplace. I thought—What happened to me? Why am I up here in a tree, hungry and cold, and that kid has the perfect life? What went wrong, Marvin?"

"I don't have an answer."

"I know you don't, Marvin, so just humor me, okay? My biological clock is ticking. I mean, really ticking."

"We better get back inside. You got thirty-three minutes. The warden might catch us out here."

"What's he gonna do? Give me some demerits? Put me on probation?"

"Don't know, but he can stick me over there in the general population with the riffraff."

Cody laughs at this. "I guess life's better here on death row."

"I prefer it."

"Thank you, Marvin, for this." He waves at the moon. "Thank you for being nice to me. Some of those other guards are assholes."

"I've always liked you, Cody, and I never felt like you deserved to be here."

"Well, thank you, Marvin, that's nice to hear now that we're down to the wire."

Vehicles approach on the road that leads to the central prison. It's a caravan of sorts, with a police car in full blue-light mode leading three identical white vans. Another police car follows. They turn in to the parking lot near the front of death row and stop. In the distance, and too far away to hear what's being said, the vans empty and the guards escort the people inside.

Cody and Marvin watch this, and when the people are out of view, Cody says, "Well, I guess the witnesses have arrived. The hour is drawing near."

"You got that right."

"Have you seen the witness list, Marvin?"

"I have."

"So, who's on it?"

"I can't say."

"Come on, Marvin. I think I'm entitled to know who'll watch me die. For Pete's sake."

"Some of the family. The Bakers had three children."

"Murray, Adam, and Estelle. Thank God they were not at home that night. I remember them from my trial. I even wrote letters to them but they never wrote back. Can't really blame them."

"Well, they're here, along with a couple of the prosecutors, some cops, I think. I don't know everybody on the list."

"And no one on my side of the room."

"That's what you want, right?"

"I guess. You want to watch me die, Marvin?"

"The answer is still no."

"Didn't think so. Just wondering, Marvin, how will they feel when it's over? Will they be relieved? Sad, maybe? Downright happy that I'm gone? I don't know. What do you think?"

"Don't know. They surely want to see you die, else they wouldn't be here."

"Well, I'll give 'em their money's worth, me and the warden." Cody paces a few steps and keeps looking toward the Gas House. "You know, Marvin, I do feel sorry for them. They lost their parents and they were good people and all that, but I swear I didn't kill anybody."

"I know."

"I even told Brian to put the gun away."

"One time, years ago, I was talking to your lawyer, Jack. I like that guy. He told me about your case, said you didn't kill those people, said it was your brother who did all the shooting."

"True, but I was there, as an accomplice, and under the laws of this great state I'm just as guilty as my brother."

"Still don't seem right."

"It was my fault, Marvin. All my fault."

(9)

The house was in a development of sorts, two-acre lots out in the country, on a paved road, with county water and sewer, neighbors too far away to meddle but close enough to help, 3,000 square feet heated with plenty of room for a pool, gardens, dogs. The neighborhood was a perfect target for unsophisticated smash-and-run thieves who could slither in from the woods and strike night or day. So far, it was virgin territory for the little Wallace gang. There were fourteen houses on the road, all built within the past twenty years, modern enough to have security systems and alarms. Along most of the driveways there were little tin signs advertising ALERT, the most popular security company in the area.

Brian and Cody watched the road for weeks. It was summer, time for vacations, always a busy period for thieves. At sunset, they raced through the neighborhood on their bikes to see which houses were dark. During the late afternoons, they climbed trees and used binoculars to check on the houses; which campers were gone, which driveways were collecting newspapers, where were the kids and dogs missing, where were the curtains pulled tight? It was easy to spot an empty house.

After a few days it became obvious that the Bakers were away. They lived on the north side of the road, Cody's responsibility. Brian was monitoring the houses on the south side.

They waited until after two in the morning, the best time to go in. With ALERT sensors on all windows and doors, the call to central monitoring would take place at about one minute, then the sirens or buzzers or whatever the Bakers had chosen would erupt inside the house. One never knew if the system included exterior alarms that would wake the neighbors. If things went as expected, at least twenty minutes would pass before any blue lights appeared.

Two minutes was more than enough time. Each carried a small flashlight because they worked in the dark. Again, those bothersome neighbors might include insomniacs. With a glass-cutting tool, Brian quickly removed a pane in the patio door, reached inside, unlocked the dead bolt, and eased the door open. He had done it so many times he could actually open a locked door as fast as anyone with a key.

Seconds later, the alarm began beeping throughout the house, but it wasn't loud. The boys had learned to remain calm amid the racket and go about their business. They had never hit a place with people inside. There was no one to hear the alarm.

However, on that fateful night everything went wrong. They were in the den when someone flipped a light switch at the end of the hallway. A man yelled, "Who's there?"

"Dammit!" Brian hissed, almost under his breath but loud enough to be heard because a woman yelled, "Someone's in there, Carl. I heard him."

For fifteen years, Cody had replayed those awful seconds and could never explain to himself why Brian had made a sound. They had reminded each other a hundred times that if anything went wrong, they were to scramble back to the door they entered and disappear like rabbits into the night. Don't make a sound, just run. They were dressed in black, even down to their sneakers, and wore black face paint and black rubber gloves. They were kids but theirs was an adult game and they took it seriously. They were proud of their successes.

And the gun? Why the gun? They had stolen a hundred of them and they had wasted a mountain of ammo target-shooting deep in the woods. Cody became a decent shot, but Brian could hit anything. They had argued over whether to pack a gun for these break-ins.

Another light in the rear of the house came on. Cody retreated and crawled into the kitchen where he knocked over a barstool.

"I gotta gun!" the man yelled.

Brian ducked behind a recliner in the den.

The shootout lasted only seconds, but Cody, the only survivor, could replay it for hours. The deafening boom of a 12-gauge and rapid shots from a 9-millimeter. The woman screamed and her husband fired again.

At Cody's trial, the ballistics expert would explain to the jury that Brian managed to get off five shots before getting hit by the 12-gauge. One shot hit Mrs. Baker just under her left eye, killing her instantly. Two shots hit Mr. Baker in the chest, but he still managed to take out Brian with his second shot.

When the shooting stopped, Cody found a light switch and gawked in horror at the carnage. Mr. Baker was on the floor, groaning, trying to get to his feet. Mrs. Baker was slumped against the bookcase, bleeding. And Brian was on the floor near the television, with half his head blown off. Cody screamed and reached for him.

When the police arrived, they found Cody sitting on the floor, holding his brother's mangled head, covered with blood, and weeping.

Mr. Baker died the next day. Cody, uninjured, at least physically, was locked away for the rest of his life. The crime scene photos were shown to the jurors, and they did not deliberate long before returning with a death verdict.

(10)

"It was all my fault, Marvin. I thought the house was empty, that the Bakers were still gone. One mistake by me and everything changed. It was just so awful."

Cody returns to the picnic table and leans on it, next to Marvin. Both stare at the moon. Seconds pass and it's time to go.

"There was so much blood. I was covered and I couldn't run. The cops threw me in the back seat and cussed me all the way to the jail, but I didn't care. I couldn't stop crying. Brian was dead. He was the only person I ever loved, Marvin, and the only person who ever loved me. And he's been dead for fifteen years."

"I'm sorry, Cody."

Another guard peeks around the door and says, "Warden's coming."

Marvin snaps to attention and moves toward the door. He opens it and waits but Cody is frozen in place. Slowly, he wipes tears from his face as he stares at the moon.

"Gotta go, Cody."

"Go where? Where am I going, Marvin?"

"I can't answer that."

"You think Brian might be there?"

"Got no idea."

Cody slowly stands, wipes his face again, and takes one long last look at the moon.

SPARRING PARTNERS

(1)

The law firm of Malloy & Malloy was well into its third generation, and, from all outward appearances, was prospering nicely, in spite of a rather shocking scandal not far in its past. For fifty-one years, it had litigated from the corner of Pine and 10th, in downtown St. Louis, in a handsome Art Deco building stolen in a foreclosure by an earlier Malloy lawyer.

Inside the doors, though, things were not going well. The patriarch of the firm, Bolton Malloy, had been gone for five years now, sent away by a judge after pleading guilty to killing his wife, an extremely unpleasant woman no one seemed to miss. Thus, the scandal: one of the city's best-known lawyers convicted of manslaughter and stripped of his license. His sentence was ten years, but he was already plotting an earlier release.

His sons were running the firm and running it into the ground. They were the only partners, equal in stature, authority, and earnings, but they disliked one another intensely and spoke to each other only when necessary. Rusty, the older by seventeen months, fancied himself a hard-charging trial lawyer; he loved the courtroom and dreamed of big, splashy verdicts that would attract even more cases and no small measure of publicity. Kirk, the quieter one, preferred a safer office practice with fat fees for estate and tax work.

Rusty bought season tickets for the Cardinals every year and attended at least fifty games. In the winter, he rarely missed a Blues hockey match. Kirk eschewed sports and preferred the theater, opera, even ballet.

Rusty adored blondes and had married three of them. Only the second produced offspring, his only child. Kirk was still with his first wife, a pretty brunette, but things were unraveling. They had three teenaged children who had been raised properly but were now pursuing different versions of breaking bad.

Bolton and his late wife had raised the boys staunchly Catholic, and Kirk still attended Mass every Sunday. Rusty had disavowed the church during its sex scandals and could become hostile whenever the Pope was praised. He claimed to have joined an Anglican church, but never attended.

Proud Irish, the boys dreamed of college at Notre Dame. Being a year ahead of his brother, Rusty got in first and strutted off to South Bend. By then, by their late teens, the boys were so jealous of one another and competitive that Kirk was secretly praying Rusty would not get accepted. When he got in, Kirk decided he would push hard for an Ivy and another jab at one-upmanship. He was wait-listed at Dartmouth then squeezed in at the last moment.

Notre Dame football versus Dartmouth athletics. The trash-talking was brutal. When Rusty informed the family that he was applying to Yale Law, Kirk went into orbit and decided to apply to Harvard. Neither quite made the cut, though both had solid undergraduate résumés. Rusty's second choice was Georgetown. Kirk's was Northwestern, which at the time was rated four notches higher by a leading magazine. Kirk, therefore, went to a superior law school, but Rusty would have none of it.

Bolton fully expected both sons to return to the family firm in downtown St. Louis, and after paying every dime of their undergraduate and law school costs, he was firmly in control of their futures. However, to toughen them up, he insisted they spend a few years in the trenches getting their noses bloodied in the real world. Rusty chose a public defenders' office in Milwaukee. Kirk became an assistant prosecutor in Kansas City.

Malloy & Malloy had always been knee-deep in politics, with Bolton playing both sides of the fence and donating to the politicians and judges with the best chances of winning. He had never cared which party a candidate belonged to. All he wanted was access, and he wrote the checks and raised the money to get it. Here, though, the boys split again. Rusty was a die-hard Democrat who despised big business and tort reformers and insurance companies. His friends were other street lawyers, tough brawlers who saw themselves as the protectors of the poor and injured. Kirk hung out with a richer crowd, lunching on the upper floors of tall buildings and playing tennis at the country club. He was proud of his record of never having voted for a Democrat.

The firm was so deeply divided that the two factions had separated, literally. Upon entering the plush lobby from Pine Street, one was greeted by a comely receptionist behind a sleek modern desk. For those seeking Kirk, she nodded to the right where he held forth in his wing of offices. For Rusty, she nodded to the left to his domain. Each kept his staff and underlings—associates, secretaries, paralegals, and gofers—on "their" side of the building. Mixing with the "other side" was frowned upon.

To be fair, there was rarely the need to mingle. Rusty's cases involved hardball personal injury litigation, and his staff was experienced in accident reconstruction, medical malpractice, pre-trial maneuverings, settlement negotiation, and the actual courtroom work. Kirk worked by the hour for the well-heeled, and his staff was adept at writing wills an inch thick and manipulating IRS regulations.

The firm had not had a party in five years, since Bolton left. The old man had always insisted on a wine and cheese reception the first Friday of each month at precisely 5:00 p.m., to loosen up the staff and raise morale, and he encouraged everyone to overdrink at the annual Christmas bash. But those gatherings left with Bolton. As soon as he was sentenced, the two sides withdrew to their respective wings and silently adopted new rules of engagement.

To avoid his brother, Rusty worked hard on Mondays and Wednesdays and Friday mornings. Unless, of course, he was in trial. Kirk was more than happy to avoid the office those days and worked hard on Tuesdays, Thursdays, and occasionally on Saturday mornings. They often went weeks without speaking to or even seeing each other.

To provide some modicum of management in the midst of such hostilities, the firm relied on Diantha Bradshaw—the rock, the mediator, the unofficial third partner. Her office was in the demilitarized zone behind the front receptionist, equidistant from both wings. When Kirk needed something from Rusty, which was rare, he went through Diantha. Same for Rusty. When an important decision was at hand, she consulted with both of them, separately, then did whatever she thought was right.

In a profession where firms explode weekly, the Malloys should have split and pursued their own callings without the burden of family complications. But that could not happen for two important reasons. The first was a harsh partnership agreement Bolton had forced them to sign before he left for prison. Each agreed, practically at gunpoint, to remain as equal partners for the next fifteen years. In the event one decided to leave, then *all* of his cases and clients and fees would remain within the firm. Neither could afford to walk away. The second concerned the matter of real estate. The building was entirely owned by Bolton and he leased it to the firm for one dollar a year. He figured he was making money from its appreciation. A fair monthly rental would be somewhere in the neighborhood of $40,000. If the firm blew up, then everybody got evicted, past rent was jacked up and accelerated, and in general life for all involved would be miserable.

Bolton had always been a controlling, scheming, even shifty father, partner, and boss. No one missed him. His comments about early parole were upsetting.

Malloy & Malloy, both wings, needed Bolton to stay in prison.

(2)

It was early on a Thursday, a workday for Kirk, and he turned off 10th Street and into the underground garage beneath the Malloy building. There were a few scattered vehicles, belonging to Rusty's staff, all there before 8:00 a.m. because the great man himself was in trial. Near the elevator were four reserved spots, with names on large signs to guard them. Rusty's was occupied by a massive Ford SUV, a vehicle so large it barely fit within the tight space. On its bumper was a new sticker that read: HAL HODGE FOR GOVERNOR, VOTE DEMOCRAT.

Kirk parked opposite the Ford and next to a shiny Audi owned by Diantha. The fact that she was at the office so early meant she was monitoring the progress of Rusty's latest court-room adventure.

When Rusty went to trial, the entire firm, both sides, held its breath.

Kirk got out, grabbed his briefcase, and began walking toward the elevator. He stopped to sneer once again at Rusty's bumper sticker. In his opinion, Hal Hodge was a useless bureaucrat who had spent twenty-plus years in the state legislature and had little to show for it. Kirk turned and admired the new sticker on the rear bumper of his own spotless BMW. REELECT GOVERNOR STURGISS, A REAL REPUBLICAN.

Kirk had supported Sturgiss four years earlier by writing checks and hosting fundraisers. He was a likeable enough politician whose greatest asset at the moment was the fact that he was already in office and likely to be reelected. Missouri was a solid red state.

In the elevator, Kirk adjusted his silk tie and straightened his collar. Attire was another flashpoint. When Bolton was in charge he ran things with an iron fist, including the dress code. He insisted on coats and ties, suits in the courtroom, and appropriate outfits for the women, though he did admire shorter skirts. The day after he went to prison, Rusty quickly caved to his younger staff and tossed aside all the rules. His associates and staff were now wearing jeans, khakis, boots, and never ties, at least around the office. In court, though, and in serious meetings, they could still look like lawyers. Kirk loathed the unprofessionalism and maintained Bolton's dress code for his side of the building. His associates seethed at what they perceived as unfair treatment.

At Malloy & Malloy there was always a group seething about something.

The elevator opened into the main lobby, and for a moment Kirk toyed with the idea of wandering into Rusty's wing to see how the trial was going. He walked over, went down the wide hallway, and realized that the lawyers and staff were in a meeting. He put an ear to the door of the conference room, then decided to leave it alone. An unexpected appearance by him would irritate his brother and disrupt the meeting.

Diantha was in there and she would brief him later. She

was not watching the trial, but word from a mole was that it was not going well for the plaintiff.

(3)

On the other side of the door, Rusty paced while he talked. The mood was tense. His staff, all properly dressed for trial, seemed fatigued at 8:00 a.m., which was not unusual several days into a big jury trial. Tall coffee cups littered the long, marble conference table. A platter of pastries appeared to be untouched.

Rusty was saying, "So Bancroft called me last night around ten o'clock. Went through the usual bullshit, then said his client would pay one mil to settle everything."

Diantha was not sitting at the table but in a corner, as if she was there because she had to be but wasn't really involved. When she heard the magic words about the settlement offer, she closed her eyes and tried to conceal a smile.

"Of course, I told him hell no. In no uncertain terms, I said we are not settling, at least not for a lousy million dollars."

Diantha, eyes still closed, frowned and barely shook her head.

He paused to look around the room, almost daring anyone to question him. "Are we all on board with this?"

Carl Salter was a jury consultant, neither a lawyer nor an employee of the firm, and an old friend of Rusty's. The two had been through many trials over the years and pulled no punches with each other. He said, "Take the money, Rusty. This jury is not with you. You may have jurors one, three, and five, but that's only half and it's far short. Take the money."

Rusty said, "I disagree. We have juror number two in our pocket. I've watched that woman for a week now and she's with us. She actually cried when Mrs. Brewster testified."

"She cries a lot," said Carl. "Hell, I saw her crying during a recess yesterday."

Rusty looked at an associate and said, "Ben?"

"I don't know, Rusty. She does cry a lot. I think we have four out of six but it takes five. I don't think we have the magic number." Ben Bush had been Rusty's top trial assistant for the past eight years. In most firms of any size he would have already been promoted to some level of partnership, but the Malloys didn't promote well. They were generous with salary and benefits but not ownership.

Rusty glared at him as if he were nothing but a spineless coward, then jerked his head and looked across the table. "Pauline?"

She knew it was coming and didn't flinch. Little caused Pauline Vance to react with anything but calm. She had been on Rusty's staff for eleven years and had earned her reputation as a gutsy litigator who'd rather fight than settle.

She said, "I don't know. The case has tried well and we've proven liability. The damages are horrific. I think the potential is still there for a huge verdict."

Rusty smiled for the first time that morning.

Carl made the smile vanish when he butted in with "May I ask a question?" Without waiting for a response, he kept talking. "Did you by chance inform your clients that the hospital made an offer to settle the case?"

"No. It was late at night. I thought I would tell them this morning."

"But it's too late. You've already rejected the offer, right?"

"We're not taking the offer, Carl. Understand? This case is worth a fortune because in about two hours I will stand before our wonderful jurors and ask them for thirty million dollars."

Rusty was never bullied by his staff, or anyone else for that matter. He had the brass balls and fearless temperament of a seasoned trial lawyer. He still held the record for being the youngest lawyer in Missouri history to win a jury verdict in excess of a million dollars. At the age of twenty-nine he had cajoled a $2 million award out of a jury of his peers in a Cape Girardeau courtroom. It inspired him to sue at the drop of a hat, eschew settlements, join mass-tort scams, advertise, network, boast about his verdicts, live large and spend foolishly. Typical trial lawyer.

His career had been on track until the verdicts stopped coming.

He lowered his voice and looked at his staff. Always the actor, he said gravely, "You guys know how much we need a big verdict. Well, today we're gonna get one. Let's go slay the dragon."

They grabbed their papers and briefcases and began to file out. At the door, Diantha said, "Say, Rusty, got a minute?"

"Only a minute," he said with a phony smile. They were close friends and shared many secrets, and Diantha was probably the only person Rusty might occasionally listen to.

She nodded at Carl, who closed the door and joined them. When the three were alone, Diantha said, "We have a problem, a rather large one."

"What is it?" Rusty snapped.

"You know damned well what it is, Rusty. You got an offer to settle the case and you did not consult with your client before you rejected it."

Carl groaned and shook his head in frustration. Rusty glared at him, then said, "It's not going to matter, Diantha. I've got this jury."

"Carl thinks otherwise, as does your team. I watched their faces."

"You're not in the courtroom, Diantha."

"But I am," Carl said. "Take the money and salvage something."

Rusty took a deep breath and seemed to stand down for a moment. Diantha moved in quickly. "Do you know how much we owe on this case for litigation expenses?"

"No, I'm sure—"

"Just over two hundred thousand dollars."

"It's an expensive game."

"And we have a fifty percent contract with the client. A million bucks covers the debt, then we split the rest with the client. That's four hundred thousand dollars for the firm, Rusty."

"The Brewsters deserve much more. You should see the jurors look at Trey. They want to give that boy a fortune."

Carl said, "Yes, they do, they're very sympathetic, but it's not going to happen, Rusty. You have not proven liability. The damages are huge, but the liability is thin. Bancroft will eat your lunch."

Such language usually ignited Rusty, but he was still breathing heavily, and listening. His shoulders sagged even more and he looked deep into the eyes of Diantha. What he saw crushed him. She had no confidence. She doubted him. She thought he was about to lose, again.

"Carl is usually right, Rusty," she said. "Let's take the money and run. We're up to our ears in bank loans."

Rusty exhaled and managed another fake smile. "Okay, okay. I hate fighting with you guys."

Carl said, "Take the money."

(4)

Diantha walked them to the elevator and watched the door close. She hustled to the right side of the building, nodded at a young lawyer who was unpacking her briefcase, and tapped on the door of Kirk's office. Without waiting, she pushed it open. He was standing behind his desk, as if waiting for her.

"The hospital offered one million to settle last night and Rusty just agreed to take the money."

"Thank you, thank you," Kirk said as he closed his eyes and raised his hands to the ceiling.

"He didn't want to but Carl twisted his arm."

"Hallelujah. Praise be to God."

"There might be a problem, though."

"What is it?"

"Bancroft called with the offer late last night and Rusty blew him off. Said no way. And of course he never thought about consulting with the client."

"Late last night means he'd probably knocked back four or five doubles by the time Bancroft called."

"I'm sure. He says he rejected the offer outright, but now plans to take the money this morning."

"I'm sure the hospital would love to get out with only a million."

"We'll see."

"How much cash do we have in the case?"

"Two hundred grand."

"Two hundred grand? How can he spend so much money on a single case?"

"He always has, Kirk. The difference is that now he can't quite seem to get the money back."

"He's lost the last three, right?"

"Four. This would be number five. Carl and Ben don't like his chances."

"We can't afford another loss. He needs to stop suing people."

"And you're going to tell him that?" she asked.

"No. It would do absolutely no good. Litigation to him is like blood to a vampire. He loves the courtroom."

"And once upon a time it loved him."

"But he's lost his touch."

"I'll check back later," she said and turned for the door.

"Are you monitoring the case?" he asked.

"No, but I have a mole inside the courtroom."

"Ben or Pauline?"

"I'll never tell."

"You're very good with secrets, Diantha."

"You have to be, around this place."

(5)

A secretary led them back to the chambers and showed them in. Judge Pollock was already robed and chatting with Luther Bancroft, the lead defense attorney. A small band of his associates huddled in one corner, sadly lacking in clout and reputation to join the conversation. When Rusty marched in with his customary purpose, all eyes turned to him and he flashed a smile. Ben and Pauline were right behind him. Carl, the non-lawyer, did not qualify for the meeting.

After a round of terse "good mornings" and quick handshakes, Judge Pollock said, "So, gentlemen, I assume we are ready for closing arguments."

Rusty smiled again and said, "Some good news, Judge. Late last night I took a call from Luther here and he made us an offer of settlement. I declined, but after a good night's sleep we have decided to accept the sum of one million dollars to settle the case."

His Honor was surprised and glared at Bancroft. "You didn't mention a settlement offer to me."

Bancroft said, "Well, Your Honor, I didn't say a word about

it because Mr. Malloy rejected my offer outright. He never even consulted with his client. Indeed, he was quite abrupt and used language you wouldn't tolerate in open court."

"I apologize, Luther," Rusty said, condescending. "I didn't realize you were so sensitive."

"Apology accepted. Anyway, I informed my client and the offer was immediately taken off the table. I was instructed to try the case to the end. We've come this far. Let's get it over with."

Ben shot a look of desperation at Pauline, who appeared unmoved.

Rusty was surprised but recovered quickly. He rubbed his hands together as if itching for a fight and said, "Great! Let's tee it up."

Judge Pollock frowned at both lawyers and said, "Well, it seems to me that one million is a fair settlement, all things considered."

Bancroft nodded gravely and said, "I agree, Judge, but my client was, and is, adamant. No settlement. The hospital firmly believes it did nothing wrong."

"Let's go!" Rusty said, ready to rumble.

"All right. Proceed to your tables. I'll have the bailiff prepare the jury."

All the lawyers filed out and headed for the courtroom. Ben Bush ducked into a restroom, locked himself in a stall, and sent a text message to Diantha: *Defendant withdrew the offer after R's rejection. Client never told. Headed for closing arguments. We're so screwed!!*

(6)

Under the steady gaze of everyone—lawyers, parties, spectators, clerks, bailiffs, and Judge Pollock—the six jurors filed in and took their seats. The seventh, an alternate, sat next to the jury box. There were no smiles, only the stressed looks of people who wished they were somewhere else.

The plaintiff's table was closer to the jury box than the defense's, and throughout the trial the jurors had been forced to look at Trey Brewster. He was positioned on their side by his lawyer, who, of course, wanted him exposed as much as possible. Trey was twenty-three years old but age didn't matter anymore. Birthdays came and went and he had no clue. His eyes were always closed, his mouth perpetually opened, his head propped awkwardly on his left shoulder. One tube with oxygen ran to his nose. Another, with formula, ran down his throat. He had a feeding portal in his stomach, but Rusty wanted the jurors to see all tubes possible. As brain-damaged as he was, Trey could still breathe on his own, so there was no noisy ventilator to grate on the jurors. He weighed 120 pounds, down 80 since his surgery two years earlier. He was nothing more than a shriveled shell of a young man, and there was absolutely no chance his condition would ever improve.

His mother sat to his right with her hand always on his arm. She had the hollow-eyed, fatigued gaze of a defeated caregiver who could never give up. His father, to his left, stared blankly ahead, as if detached from the proceedings.

Judge Pollock pulled his mike closer and said, "Ladies and gentlemen of the jury, we have now made it to the end, or something very close to it. You've heard all the witnesses, seen all the exhibits, listened to the law as I have instructed you. This has been a long trial and it's almost over. Again, I thank you for your service and patience. Both sides will now be allowed to make their closing arguments, and then you will retire for your deliberations. For the plaintiff, Mr. Malloy."

Rusty stood and walked to the podium with great confidence. He looked at the six jurors and offered them a business-like smile. Three met his gaze. Three looked away. Number two appeared to be ready to cry. He began without looking at notes.

"When my client, Trey Brewster, was admitted to GateLane Hospital for a routine appendectomy, no one in his family, no one on his medical team, no one in the world could have predicted that he would never regain consciousness, that he would spend the rest of his life paralyzed, brain-dead, in a wheelchair, fed by a tube, his bladder drained by catheters."

Rusty's voice was rich and heavy, his cadence dramatic. He was the only actor on the stage, and relished the moment. His opening was powerful. The courtroom was still and silent.

On the third row of the gallery, Carl Salter looked in the general direction of Rusty, but he was really watching all six faces, all twelve eyes.

And he didn't like what he saw.

During the trial, Bancroft did a masterful job of passing the buck. The negligent party was not in the courtroom. An anesthesiologist with emotional and financial problems had been asleep at the switch. No, worse than that: he wasn't even present for most of the routine surgery. He administered three times the customary level of ketamine, knocked the kid out, then failed to monitor anything during the thirty-minute operation. A week before, he had allowed his medical malpractice insurance to lapse. A week after, he filed for bankruptcy and fled the area. The hospital could be blamed for hiring him, but for his first eight years his work had been stellar. A terrible divorce ruined him, and so on. The bottom line was, he wasn't in the courtroom. GateLane Hospital was, and it had done nothing wrong.

Carl knew the jurors were sympathetic—who wouldn't be? But Rusty had proven a weak case of liability against the hospital.

(7)

For the second time in an hour, Diantha barged into Kirk's office with hardly a knock. She announced, "The hospital withdrew the offer. They're doing closing arguments."

As always, Kirk was buried in paperwork. He shoved some of it away and threw up his hands. "What happened?"

"How am I supposed to know? Just a quick text. No deal, offer withdrawn, closing arguments."

She fell into a leather seat on the other side of his desk and shook her head.

Kirk said, "So, let's keep things clear. The offer came late last night and Rusty, drinking as always, rejected it. Said no, or something to that effect. He did not inform his client. So, if he loses again, then the client will have a beautiful lawsuit against Malloy & Malloy. Right?"

"That's pretty clear, isn't it?"

Kirk exhaled in defeat and frustration and slid lower in his chair. He shook his head at Diantha, who looked just as irritated.

Kirk said, "Well, maybe Rusty can win one for a change."

"Maybe so. A win would be nice. We could pay off some of his litigation loans."

"I think you should go watch the trial. It's just around the corner."

Diantha actually laughed at this. "You couldn't pay me to get near that courtroom."

"I wasn't serious. This is probably catastrophic, don't you think?"

"Probably, yes. I got a bad vibe in the meeting early this morning. The jury is not with him."

(8)

The jurors watched him closely. About half seemed convinced. The other half, skeptical.

He stood at a large whiteboard and held a blue marker. "Now, according to our experts, Trey has a life expectancy of fifteen years. That's pretty sad for a young man who's twenty-three years old and was racing dirt bikes before he encountered GateLane Hospital. So, give him fifteen years. To properly care for Trey, he needs to be in a facility with round-the-clock monitoring. His parents can no longer do it. That's plain and simple. I mean, how much more convincing could a witness be than Jean Brewster? The poor woman is exhausted and cannot go on. So, let's put Trey in an adequate facility, one with nurses, orderlies, housekeepers, technicians, plenty of medicine and that formula that somebody calls food. The average rate for such a place in the metro St. Louis area is forty thousand dollars a month, half a million a year, for fifteen years."

Rusty masterfully scrawled on the whiteboard, tallied it all up, and showed the number of $7,500,000. But he wasn't finished.

"Factor in inflation at three percent a year over fifteen years and the figure comes to . . ." In bold numbers he wrote and said, "Nine million dollars."

He paused and walked away to allow that number to rattle around the courtroom. He took a drink of water from a paper cup at his table, then took his time returning to the podium. "Nine million dollars just to take care of Trey."

The courtroom was silent because everyone knew bigger numbers were on the way.

(9)

Kirk said, "The old man called last night."

"Whose phone?" Diantha asked.

"His. He has another cell phone."

"I thought he was in solitary because they caught him with a cell phone."

"They've caught him with several. He bribes the guards and they sneak in cell phones. Evidently it's a big business in prison."

"I'm sure he's bribing everyone."

"No doubt. One minute he's playing poker with the warden, the next minute he's in solitary, phoneless."

"Why'd he call?"

"You know Bolton. I think he just wanted me to know that he has another cell phone. And, he's expecting me tomorrow. It's my turn to visit. We talked about that. We talked politics. We talked about his chances for parole next year."

"He's only served five years."

"Yes, but he's dreaming."

"I like him better in prison."

"Don't we all?"

"What's his plan?"

"He wouldn't say over the phone, but I'm sure it involves bribery and politics."

(10)

Rusty stood at the podium and aimed a red laser pointer at a large whiteboard. He looked at the jurors, then the whiteboard, and said, "Now, before Trey made the fateful decision to have routine surgery at GateLane Hospital, he was pursuing a rewarding career as a software designer and earning eighty thousand dollars a year. That career is gone. That salary is gone. Everything is gone, except your verdict. Under our laws, he is entitled to recover his lost income. Eighty thousand dollars times fifteen years comes to one point two million. Inflation will take it to two million. Add that to the future cost of his care, and his pain and suffering, and our total becomes seventeen million dollars."

He put away the red laser, took a black marker, and carefully added the sum of $2,000,000 to $9,000,000 for "Care" and $6,000,000 to "Pain and Suffering." He totaled it up nicely at $17,000,000.

All six jurors stared at the amount. It was a shocking sum of money, but seeing it in bold print lessened the impact. Rusty was making a case that the money was justified.

He walked to his table, found a report half an inch thick, and flipped pages as he returned to the podium. "According to its own financials, last year GateLane Hospital System had six hundred million more dollars in revenue than expenses. We don't dare refer to the difference as 'profits,' because we know that GateLane is proud of its nonprofit status. That means it doesn't pay any state or federal income taxes. So, after all of its expenses, including the seven million dollars it paid its CEO and the five million dollars it paid its chief operating officer, after all the fat salaries were paid, GateLane had six hundred million more dollars in the bank than when the year started. What does it do with all that extra cash? It buys other hospitals. It wants to be a monopoly so it can continue to raise prices."

Luther Bancroft stood, shaking his head. "Objection, Your Honor. This is not an anti-trust case."

"Sustained. Move along, Mr. Malloy."

Without so much as a glance at the two, Rusty continued, "The only way to get the attention of a defendant like GateLane Hospital System is to slap it in the face with punitive damages."

He paused for dramatic effect and stepped to the side of the podium. "Punitive damages. Damages imposed to punish a corporation, for-profit or otherwise, for wrongdoing. For gross negligence. How much would it take to get the attention of a mammoth hospital system like GateLane? One percent of its annual profit? Oops, sorry, can't use that word, can we? Let's call it something else. Let's call it the 'cushion.' One percent of the cushion would be six million dollars. That's a lot of money but it probably wouldn't bother the CEO because he makes more than that. Two percent would be twelve million. You know what? I think three percent sounds better because that's eighteen million bucks, and I'll bet you that when you hit 'em with eighteen million bucks in punitive damages they'll get the message. They'll feel the pain. They'll be more cautious about who they hire and keep on staff."

Slowly, he uncapped the marker again and added $18,000,000 to the total.

All six jurors stared at the board and tried to comprehend handing over $35,000,000 of someone else's money.

Rusty left them with "It's a lot of money, ladies and gentlemen. I've been here many times before. I've tried a lot of cases and I've stood here before hundreds of jurors. And I've never asked for this kind of money."

He stepped over and put a hand on Trey's right shoulder. He looked at him pitifully, and, with a breaking voice, said, "But I've never had a client as deserving as my friend Trey."

Fighting tears, he looked at the jurors and said, "Thank you."

(11)

Diantha was behind her desk reading a document when someone tapped lightly on her door. Before she could respond, Kirk opened it and closed it behind him. He looked at her and said, "I can't concentrate."

"Neither can I," she said.

"I hate it when he's in trial," Kirk said as he fell into an oversized leather chair.

"I hate it when he loses," she said. "It's okay when he wins, as I seem to recall."

"No word from the courtroom?"

"No. My mole can't use a phone in the courtroom. He or she should text me shortly."

"Look, Diantha, I know tomorrow is my day to visit the old man, but I can't go. Rusty went last month, and besides, he's tied up with the trial."

She gave him a look and asked, "Why can't you go?"

"Because I have an appointment with my divorce lawyer."

"Kirk, I'm so sorry. I thought you'd found a good therapist."

"We've found all the best therapists, Diantha, but nothing can save us. It's over. Or, I suppose it's just beginning. It won't be easy."

"I was just hoping . . ."

"Yes, so were we. The truth is, we've known for a long time. Things just keep getting worse and we're worried it might be affecting the kids."

"I'm so sorry, Kirk."

"I know. Thanks. Chrissy plans to file next week."

"On what grounds?"

"She hates my guts. I can't stand the sight of her. That good enough?"

"Depends on your lawyer. Who'd you hire?"

"Bobby Laker. A hundred thousand bucks for the initial retainer."

"Who did she hire?"

"Scarlett Ambrose."

"Wow. This should be a doozy. You guys have lawyered up with the two nastiest pit bulls in town. Can I come watch the trial?"

"Maybe. We might sell tickets." He closed his eyes as if in pain and pinched the bridge of his nose. About a year earlier he had first confided in Diantha that the wheels were coming off at home. He felt she should know because it would eventually affect the firm. At his direction, she had informed Rusty, who, with three divorces under his belt, had no sympathy whatsoever.

He ran his fingers through his thick hair, offered her a fake smile, and asked, "Can you go see the old man?"

"Why me?"

"Because there's no one else. It's my turn and Rusty wouldn't dare offer to pinch-hit, even if his trial is over. I could put it off a week, I guess, but you know how he is about the visits. He's trying to control the firm from a prison cell."

She frowned and studied a wall.

He continued, "Look, it's a huge favor, okay? So I'll owe you one. I swear I'll pay you back in some marvelous fashion."

She shook her head and mumbled, "You certainly will."

(12)

Luther Bancroft buttoned the top button of his fine black linen jacket as he walked to the jury box. He didn't bother with phony smiles or gushing praise for jobs well done. Instead, he went straight to the heart of the matter.

"Mr. Malloy here has you, the jury, confused with an ATM. He's standing before you, smiling, dreaming, having far too much fun pushing buttons and waiting for a pile of cash to suddenly appear. He wants, let's say, a million bucks for this, and a million bucks for that. He pushes some more buttons, more cash spits out. It's all fun and games, free and easy money. Pain and suffering? How about five or ten million? Just push a button. Future medical expenses? How about five or ten more? How beautiful it is, growing on trees, just waiting to get picked. And the biggest one of all—punitive damages! The sky is the limit. Eighteen million has a nice ring to it, so push that button. And what's the grand total? How much cash will the plaintiff's ATM fork over? Thirty-five million! Isn't this fun?"

The jurors absorbed this, at least three with some semblance of a smile.

Bancroft turned and took two steps toward Trey, and looked down at him with great compassion. He shook his head, looked to be on the verge of tears, and said to the jurors, "Ladies and gentlemen, who does not have great sympathy for this young man and his family? Their ordeal is ongoing and heartbreaking. Yes, they need a lot of money, for care and living expenses and everything else Mr. Malloy mentioned. Sure, Trey needs money, and lots of it."

He paused and returned to the podium. "But, sadly, Trey Brewster is in the same boat with his lawyer. Neither has an ATM card. Neither has the right to expect GateLane to hand over a fortune. Why not, you ask?"

He let the question rattle around the courtroom for a second or two, then walked to the defense table and rather ceremoniously yanked up a pile of papers, which he waved at the jurors. "These are called jury instructions. This is the law, as agreed upon by both parties and the judge. In just a moment, when the lawyers are finally finished and we all sit down, the judge will read the law to you. And you took an oath to follow the law. And the law here is quite simple. Before you can consider damages, or in my terminology, before you can start having fun with the ATM, you must first determine liability. You must first decide that my client, GateLane Hospital, was negligent and deviated from the standard of care. Without liability, there can be no damages."

The courtroom was silent. Bancroft had everyone's attention, including Rusty's, who was listening while pretending not to.

"Ladies and gentlemen of the jury, this is a tragic case with horrendous injuries and damages, but, and please forgive me for saying this, but it is the cold hard legal truth, in this case, the damages do not matter. Because . . . there is no liability."

He tossed the jury instructions onto the defense table, took one last look at the jurors, and said, "Thank you."

Carl studied the faces of the jurors, then closed his eyes and slowly shook his head.

(13)

The reservation was for four people at noon. Tony's, a swanky Italian place downtown, was Rusty's favorite any day of the week, but especially at the end of a tough trial when good food and wine were needed. During a trial, the meals often deteriorated to stale pastries in the morning, cold sandwiches while working at lunch, and by dinner the nerves were shot to hell and nothing tasted good. When the jury disappeared to ponder its verdict, Rusty was always ready for a fine meal.

His little team followed the black-jacketed host to a choice table and took their seats. As soon as they were alone, Rusty, with a huge smile, said, "Okay, let's have it. How great was my closing argument?"

It was not the time to be shy, because the boss was craving accolades. Pauline went first and said, "All six are incredibly sympathetic and you did a masterful job taking the sting out of such a huge amount of damages."

"Were they shocked at the thirty-five million?"

Ben said, "I think so, at least initially, but they got over it. Number four rolled his eyes."

"He's been rolling his eyes from the beginning. He's the last one we'll get. Remember, I wanted to cut him. But I think we have a shot at the other five."

Carl glanced at Ben with a look of exasperation.

The waiter appeared and said, "Good afternoon, Mr. Malloy. Always a pleasure to have you here."

Rusty smiled at him, and the diversion gave the other three a chance to exchange frowns.

"Hello, Rocco," Rusty said. "How's the wife and kids?"

"Doing great, sir. Thanks. Something from the bar to start with?"

"Well, as a matter of fact, we've just finished a big trial and the jury is out. We're parched, and hungry too. How about some champagne?" He smiled at Ben and Pauline, as if they could say no.

Carl said, "Might be a bit premature."

Rusty ignored this and said, "Veuve Clicquot, two bottles."

"Excellent choice, sir. I'll have them right out."

Rusty frowned at Carl and said, "I'm getting a bad vibe from you, Carl. What's on your mind?"

"The same thing that's on your mind. That damned jury. I'm not nearly as confident as you."

"Just wait. You'll see."

(14)

With the courtrooms empty and everyone—lawyers, judges, jurors, litigants, bailiffs—away for lunch, the grand hall on the main floor was almost empty. It was a long solemn corridor with a row of stately courtrooms on one side and tall stained-glass windows on the other. The walls were covered with portraits of the city's greatest judges, all white, all male, all old and stuffy. Not a warm face to be found. Ancient and worn wooden benches lined the walls and between them were bronze and granite busts of governors, senators, and lesser politicians. Another white world.

On a bench at the far end of the corridor, almost hidden and certainly not wanting to be seen, the Brewster family prepared for lunch. Trey sat sleeping with his tubes still exposed. His mother gently selected one and began loading it with formula from a syringe. When he was fed, she sat back on the bench and put away her syringe. Mr. Brewster sat next to her, staring as always at a spot on the floor a few feet away, his sad eyes forever locked into a stare of thorough defeat.

From a shopping bag, Mrs. Brewster removed two small sandwiches wrapped in foil and two bottles of water. Lunch for the poor folks.

Nearby an elevator pinged and its doors opened. Luther Bancroft and an associate stepped out, both hauling bulky briefcases. They saw the Brewsters at the same time, and for a long second took in the family having lunch. Then they quickly continued walking down the long corridor. The Brewsters did not seem to notice them.

At the doors, the associate stopped and said, "You know, Luther, it's not too late to settle. We should call GateLane and try to get those folks a few bucks."

Bancroft scoffed and said, "We tried that yesterday and Malloy gave us the finger."

"I know, I know. But they're gonna be devastated when they leave here with nothing."

"So you smell a big win for the home team?"

"Sure. Malloy got greedy and alienated the jury. You could

see it in their eyes." He nodded to the far end, toward the Brewsters. "But it's not their fault. Let's get them a million bucks to cover some of their expenses."

Bancroft scoffed at the idea. "Malloy would just take all the money. Those poor folks wouldn't see a dime."

"It's the fair thing to do, Luther."

"I'm surprised at you. It was a trial, and since when are we concerned with fairness? This is about winning and losing, and we're about to kick Malloy's ass. Buck up, ole boy. This is hardball litigation and it's no place for the sympathetic."

Bancroft huffed away. The associate took one last look at the family, then followed his boss.

The Brewsters ate their sandwiches, in another world, oblivious to the conversation far down the hallway.

(15)

Rusty held a bottle of champagne and offered to pour more around the table, but everyone declined. So he filled his own glass for the last time.

Rocco stopped by and said, "Dessert, Mr. Malloy? Today's special is chocolate mousse, your favorite. It is delicious."

Ben grabbed his phone, gawked at it, and blurted, "It's the clerk. The jury has a verdict."

Dessert was instantly forgotten as the four exchanged looks. Rusty said, "Sorry, Rocco, we need to hustle back to court. The jury is ready."

"Very well. I'll fetch the bill."

Rusty looked at his team and said, "That was quick, don't you think?"

Their nervous glances said it all.

Thirty minutes later, they were in place at the plaintiff's

table, with the Brewsters close by. A door opened and the bailiff led the jurors to their seats. As they settled in, not a single one dared to look at the plaintiffs and their lawyers.

The judge pulled his mike closer and asked, "Ladies and gentlemen of the jury, have you reached a verdict?"

The foreman stood and said, "Yes, Your Honor. We have." He handed a slip of paper to the bailiff who, without looking, handed it up to the judge. He read it without expression, and, taking his time, said, "The verdict appears to be in order. It is unanimous and it reads: 'We the jury find for the defendant, GateLane Hospital.'"

The courtroom was silent for a few seconds, until Mrs. Brewster collapsed into her husband's arms. Rusty closed his eyes and tried to absorb the disaster. Then he glared at the jurors and wanted to lash out.

The judge said, "Both sides will have thirty days for post-trial motions. Again, ladies and gentlemen of the jury, thank you for your service. You are excused. Court's adjourned." He tapped his gavel and disappeared from the bench.

(16)

Kirk stood at his window, hands on hips, staring at the glass, staring at nothing, speechless. Diantha sat in one of his leather chairs, looking at her phone, as if the bad news might somehow change into something good.

Kirk mumbled, "Another two hundred thousand dollars down the drain. We can't afford his career as a high-flying trial lawyer."

Diantha said, "We have to keep him out of the courtroom."

"We need to keep him out of this law firm. Any ideas?"

"Nothing short of murder."

"I've thought about that too."

Kirk turned and walked to his desk and fell into the executive swivel. He looked at her with disgust and said, "When is his next trial?"

"I don't know. I'll check the calendar. Hopefully it's a few years from now."

"At the rate he's losing, no defense lawyer will offer him a dime in settlement. Would you?"

"I don't know what I would do, Kirk. I really don't. This place is spinning out of control."

"Well, maybe so, but when you see the old man tomorrow you gotta keep things positive."

"He's not stupid. I'll go tomorrow, Kirk, but never again. It's up to you and Rusty to visit your father in prison. It's not fair to dump it on me."

"I understand."

"Do you?" She got to her feet, walked to the door, and left without another word. Passing through the hallway on Kirk's side of the firm, she caught a few glances from the staff. By now everyone knew that Rusty had bombed with another jury. It took only a matter of minutes for the news to spread. On his side of the building, things would be even gloomier.

Diantha needed to stay away from there. She had a desk covered with paperwork and her phone was ringing, but she needed to hide somewhere for a few minutes. She got on the elevator and punched the button for the seventh floor. When the door shut she closed her eyes and breathed deeply. A bell rang as she passed each floor. The first three were Malloy territory, the fourth was a real estate company, the fifth was a bunch of architects and accountants. As she went up and got away from the firm, the air seemed to lighten as the tension decreased. The seventh floor was a hodgepodge of small suites leased to engineers, insurance agents, and any number of professionals who came and went.

At the end of a long hall was the office of Stuart Broome, the unlicensed accountant who kept the books for Malloy & Malloy. Old Stu preferred the seventh floor because it was as far away as possible from the rest of the firm. He was not an elderly man but moved about as if he longed to be. He was sixty-two, to be exact, but with his unruly gray hair and white bushy eyebrows and waves of wrinkles across his forehead, he could easily pass for a man twenty years older. Tall by nature, but with a hump in his back, he worked standing at a treadmill desk that never moved. Someone should have suggested that Stu turn on the damned thing so he could burn some calories, as was the design, but they were not being burned and he had been adding at least five pounds a year for decades. With the potbelly up front and the hump in the rear, Stu was a model of human deformity and tried to conceal it under an oversized black blazer that he refused to take off. He wore it every day, along with a white shirt and the same black tie, same black trousers, and same unpolished black shoes.

Thirty years earlier, when Bolton Malloy made a killing by suing Honda for its defective three-wheelers, he hired Old Stu to keep him out of trouble with the IRS. As things evolved, the IRS wasn't the problem. Bolton's wife, the late and forgotten Tilda, routinely terrorized the office looking for money. Colluding with Bolton, Stu learned to hide as much as possible from Tillie. Shifting fees here and there became an established practice at Malloy & Malloy.

To avoid prying eyes, Old Stu worked alone in his little hidden corner of the building. He had fired so many secretaries and assistants over the years that even the thought of training another one was exhausting. He relished his privacy and did his work without the slightest hint of supervision. No one from the firm ever went near him, primarily because no one from the firm was welcome. Except Diantha. He had a soft spot for her and they could talk about anything.

These days the hottest topic was the firm's survival.

She tapped on his door and entered before he said anything. He was standing on the treadmill, staring at the screen of an antique computer, crunching numbers. He rarely smiled but always managed one for her.

"Come in, dear," he said, suddenly warm and welcoming. He stepped down from the treadmill and waved his hand at a dusty sofa in a corner.

"More bad news," she said as she sat down.

"Rusty lost another one?"

"Yes. He asked the jury for thirty-five million dollars. He got nothing. Zero. Defense verdict."

Stu sighed as his shoulders sagged. He fell into a chair and looked at her in total defeat. "Two hundred and seventeen thousand dollars, at last count. Not including the final bill from Carl, and we know that Carl's final bills are always suitable for framing, don't we?" He threw up both hands and said, "Poof."

"This one will get worse. Rusty had a chance to settle last night for a lousy million, but he said no. Said it quickly before he thought about running it by his client. A million bucks would have covered our expenses and given the clients some change. I expect a malpractice notice very soon."

"Well, we've certainly seen them before, haven't we?"

"Too many. Rusty's out of control and I'm not sure how to rein him in."

"It's in his blood, Diantha. Not too many years ago he was the most feared courtroom lawyer in the state, at least in civil cases."

"Oh, I remember. Those were the days. Now he's lost his touch."

They studied the dust on the coffee table. After a moment she said, "Even more bad news. I'm going to see Bolton tomorrow."

"Why?"

"It's Kirk's month to go but he's meeting with his new divorce lawyer in the morning. The divorce will be a mess. I'm sure all of your records will be put on the table."

"Bring 'em on. Which set should I show them?"

She smiled at his candor and knew he wasn't joking. She asked, "When Kirk and Rusty go visit Bolton, don't they take the current financials?"

"Among other things. Bolton wants the prior month's profit-and-loss, and year-to-date. Says he wants to know what's happening in 'his firm.' Rusty went last month and according to him the old man wasn't too happy with the numbers. Rising overhead. Declining income."

"Why does he worry? He's not coming back here. He'll never get his license back, plus he'll have the tobacco money."

Old Stu smiled and repeated, "The tobacco money."

(17)

The tobacco money.

In 1998, the four largest tobacco companies in America agreed to settle a series of massive lawsuits brought by forty-six states to seek reimbursement for the medical costs of smoking. The amount was over $300 billion, the largest civil settlement at that time. The companies also agreed to pay over $8 billion to the lawyers who had cooked up the litigation and brought the industry to the bargaining table. This, obviously, was an unheard-of bonanza for the plaintiffs' bar, or at least for those lawyers who had rolled the dice and signed on early.

A trial lawyer friend he admired had convinced Bolton Malloy that the litigation was worth the risk. In the beginning, the lead lawyers desperately needed cash to fund the ever-expanding litigation, and they were passing the hat and rounding up investors. Bolton wrote a check for $200,000, over the objections of his two sons and everybody else in the building. Four years later, the tobacco companies, always on the defensive, wanted a truce and were willing to pay for it.

In the frenzy that followed, some lawyers got filthy rich. Those at the top of the pyramid had put serious skin in the game and taken enormous risks, and they were compensated first. One small firm in Texas was awarded $500 million. The money flooded down to the others and the payouts were based on the amounts invested. Bolton's share came to $21 million, money he planned to keep for himself.

As usual, his wife knew little of the firm's inner workings because Bolton had always tried to keep her in the dark. He put a lid on the settlement gossip and refused to talk about it, though he privately reminded his two sons that they had scoffed at the tobacco litigation and warned him to stay away from it. Bolton wanted a divorce but couldn't stomach the thought of a protracted fight with hungry lawyers poring over his records.

Buying into the lawsuit proved to be his first brilliant move. His second was to defer payments of his fees and structure them so that they would be invested but not paid for ten years. Maybe in the meantime he could get a divorce, or even better, maybe his wife would just up and die. Her health was fragile.

Then she did die, rather mysteriously, without ever seeing the money, and Bolton went to prison for manslaughter. He'd been there for a month when the tobacco checks started arriving—$3 million a year for at least twelve years. Old Stu set up offshore accounts around the world and routed the money through a maze of entities that a hundred IRS agents couldn't follow. He showed enough real income on the firm's books to placate the tax collectors, but the vast majority of the tobacco money was piling up in shady havens where there was little regard for U.S. tax treaties.

Their secret plan was simple. As soon as Bolton got out of prison he would disappear, hopefully with a young blonde on his arm, to some exotic playground where he would retrieve his money and watch it grow. For his troubles, Old Stu would be handsomely compensated and retire in style as well.

Legally and ethically, the money belonged to Malloy & Malloy. All of it. And, technically, it was unethical for lawyers—Rusty and Kirk—to split fees with non-lawyers—Bolton. But the legal and ethical niceties were being ignored and the sons were simply unable to agree on how to confront the father.

A confrontation, though, was inevitable.

(18)

Diantha said, "It's only a matter of time before they'll want some of the money, you know?"

"I'm sure they will," Old Stu said with a smile. "But they can't find it."

"Well brace yourself, because they're coming. The firm is losing money. Both of them are heavily mortgaged. And now Kirk wants a divorce, which means some nasty boys will soon be going through your books."

"Listen to me, Diantha. There's a lot of shady stuff in those books. I know because I put it there, at my client's insistence, of course. But I am not going to prison like my client, or because of my client."

"That's good to hear, Stu. Just make sure the rest of us are okay."

(19)

By five each afternoon, the bar of the Ritz-Carlton was usually bustling with a well-heeled crowd of business travelers happy to pay twenty dollars a drink and hide it somewhere on their generous expense accounts. For this reason, attractive young women who worked in the downtown offices frequented the bar and its sweeping lounge. And because it had a reputation for attracting upscale local women, it also attracted upscale local professionals in need of a drink.

Rusty loved the place and was there at least once a week. Usually, he met other lawyers and judges to knock back a few before heading for the suburbs. Because he was single, he hung around after his pals headed home, and began hitting on women. That was his customary routine.

However, tonight he was at the bar alone, nursing his third Scotch and cursing another jury. He had been foolish to ask for so much money. He knew St. Louis as well as anyone, and he knew it was a conservative town with no history of jaw-dropping verdicts. Some cities were known for their freewheeling style of tort litigation and stunning awards. Miami, Houston, Boston, and San Francisco came to mind. But not St. Louis. He should have throttled back and asked for only $10 million. He had a $5 million and a $6.4 million under his belt, in years past, and ten would have made more sense. The problem, though, and he admitted this as he drank, was that his ego wanted more, much more. He wanted to single-handedly bring St. Louis into the modern era of staggering verdicts. He, Rusty Malloy, would be the King of Torts in town and smile as the lesser lawyers ran to him with their cases. He would pick and choose.

Three young women made a noisy entrance and Rusty looked them over. One he'd seen before, maybe even bought her a drink. They were about thirty, probably married and looking for some fun before heading home. Short skirts, heels, no sleeves, a lot of flesh on display. They sat in a corner and surveyed the bar scene. One glanced at Rusty, and when a second one did too, he nodded at Jose, the bartender, and nodded at the women. Jose knew what to do for Mr. Malloy—keep the tab open.

They were giggling when he walked up and said, "I'm buying the first round. What'll it be?"

If they were expecting their husbands or boyfriends, they would have waved him off. They did not. The two on the couch moved a few inches apart and one patted the cushion. He fell in between them and quickly admired their legs. A waiter appeared and took their orders.

He had tried marriage three times and simply wasn't cut out for it. He had never been faithful to any woman and it was too late, at the age of forty-six, to change his ways.

(20)

Diantha left the city at dawn and for once enjoyed the drive, for the first few minutes anyway. It was a pleasant change to zip along in no traffic and see it all over there on the other side headed inbound. She busied herself by sipping coffee and listening to the BBC on Sirius.

Saliba Correctional Center was two hours away and off the main highways. The roads got narrower until she approached the town of Kerrville, a deserted outpost in the heart of Missouri's farm country. Large signs pointed this way and that, and it became obvious that the prison was vital to the community. There was little else in Kerrville. It was called a medium-security facility, designed to house 900 inmates. According to the internet, it currently housed almost twice that number. It was built in the 1980s when the War on Drugs was launched by tough politicians and all fifty states joined the prison construction boom as incarceration rates soared. To keep the softer inmates away from the drug traffickers, a minimum-security wing was added in 1995, and somewhere deep in its bowels resided the once Honorable N. Bolton Malloy.

Diantha parked in a vast lot and inspected her face in the mirror. No makeup, no jewelry, nothing to attract attention. Slacks, flat-sole shoes, a jacket, no skin showing from the neck down, as per the website. For a stylish woman who loved fashion and took plenty of time each morning putting herself together, she was surprised at how plain she looked.

Back in the early days when she was fresh out of law school and the first female associate at Malloy & Malloy, she had always made the effort to dress up for the office. The men appreciated it and Bolton especially enjoyed her company. The clerical staff was all young women and Bolton paid them well. He was a demanding boss who favored linen suits, silk ties, French cuffs, and Italian shoes. The unwritten dress code around Malloy & Malloy was that to succeed you'd better look good.

She left her cell phone and briefcase in the car and locked it. At the entrance of the administration building she paused for a second to look at the cheap bronze plaque the state had screwed into a cinderblock wall. It commemorated the distinguished career of an old warden who'd been dead for forty years. Winston Saliba.

Who finished high school with the dream of having a prison named in their honor?

Inside the doors was a grungy reception area and two guards who appeared ready to pounce on the next visitor. They took her driver's license and ran her through the metal detectors. She filled out forms and was sent to a holding room where she waited half an hour. The chairs were plastic and unbalanced. The magazines were three years old. The place smelled of cheap antiseptic and gas heat. When it was her turn, a guard led her down a hallway, through locked doors, and into a pen where a golf cart awaited. He pointed to the back seat and they climbed in. He drove without a word, and she had nothing to say as well. Their pathway was a narrow paved road lined with chain-link fence ten feet tall and topped with glistening razor wire. On the other side were dozens of inmates out in the yard, staring at her.

How anyone, especially an older white guy like Bolton, could survive in such a dismal place was unfathomable. She saw a sign for Camp D and knew she was close. The mail she sent him went to Camp D.

Inside, the guard grunted this way and that and they entered a large visitation room with plastic tables and chairs scattered about, and vending machines lining the walls. There were no other visitors. Lay people visited only on the weekends. Lawyers could come and go as they pleased. He pointed to a corner where there were four doors under a sign that said ATTORNEY VISITATION ROOMS. He opened a door, showed her a seat, and said, finally, "He'll be out in a minute. You got anything to hand over to him?"

"No."

The narrow room was divided by a wall four feet high, and on top of it was a thick sheet of glass that ran to the ceiling. The minutes dragged on, and she reminded herself of how much she resented Rusty and Kirk for forcing her to be there. Bolton was their problem, not hers. She had not seen him in five years and that was not long enough.

His door opened and a guard appeared. Bolton was behind him and ignored her as the cuffs were removed. The guard left and closed the door. Bolton sat in his plastic chair and smiled at her. He picked up his receiver and said, "Hello, Diantha. I wasn't expecting you."

His first words were lies. Kirk had told him the night before, on his illegal cell phone, that she would be pinch-hitting.

"Hello, Bolton. How are you?"

"Swell. The days and weeks are passing. I'll be out soon enough. How are you these days, Diantha? It's so great to see you. What a pleasant surprise."

"I'm well. Phoebe's growing like a weed. Fifteen now and trying to drive me crazy." She managed a quick smile, but it was difficult.

"And Jonathan?"

She nodded for a second and decided to tell a fib of her own. "Jonathan's fine."

"You look great, aging beautifully, which is not unexpected."

"Thanks, I guess. You look almost dapper in your prison fatigues."

And he did. Thin as a rail, fit, lean, and his matching khaki shirt and pants had obviously been starched and pressed. Those in the general population she had just driven past all wore white pants with blue stripes down the legs, and white shirts. Evidently the softer ones in Camp D got better clothes if they could afford them. Every month she deposited $1,000 in his account and the money went for food, clothing, books, and such luxuries as a color TV and portable AC unit. She would be sending more, per Rusty and Kirk, but the prison max was $1,000.

With plenty of time to sleep and rest and almost unlimited access to the outdoor gymnasium, Bolton looked younger than he had five years earlier when they said goodbye. That, plus no alcohol, no women, no eighteen-hour days at the office, and he appeared to be thriving in prison, at least physically.

And no complaints. According to Rusty and Kirk, the old man had never once blamed anyone for his bad luck. Nor had he shown the slightest remorse for the death of his wife. He had always maintained that he did not murder her. He had pled to manslaughter, a far less serious charge.

"So where's Kirk?" he asked.

He knew damned well, but she played along. "He had an important appointment with his new lawyer. Things are not going well with Chrissy."

"No surprise there. And Rusty?"

"He was in trial all week and couldn't get things organized."

"How'd the trial go?"

"He lost again. Asked the jury for thirty-five million, got zero. Big loss."

He shook his head and seemed irritated. "I don't know what's wrong with that boy. Ten years ago he could pick a jury's pocket for anything he wanted, now he's washed up."

"He'll turn it around. As you know with trial work, there are hot streaks and cold ones."

"I suppose. Did you bring the financial statements?"

"No, I did not."

"May I ask why not?"

"Sure, you can ask. The answer is that I didn't exactly volunteer to be here, Bolton. And I'm certainly not going to be told what to do by you, of all people. I don't work for you anymore and I'll never work for you again. You thought you owned me once, when I was a kid, and I still resent the things we did."

"It was always consensual, as I recall."

"I was a twenty-five-year-old kid fresh out of law school and you gave me a job. What happened after that was hardly consensual. You were all over me from day one and left little doubt that any resistance might lead to a termination. That's what I remember."

He smiled as he shook his head. "Well, well. Venus and Mars again. What I remember was a sexy young lady in short skirts who thought screwing the boss was the ticket to a partnership. Didn't we have this conversation years ago when we reconciled? I thought this was all water under the bridge."

"Your bridge maybe, Bolton. We carried on for three years and it was me, not you, who finally stopped it."

"True, then we sat down and hashed through it and decided to remain friends. I've always treasured your friendship, Diantha, and your wisdom. I know that we reconciled."

"Oh really. If our relationship is so cool, then why have I been in therapy for the past fifteen years?"

"Oh come on. You can't blame me for all your problems."

Both needed a truce, so they sat and ignored each other. After a long gap, she said, "I'm sorry, Bolton. I didn't plan to say all that. I didn't come here to beat you up over something that happened a long time ago."

"You have a lot of anger and resentment."

"I do, and I'm trying hard to overcome it."

"Well, I would say I'm sorry but that's already been said. Obviously it didn't mean much. I have great memories of you, Diantha. I want you to like me. I swear."

"I'll try. Look, we're here in prison and I'm supposed to be bringing smiles from the outside world. Not causing trouble. My problems are small compared to yours, Bolton. How do you survive in a place like this?"

"Day by day. Before long it's a week, then a month, then a year. You stop crying, get tough, realize you can survive. You make sure you're safe. Me, I'm lucky enough to have a little cash to spread around. You can buy almost anything in here."

He smiled and clasped his hands behind his head, looked

at the ceiling. "Almost anything, except what really matters. Freedom, travel, women, golf, good food and wine. But you know what, Diantha, I'm okay. This is almost over and I'll be out soon enough. Statistically, I'll have about twenty more years to live, and I plan to have a ball. I'll leave St. Louis and all the bad memories, and I'll go somewhere nice and quiet and start over again."

"With plenty of money."

"Damned right, with plenty of money. I was smart enough to buy into the tobacco settlement when you and the boys and everybody else in the office said don't do it. The gamble paid off, then I was smart again and kept the money away from Tilda. May she rest in peace. I'm going to take the money and run away. Wanna go with me?"

"Is that another proposition?"

"No, it was a joke. Lighten up, Diantha, you seem to have more troubles than me and I'm the one socked away in this shithole."

"How do you plan to get out?"

"Wouldn't you love to know? Let's just say I do indeed have a plan and things are coming together."

"Let's talk about something else. I've only been here for fifteen minutes."

"Please don't hurry, Diantha. There are no time limits on attorney conferences and you're a rare bright spot for me."

"What about the law firm? I'm sure you're curious."

"Great idea. How many associates do we have now?"

"Twenty-two. Eleven on each side. If Rusty hires one, then so does Kirk. Same for secretaries, paralegals, janitors. As always, the expenses and the net draws must remain perfectly equal. If one feels the other is somehow getting ahead, then there's trouble."

"What's wrong with those boys?"

"You've been asking that question as long as I've known you."

"Yes I have. I cannot recall a period of time when they got along. It was like a sibling war from the crib. They're trying to destroy the firm, aren't they, Diantha? I've seen the financials. I know what's going on. Far too much overhead, far too little in revenue. As you remember, I ran a tight ship and watched every penny. I hired good people and I was generous with them. These two guys don't have the sense to run a law firm."

"It's not quite that grim, Bolton. We have some talented lawyers that I've hired over the years and they are developing nicely. I'm still in charge, albeit by default. Since Rusty and Kirk don't speak, everything crosses my desk and I manage the firm. The business is always up and down."

"I suppose."

He gazed wistfully at the ceiling and let some time pass. After a spell, he asked, "What do people say about me around town, Diantha?"

"That's a funny question, coming from a man who never cared what others said or thought."

"Don't we all think about our legacy?"

"Well, to be honest, Bolton, when I'm asked about you it's always in reference to Tillie's death and your incarceration. I'm afraid that's how you'll be remembered."

"Fair enough, I guess. Truthfully, I really don't care."

"Attaboy."

"The odd thing, Diantha, is that I have no remorse. I have not missed that woman for a moment. In fact, when I think of her, and I try mightily not to, her death always brings a smile. Yeah, sure, I wish I hadn't got caught and all that, and I made some dumb mistakes, but knowing that Tillie is in the ground brings me great joy."

"I can't argue with that. No one misses her, not even her two sons."

"She was just awful. Let's leave it at that."

"You and I have never talked about her death, have we?"

He smiled and shook his head. "No, and we can't talk about it now. These little rooms are not always secure. There could be leaks."

She glanced around and said, "Sure. Maybe one day when you get out."

"Are we going to be friends when I get out, Diantha?"

"Why not, Bolton? Just keep your hands to yourself. That was always your problem."

He laughed and said, "It was, but now I'm too old for the chase, don't you think?"

"No, I think you're incorrigible."

"No doubt. I've already planned my first trip. I'm going to Vegas to rent the penthouse at a tall shiny hotel, play cards all day, bet the games, eat steaks and drink good wines, and enjoy the young ladies. I don't care how much they cost."

"So much for rehabilitation."

(21)

The death of Tilda Malloy had been imagined many times, and, not just by her husband, though Bolton for decades had been by far the most active schemer. After ten years of tumultuous marriage, with no peaceful way out, he began to plot her demise.

It began with a sudden interest in trout fishing the rivers of the Ozarks, something he enjoyed but not nearly as much as he let on. Several times a year he and some friends, and later Rusty and Kirk, would drive three hours south from St. Louis into the mountains, rent cabins, and fish and drink like frat boys.

This led to the purchase of a log house retreat on Jack's Fork River in southern Missouri. Bolton went through an elaborate and prolonged ruse of feigning a newfound love of the outdoors, and, with time, did in fact acquire a certain fondness for quiet weekends, especially when Tillie refused to join him. She had no interest in any activity that could not be undertaken within ten miles of her beloved country club. She thought the hills were full of hicks, fishing was a weird sport for boys only, there were bugs and crickets everywhere, and besides there wasn't a decent restaurant to be found anywhere.

When she was diagnosed with coronary heart disease at the age of fifty-seven, Bolton was secretly delighted but maintained a passable front of the nurturing caregiver. Much to his dismay, she whipped herself into better shape, pursued a plant-based diet, exercised two hours a day, and claimed to feel better than ever. When one test after another showed better results, it became apparent that she was not dying anytime soon. Bolton went into a funk and resumed his decades-long fascination with her premature death.

Her first heart attack, at the age of sixty-two, had given her family a renewed hope. Though the topic was never discussed, life without Tillie was a constant dream for Bolton and his sons, and especially their wives. Tillie the mother-in-law was a meddling, conniving troublemaker.

Months passed, then years, and the old gal not only hung on but continued her evil ways with gusto. A second heart attack, at sixty-four, failed to slow her, and the entire family became depressed.

Yielding to pressure from Bolton, her doctor ordered her out of the city and into the hills for a two-week retreat—no phones, no internet, no television. Nothing but rest and bland food and lots of sleep. She had in mind a luxurious spa in the Rockies where her friends went to dry out, but Bolton insisted on his fishing cabin. She loathed the place and squawked for three hours as Bolton drove and fumed and fought the urge to whip the car over onto a gravel road and strangle her in a ditch.

For dinner, they ate civilly at the small, rustic table. Frozen fish entrees, plus a glass of wine for him. She said she wasn't feeling well, the drive fatigued her, and she wanted to go to bed. As she prepared herself, Bolton, wearing thick gloves and sweating and scared out of his mind, removed an eight-foot king snake from a crate hidden in a closet and put it in their bed, on her side, under the blanket. He had mentally rehearsed this a thousand times, but who in hell knows what will happen when a king snake, one well fed and supposedly tame, whatever that meant, gets thrown onto cotton sheets he's never felt before, then covered with a blanket. Would he freak out and slither out of bed and onto the floor and force Bolton to crawl crablike under the bed trying to catch him? Or would he freeze in place for a few seconds in anticipation of being discovered and the high drama to follow?

The snake cooperated and stayed put. Bolton managed to peel off the gloves before she came out of the bathroom, griping about the temperature. As she was preparing to pull back the covers, Bolton yanked them and screamed at the monstrous black, spotted snake lying on their beautiful white linen sheets. Tillie was so stricken that her vocal cords froze in terror and she could not utter a sound. She recoiled and fainted as she fell back and landed hard against a wall.

For a moment no one moved. Bolton kept one eye on the snake and glanced at his wife, who appeared to be unconscious. The snake raised his head slightly and looked down at Tillie, then turned to check on Bolton. Suddenly, he'd had enough and quickly weaved his way off the bed and onto the floor. When Bolton gave chase, the snake picked up speed and slid faster over the pine flooring. It was imperative to get the damned thing back in its crate, and out of desperation Bolton grabbed its tail, which caused the snake to immediately coil and strike. Bolton yelled as the tiny, razor-like teeth sunk into his left hand. Of course the snake was nonpoisonous—Bolton wasn't that stupid—but he could still bite and it hurt like hell. Bolton backed away holding his hand and noticing blood. He went to the kitchen, each step careful now that the snake was on the loose, and put some ice in a bowl for his hand. He sat at the table and tried to collect himself. His breathing was labored and he was still sweating. He had to think clearly. Think of it as a crime scene, which in effect it was.

The bleeding stopped but the swelling did not. He wrapped his hand tightly with a dish towel and went to check on his dear wife. She hadn't moved but had a faint pulse, much to his chagrin. Almost dead presented several scenarios, all of which he had walked through a thousand times. None, though, involved a damned snakebite that would be impossible to hide. He splashed some cold water in her face but she did not respond. The pulse grew fainter but wouldn't go away. He circled wide to avoid another encounter with the snake, who when last seen was disappearing under the sofa.

Bolton's future depended on the next few decisions. He would get only one chance to make things work. He checked his wristwatch. 9:44. She had been out for maybe ten minutes. What was the snake doing under the sofa, or had he moved on to another hiding place?

Bolton knew from his careful research that the nearest EMT unit was in the town of Eminence, the county seat, population 600, and it was a volunteer outfit. A prompt response by a well-trained team of medics was unlikely. However, failure to call 911 would only raise suspicions.

He really wanted a shot of bourbon but fought the temptation. There was a decent chance he would be talking to doctors and nurses and he did not want alcohol on his breath.

Her pulse grew weaker.

He opened the doors and with a broom tried to sweep under the sofa. No sign of the snake and it was important to find the damned thing.

At 11:00 p.m., Bolton finally called 911 and reported that his wife was having breathing problems and complaining of chest pains. He thought she might be having a heart attack. The dispatcher sounded as though she had walked in off the street and was taking her first call. Bolton gave his name and the address of his cabin, which, like many in the area, was hard to find in broad daylight. He intentionally neglected to mention a crucial left turn at an intersection, thus guaranteeing the ambulance would take forever.

He loaded the snake's empty crate into the trunk of his car, to dispose of later. He spoke to Tillie again as he squeezed her wrist. She wasn't making this easier. Because of her dedication to fitness she weighed only 110 pounds, and for this he was grateful. He managed to fling her over his shoulder, stagger down the front steps, and toss her into the rear seat. She did not make a sound.

Poplar Bluff was an hour away and had a nice regional hospital. He planned to arrive well after midnight and hopefully the A-team would be gone. He drove as slowly as possible and took several wrong turns. Not a sound from the back seat. At the edge of town, he stopped at an all-night convenience store for a coffee to go. With no one looking because there was no one else to be seen, he reached into the rear and checked her pulse again. He breathed a sigh of relief.

Tilda Malloy, his quarrelsome wife of forty-seven long and unhappy years, was finally dead.

Bolton hurried on to the hospital and wheeled into the emergency entrance.

(22)

The snake had not fled the house. He was coiled on the kitchen floor having a snooze when the crew arrived and saw him. They kept their distance as they searched the house and found no one. Oddly, all doors were open, all lights were on.

The dispatch log would reveal that the call from Mr. Malloy came in at 11:02. The EMTs reported arriving at 11:55, after several wrong turns. They secured the house, closed the doors, and checked out at 12:20.

And they took the snake with them. The unit chief had a thing for reptiles, enjoyed collecting them, and often did a Serpent Safety routine at area schools. He had never seen such a beautiful, and rare, speckled king snake and had no trouble capturing him. He assumed he was not a pet, but would readily bring him back if so requested. No request would ever be made.

The ER records would show that Mr. Malloy arrived at 1:18 a.m., with his nonresponsive wife in the rear seat. She was put on a stretcher, rushed into an exam room, and promptly declared dead.

A nurse quizzed Mr. Malloy and got the basics. She noticed his swollen and bandaged hand. He waved her off and said he had injured himself working on the deck the previous afternoon. A doctor insisted on looking at his hand and was intrigued by the odd semicircle of bite marks. Mr. Malloy insisted he had not been bitten by anyone or anything, and became uncooperative. The nurse noticed blood on the deceased's nightshirt and asked Mr. Malloy about it. Of course it was his. His hand was bleeding when he had no choice but to haul her from the bedroom to the car. The doctor asked if they could take photos of his wound and he refused.

Two deputies arrived with an injured drunk driver, and

their presence emboldened the doctor. He asked Bolton again if he could photograph his wound, and when he angrily declined the doctor nodded at a deputy. The two came over and had a look at Bolton's left hand.

"Looks like a snakebite," one of them said. "Nonpoisonous. A rattler and you'd have two deep fangs and swelling out your ass."

The other deputy concurred and said, "A perfect row of tiny teeth. Big constrictor. I'd say either a corn snake or a king snake."

Bolton waved them off with "Please, guys, I've just lost my wife. Could I have some privacy here? I have no idea what you're talking about."

"Sure. Sorry."

"Yes, sir. Sorry."

They left and Bolton puttered around the hallway, waiting for someone to tell him what to do next. The hospital wasn't busy and he grew irritated at the delay. About an hour after he'd arrived, the same doctor pulled up a chair and asked if he wanted coffee. It was almost 2:30 in the morning, not his usual coffee hour. The doctor explained the protocol: At around 8:00 a.m., the funeral home director would come to the hospital and discuss the death. Bolton would be needed to verify the identity of the deceased and discuss her medical history. When satisfied with the cause, the funeral home director would then prepare a death certificate.

"She wanted to be cremated," Bolton said gravely. She did not. Tillie wanted a full-blown Catholic Mass, with communion. Bolton was secretly opposed to this because he was afraid of a sparse crowd.

The doctor replied, "Well, under Missouri law you have to wait twenty-four hours before you can cremate a loved one."

"I know Missouri law," Bolton said rudely. "I've practiced it for forty years." Which was true, though he had never specialized in cremations. He was now sharp on that little niche in the law, because he had mentally rehearsed this scenario a hundred times.

The doctor was patient and said, "Okay, why don't you get some sleep and meet me and the funeral home director here at eight?"

"I'll do that."

He left Poplar Bluff and returned to his cabin. Fifty-one minutes, no traffic at all. He was trying to anticipate trouble. The EMTs had left a sticker on the cabin door giving the times of their arrival and departure. Bolton tiptoed through the house, holding a broom as a weapon, searching high and low for the damned snake. It was quite possible he had returned home and slithered up through the walls to the attic, but Bolton wasn't about to poke around up there. He closed the doors and turned off most of the lights. He gathered all of Tillie's shoes and clothing and packed them into her suitcase. Her other stuff—old pajamas, a bathrobe, underwear, toiletries, hiking boots she'd never worn—he loaded into a cardboard box and placed next to the suitcase in the trunk of his car. He wanted no sign of her left in his cabin.

Though he was calm and in no hurry, he felt a bit on edge and needed a strong shot of bourbon. He stretched out on the sofa in the den, sipped for a while, got sleepy and almost nodded off, then remembered it was the snake's first stop when he was fleeing the scene. He jumped up and walked around the cabin and finally eased onto the bed, but he smelled something odd and was certain it was an oil or some other bodily fluid left behind by the slimy reptile. Convinced the house was uninhabitable, he got a quilt and retired to a wicker rocker on the porch where he, with the help of a second bourbon, fell asleep in the chilly air.

Promptly at six a coyote howled from somewhere close and Bolton jumped out of his skin. He showered, changed clothes, loaded the car, and left at seven. It was early Sunday morning and no one else was awake. Near a country store, he stopped at a county dumpster and threw away all evidence of Tillie, as well as the crate the snake had lived in for the past four months. Lighter now, he hurried back to Poplar Bluff. Fifty minutes even.

At the hospital, he met with the same doctor and nurse, along with the funeral home director. He showed them his driver's license and swore he was the husband of the deceased. He even produced their current passports that he had packed just in case his scheme got this far. Once they were convinced he was indeed the husband, they asked him about her medical history. Without a doubt, in his opinion, the cause of death was cardiac arrest. In great detail, he listed Tillie's health problems: the coronary disease, the two heart attacks, the long list of doctors who had treated her, the hospitalizations, the avalanche of meds. His recall was impressive and he proved his case. His only embellishment was a fictional account of their last hours together when she complained of chest pains and he insisted on rushing her to the doctor. But she wouldn't go. At the end, at the most crucial moment, she had gasped and flung both hands over her chest as she fell to the floor. He tried mouth-to-mouth but it didn't work.

Of course, the snake was never mentioned.

The doctor, nurse, and funeral home director unanimously agreed. The cause of death written onto the certificate was cardiac arrest.

They loaded her into a simple metal casket, one used for such occasions, and rolled her into the back of the hearse. Bolton followed it to the funeral home across town where she was put on ice while time passed. Bolton's idea of a productive day was not one wasted hanging around a funeral home.

The director had a busy afternoon planned because there were three "clients" waiting to be viewed that afternoon, after church let out. All three had been properly embalmed and two of the wakes would involve open caskets. Bolton managed to ease into the visitation rooms and take a peek at the corpses. He was not impressed with the mortician's talents. After killing an hour, he managed to catch the director in his office and said, "Look, I know the law requires you to wait twenty-four hours before cremating someone, but I'm in a hurry. I need to get back to St. Louis and start planning a funeral. My family is waiting for me now and everyone is terribly upset. It's sort of cruel to make us wait. Why can't we do the cremation now and I'll be gone?"

"The law says twenty-four hours, Mr. Malloy."

"I'm sure there's a loophole somewhere that allows for an expedited procedure for the health and safety of those involved. Something like that."

"I'm not aware of such a loophole."

"Look, who'll ever know the difference? Go about it quietly now and I'll be on the road. No one from the State of Missouri will come around checking your records. I'm in a real bind here and need to get home and see my family. They are distraught."

"I don't think so, Mr. Malloy."

Bolton pulled out his wallet and slowly opened it. "How much does a cremation cost, anyway?"

The director smiled at his ignorance and said, "Depends on several factors. What type of cremation do you have in mind?"

Bolton huffed and rolled his eyes. "Well, I don't have anything in mind, except for the process of your putting her into the oven and then giving me a box of ashes to take home."

"So, a direct cremation?"

"Whatever."

"Do you have an urn?"

"What an idiot. I forgot to bring one. Hell no, I don't have an urn. I'll bet you've got one for sale."

"We have a selection, yes."

"Okay, back to the question. How much does a cremation cost?"

"A thousand dollars for a direct cremation."

"How much for an indirect?"

"I beg your pardon."

"Forget it." Bolton handed over his silver American Express card and said, "Ring me up. And I want the cheapest urn."

The director took it. Bolton pulled out some bills, counted ten $100s, and laid them on the desk. "An extra thousand if you'll get it done by noon today. Okay?"

The director looked at his closed door and cut his shifty eyes around the room. Then he scooped up the cash and made it disappear faster than a blackjack dealer. "Come back in two hours," he said.

"You got it." Bolton drove around for a while and finally remembered to call his sons with the news that their mother was dead. Both kept their composure and there were no breakdowns. He found a waffle house and had pancakes and sausage with the Sunday edition of the *Post-Dispatch*. He ate as slowly as possible and downed four cups of coffee. He enjoyed the obits and wondered if they might soon include his late wife.

By 12:30 he was racing back to St. Louis with her remains in a cheap plastic urn in the trunk. He could not remember such a feeling of exhilaration, of complete freedom. He had pulled off the perfect crime, disposed of a woman he'd wished a thousand times he'd never met, and his future was suddenly glorious and unburdened. He was only sixty-five years old, in perfect health, and within a year his tobacco fees would start arriving like golden eggs. His forty-year career as a hard-charging lawyer was over and he couldn't wait to travel the world, preferably with a younger woman. He had two in mind, both lovely divorcées he'd been itching to take to dinner for a long time.

(23)

A week after Tilda's funeral, a small private affair that drew little interest, Bolton moved aggressively to collect $5 million in life insurance. He and his wife had purchased matching joint policies years earlier, primarily because he was convinced she would meet an early demise, though he assured her at the time it was in her best interest because, according to the actuaries, he would likely die first. When the insurance company dragged its feet, Bolton, with typical trial lawyer bluster, threatened to sue for bad faith and all other applicable torts. It was a rare strategic blunder.

The insurer decided to investigate the death and hired a security company known for its bare-knuckle tactics. Its investigators, most of whom had military and CIA experience, were immediately suspicious because of the timing of Bolton's movements that fateful night. Two hours and sixteen minutes elapsed from his 911 call to his arrival at the ER in Poplar Bluff. Several test runs proved that the average driving time was only 52 minutes, and that was obeying all traffic laws. It was easy to assume that a reasonable person might push the speed limit a bit when hauling in a heart attack victim. It seemed as though Bolton had certainly taken his time.

He would be questioned about it, but much later.

Another factor was the day and time. It was late on a Saturday night in rural Missouri, not exactly the time and place for heavy traffic.

The ER doctor and nurse told the investigators that, in their opinions, Mrs. Malloy had been dead for at least an hour. Minimal rigor mortis was setting in with the muscles beginning to stiffen. In her notes, the nurse described Mr. Malloy as "uncooperative" and the doctor remarked that he seemed unbothered by his wife's passing. Both described the mysterious bite wound to his left hand. He refused treatment for it and would not allow the deputies to photograph it. One deputy was certain it was a bite from a large constrictor.

The break came in an encounter at the Ozark Mountain Snake Roundup, an annual event in Joplin that drew fans, handlers, collectors, charmers, and aficionados from the mountains and hollows and beyond. The unit chief from the Eminence Volunteer Fire Department was a regular and was proudly displaying his snakes, including two new additions: a five-foot timber rattler he had trapped in a ravine, and the eight-foot speckled king snake he had taken from the Malloy cabin a month earlier.

A handler from Kansas City seemed particularly enthralled with the king and finally asked, "He sure looks familiar. Mind if I ask where you got him?"

"Found him in a cabin on an ER call."

"He sure looks like Thurman."

"Who's Thurman?"

"Thurman's a king I bought from a dealer in Knoxville when he was only a foot long. He kept growing and growing, never seen a speckled king eight feet long before. You?"

"No, not even close. Five feet is about the longest. How long did you raise him?"

"Three years. Got pretty attached to him. Guy stopped by the shop last year and just had to have Thurman. I said what the heck, shot him a big price, and he paid me six hundred dollars."

"Six hundred dollars? Never heard of that much."

"Guy had plenty of money. Drove a big German car. I think he was from St. Louis."

"Don't remember his name, do you?"

"No. You said the snake was in the cabin."

"Yeah, all the doors were open, nobody at home. There was a 911 call and by the time we got there the place was empty.

Thurman here was coiled up in the kitchen like it was home. I'm just sort of babysitting him."

"So you wouldn't want to sell him?"

"Not now. Maybe in a year if he's not claimed."

"Why would anybody abandon Thurman?"

"Hell if I know."

The handler left and the unit chief forgot about him. Thirty minutes later he was back. "Say, you asked me the name of the guy who bought Thurman. I called the shop and my son checked the records. Guy's name was Malloy. Ring a bell?"

"Yep, that's him. He owns a cabin on Jack's Fork River."

In due course, the investigators for the insurance company made it to Eminence and checked the 911 logs and recordings. They bumped into the unit chief who told them all about Thurman. He invited them to his farm out in the country where he kept his snakes, but they politely declined. Just send some photos, if you don't mind, they asked.

They sped off to Kansas City and tracked down the handler, who identified a photo of Bolton Malloy as the customer and also provided them with a copy of the sales receipt.

The insurance company then sent its lawyers to meet with the Missouri Attorney General, a longtime political hack who was not a fan of Mr. Malloy. The lawyers laid out a purely circumstantial case claiming that, while Bolton may not have actually killed his wife, he was certainly complicit in her death. Murder could never be proven, but they had a good chance with manslaughter. In addition, Bolton may have possibly committed insurance fraud by filing a claim after her death.

The investigation, as well as the actions by the Attorney General, were kept secret and Bolton had no clue what was happening. The insurance company continued to stall with the strategy of forcing Bolton to file suit. He finally took the bait and sued, and was immediately bombarded with an avalanche of discovery requests. The insurance lawyers couldn't wait to get him in a big conference room for an all-day deposition.

Before that happened, though, Bolton was ambushed early one morning in the reception foyer of his beloved law firm when a gang of policemen surrounded him. As they walked him outside in handcuffs, the cameras were waiting. The scandal erupted with a media explosion and for days the legal community talked of nothing else. Front page, six o'clock breaking news, the works. He bonded out quickly and fled to his cabin where he holed up with a shotgun and tried in vain to sleep amid nightmares of snakes crawling under the covers.

His lawyers proclaimed innocence but said little else and stayed busy behind the scenes. The tabloids pounded the story for weeks but it eventually grew old. The State pushed hard for a twenty-year sentence, the max, but Bolton quietly insisted on a trial. When the date was a month away, his lawyers convinced him to plead guilty to manslaughter and take ten years. Otherwise, he might die in prison.

His lawyers painted a grim picture of what would happen when Thurman made his appearance at the trial. Imagine an experienced snake handler, maybe even the unit chief himself, removing the snake from his crate and holding him up in front of a mortified jury. This is the snake, ladies and gentlemen, that Bolton Malloy purchased for $600, took to his cabin by the river, kept him there for four months, for the right moment when he could show him to his wife, Tillie, a woman with a bad heart, a woman who, like virtually everyone, was deathly afraid of snakes.

Can you imagine, his lawyers went on, what the world would think when large color photos of Thurman got splashed across front pages from coast to coast? And what if the judge allowed cameras in the courtroom? There would never be a snake as famous as Thurman.

He took the ten-year offer.

Disgraced, humiliated, convicted, banished to a prison like a common criminal, he went away. Two months after he began serving his time, the first installment of the tobacco money landed in a foreign bank account Old Stu was guarding. Its arrival softened the harshness of prison and gave new meaning to his life.

(24)

It is three days after her trip to the prison. Diantha sits in a deep, well-worn leather chair with her stocking feet resting comfortably on a low, padded ottoman. The chair and the ottoman are expensive, as is everything else in the office. She appreciates the fine things because she's certainly paid for them. Mimi is now at $250 an hour, certainly less than what Diantha bills, but on the high side for therapists in the Midwest. When they met fifteen years earlier, they were beginning their careers and their rates were much lower. They have grown up together, succeeded in their careers, and could almost be close friends but for the fact that Mimi is the therapist and Diantha is the patient. Years earlier they decided it was more important to stick with the professional relationship than to jettison it and become pals.

Mimi is saying, "I didn't like the idea of you going to prison to see him."

"I know. We had that discussion. I went."

Mimi sits in her chair, a modern funky executive swivel with wheels, and she likes to roll around on the birch floor. They talk slowly and softly and seldom make eye contact once the session starts, once the initial pleasantries are dispensed with.

"And how did you feel when you saw him? What was your first thought?"

"There were so many."

"No, there was only one first thought."

"Oddly enough, I was struck by how good he looks. He's seventy-one, been locked up for five years, but he's trim, tanned, in shape. Then I felt guilty for dwelling on his looks."

"Nothing wrong with that. You once found him attractive and the feelings were mutual."

"Yes, and then I asked myself how I could've slept with this old guy for so long. He was married, everybody knew what we were doing. Why did I do it?"

"We've spent the last fifteen years talking about that, Diantha."

"Yes, we have, and I still can't believe it."

"We can't go back there, Diantha, or change what happened. We've moved on. That's the reason I advised you not to go. Seeing Bolton again brought back memories and issues that you have confronted and vanquished. Now I worry that in many ways we'll have to start over."

"No, I'm okay, Mimi. I had my reasons for going. I wanted to see the great man in prison, dressed like an inmate, moved around in handcuffs, the works. I wanted to see him humiliated, stripped of all his assets and titles and trial lawyer glories. And for that reason it was worth the trip. I won't do it again, but I'm glad I went."

"He's not exactly broke, from what you've said."

"Oh no. Bolton is getting money these days from some old settlements. That brings up another issue."

"And it is?"

"Compensation. Bolton owes me for what he did. He took advantage of a naive young lady who worked for him. I felt trapped and thought there was no way to say no. It was never entirely consensual."

"Please, Diantha. You're reverting and that's dangerous."

Diantha says, "I've made my decision, Mimi. I made it driving home from the prison. Bolton owes me, and it's time to collect."

(25)

Neither partner could remember the last attempt at a private meeting. They had worked so hard to avoid one. At the moment, though, the issue was too critical to dump on Diantha's desk and hope for the best. The dumping had become routine and both partners were ashamed of it, though neither would dare admit this. And neither had the spine to stop it.

An agreement as to time and place took almost a week to iron out. They agreed initially that they would not meet in the office, but after that simple matter was locked up everything else became complicated. Kirk suggested a private room at one of his country clubs, but Rusty despised all of them and all of the members as well.

"What do you want, a strip club?" Kirk had retorted in an email.

Since both loathed the sound of the other's voice, they avoided phones.

"Not a bad idea," Rusty wrote back, hours later.

For several reasons, they did not want to be seen together.

Eventually they agreed to meet in a hotel suite in Columbia, two hours away. Of course they drove separate cars and traveled alone.

Since Kirk's travel expenses were about to be picked through by his wife's divorce lawyers, they managed to agree that the room would be reserved by Rusty, who, at the moment, was between wives.

They met at 3:00 p.m. on a Thursday afternoon and no one

from the office had any idea where they were, no small feat for two important men who kept themselves surrounded by staff. Rusty arrived first, checked in, and found a diet soda in the mini-bar. Fifteen minutes later, Kirk knocked on the door. They managed to say polite "hellos" and shake hands. Both were determined to act civilized and speak in measured tones. Both knew that one stray word could cause a brawl.

They sat at a small table and sipped sodas. Kirk asked, "You talked to the old man lately?"

"Last week, briefly. You?"

"He called last night. Proud of his latest cell phone. Said next time not to send Diantha. He wants one of us. As you know, I had to beg off."

"Yeah, sorry about the divorce and all. I've been down that road several times and it's never pleasant. No chance of a reconciliation?"

"No way. We're too far gone."

"I hear she's hired Scarlett Ambrose."

"Afraid so."

"It'll get nasty."

"It's already nasty. I'm moving out this weekend."

"Sorry to hear that. You know, I've had three divorces, nothing to brag about. But I managed to settle all of them without the messy fighting."

"I know, I know. Look, we didn't drive here to talk about our divorces. The topic is money. We're both in rough shape financially. Because of the divorce, I'm probably in more of a jam. The law firm is bleeding cash and the future isn't looking too good. Can we agree on this?"

Rusty was nodding along. A pause, and he said, "Meanwhile, the old man is sitting fat in prison and counting the days until he gets out. The tobacco money is piling up and we can't touch it. Can we?"

"Of course not. Stu controls it and he keeps it hidden. Here's the rub. That money belongs to this law firm, not to Bolton Malloy. He's been disbarred, disgraced, sent to prison, and he'll never practice again. It's against all manner of ethics for this firm to split fees with a non-lawyer. That's understood. What worries me is that he and Stu are hiding the money and evading taxes. What if the IRS comes in with guns blazing and wants to dig through the books? What if they find the hidden loot? Guess who gets indicted. Probably not Bolton, though I'd point the finger at him pretty damned quick. It's more likely that they'll come after the two of us."

"Agreed. What are you saying?"

"I'm saying exactly what you and I have been thinking ever since the tobacco money hit the table. We are entitled to a chunk of it. We were partners in this firm when the tobacco litigation was settled and we should get a share."

"How much?"

"I don't know. You got a number?"

Rusty stood and walked to a credenza where he riffled through a briefcase. He pulled out some papers and dropped them on the table in front of Kirk. "I ran some numbers last night, something I'm sure you do all the time. At the settlement, the court approved fees for Malloy & Malloy to the tune of twenty-one million. The old man wisely deferred his share and structured a deal to postpone it for ten years, hoping of course that our dear mother would pass in the meantime. We all know that story. So for ten years the money churned at a rate of about five percent a year. Five years ago, the annual payments of three million hit home, or hit somewhere in Stu's world. At that moment, the pile was just over thirty-five million. Now, assuming the money is earning only five percent a year, and paying out at three million, then the payments will continue for another fourteen years. Bolton is almost seventy-two. What the hell is an eighty-year-old man going to do with that much cash?"

"I know all this, Rusty."

"Sure you do. I'm just repeating myself so I can justify taking some of the money now."

Kirk frowned and looked out the window. "What about Stu?"

"We make him rich. Give him a slice, enough to get a smile, enough to let the old fart quit and go home and water his roses. The conspiracy will take the four of us working together."

"Diantha?"

"Of course."

Kirk stood and paced to the door and back, rubbing his jaw with every step. "I had a long talk with her last night. The meeting with the old man was not a good idea. It brought back a lot of old issues that I thought they had resolved. Evidently not. To put it bluntly—she wants some of the money. She figures she's entitled to it after all these years."

"How convenient," Rusty said.

"Whatever. She's determined and she will not be denied."

"Great. Let's cut her in. How do we get Stu to cook the books for us for a change?"

"She thinks it'll be easy. She thinks Stu might be getting cold feet with all the money he's hiding and the taxes he's evading. He even mentioned something about not going to prison on behalf of the old man's schemes."

Rusty smiled and said, "I love it. What's her figure?"

"We're equal, okay? All four of us. We take a million each to start with, keep it offshore where it's hiding right now. Next year we take half a million each and leave one mil for the old man. Same for the following year. If it goes well, and there's no reason it shouldn't, we'll split the fees until the payments stop, or until he gets out of prison. We can adjust the distributions any way we like. But we gotta stick together."

"How do we snooker the old man?"

"Get Stu to dummy up the monthly financials. As long as Bolton's in prison he won't know the truth. When he gets out, he'll certainly cause trouble, but we'll have the money. What's he gonna do, sue us for taking fees we're entitled to?"

Rusty stopped smiling and said, "He'll evict us from his building."

"So what? If he does, we'll go somewhere else, or maybe just shut it all down. That's not a bad thought. Take a break from the law."

"While we count our money."

For the first time in years the Malloy boys enjoyed a moment together. The gorilla in the room had finally gone away. They had confronted Bolton and his monstrous fees, and they were not afraid. Driving home, Kirk was all smiles as he listened to Bach and dreamed of a far more pleasant life away from Chrissy and away from the law.

Rusty decided to hang around the hotel. He'd paid for the room, no sense hustling back home to an empty house. At five he entered the hotel lounge, got a drink at the bar and kept one eye on the door, ready to pounce on the first attractive prospect.

(26)

But Old Stu would have none of it.

He listened somewhat attentively as Diantha walked him through her tortured history with Bolton. She thought she was convincing but his homely old face became stone cold when she broached the subject of money. Damages. Compensation for sexual harassment. Since there was never spare cash lying around the firm, at least not above the table, Old Stu knew immediately that she had her eye on the treasure being accumulated offshore.

She plowed on and explained that the "boys" were getting restless and needed an "increase" in their compensation. He was nonplussed.

She wanted to remind the unlicensed accountant that he was an employee of the firm and could be terminated at any moment for any reason, or no reason at all, but she decided to keep the big arrows in her quiver and fight another day. She would regroup with the partners and plan their next move. The first, at least in her opinion, had been a disaster.

She left Stu's office on the seventh floor and rode the elevator alone all the way down. She told her secretary to hold all calls and locked herself in her office. She kicked off her heels and stretched out on the sofa. Napping was impossible. The stress was too great. She had failed miserably in her first attempt to convince Stu to join their secret raid on Bolton's beloved tobacco money. Who would she call first, Kirk or Rusty?

The answer was obvious. Kirk was a buttoned-up office guy who never got his hands dirty. Rusty was a street brawler who knew how to charm and negotiate. If the sweet-talking didn't work, then he was always ready to twist arms, or kneecap an enemy if necessary. If anyone could bully and threaten Old Stu, it was Rusty Malloy.

Early that morning, Stu had emailed to her, Kirk, and Rusty the previous month's financials. Things were bleaker than she'd thought. The banks would be calling soon and there would be the usual tense meetings.

She walked to her desk, sat with her feet on it, and studied the financials. Each year, Kirk and Rusty paid themselves

$480,000 in salaries, with year-end bonuses based on the firm's performance. The bonuses, always equal, per Bolton, were hammered out in a closed-door session each year on December 30. It was by far the most dreadful day of the year. Both partners came loaded with endless numbers, and Diantha had to referee. For the past three years, Kirk had raised hell because his side of the firm, the "right side," had grossed far more than Rusty's. Rusty fought back with five- and ten-year trends clearly proving that his personal injury practice was far more lucrative than Kirk's. Only four years ago, his "left side" had doubled the gross revenue from his rival.

That was before he began losing jury trials, and losing big.

Rivals? Why were they rivals and not partners paddling the same boat? Bolton said they had never pulled together. And now the boat was sinking.

If the business continued on course for two more months, there would be no year-end bonuses. Indeed, the gap between revenue and expenses was large enough to require Kirk and Rusty, again bound by a partnership agreement, to step up and cover the deficit, an ugly scene that had never happened before.

It was obvious to Diantha that the only smart moves were to drastically cut expenses, fire associates, get rid of staff, reduce the salaries of the two partners, and somehow convince Rusty to stop taking risky cases. None of which was remotely possible, and she was not about to make suggestions.

As she studied the financials, she asked herself again how a once prosperous firm could work its way into such a mess. She was about to leave for the day and go shopping when her secretary tapped on the door.

A process server was waiting in the lobby, a kid with a hoodie and oversized sneakers. "You Diana Bradshaw?" he asked rudely.

"The name's Diantha Bradshaw."

He looked at his paperwork and seemed to struggle with the words. "Right, and you're the registered agent for Malloy & Malloy, right?"

"That's correct."

"I'm a process server for the law firm of Bonnie & Clyde. Here's a lawsuit we filed two hours ago."

He handed it over. She took it without saying thanks. The kid disappeared.

Bonnie & Clyde were nothing but trouble. They were perhaps the most famous lawyers in St. Louis and not because of their legal talents. Husband and wife, they had been small-time divorce sloggers out in the suburbs until Clyde settled a tractor-trailer case and netted some money. His wife had always gone by the name of Bonita. Their teenaged son watched too much television and particularly enjoyed the schlocky ads run by personal injury firms. He came up with the idea of renaming his mother and blasting the airwaves with "Bonnie and Clyde" ads that featured them dressed like Warren Beatty and Faye Dunaway and holding submachine guns as they shook down slimy insurance executives for mountains of cash that went to their clients. They changed the name of their law firm to Bonnie & Clyde.

At first the local bar was horrified by the ads and sent a letter, but by then lawyer advertising was out of control, and it was protected speech anyway.

The injured clients poured in and Bonnie and Clyde got rich. They expanded their firm, hired a bunch of associates, and became infatuated with billboard advertising.

They had been hired by the parents of Trey Brewster, and they were suing Rusty and the firm for legal malpractice. Ten million compensatory and ten million punitive.

Diantha read the poorly drafted lawsuit and mumbled to herself, "I'd rather have their case than ours."

(27)

For the dirty work, and there was no small amount of it around any credible personal injury firm, Rusty had several contacts to choose from. The most experienced was an ex-cop named Walt Kemp, an investigator with his own firm of case runners, accident hounds, ambulance chasers, witness locators, and so on. Walt knew the streets and had feelers in many dark places, including prisons.

They met for egg-and-sprat sandwiches at a Russian deli in Dutchtown in the old part of the city. Walt's nondescript office was around the corner where the rent was cheap.

"I gotta weird one for you," Rusty said in a low voice.

"Won't be the first time," Walt said with a smile as he wiped beer foam off his mustache.

"You know someone at Saliba Correctional?"

"You mean, like your father?"

Rusty coughed up a nervous laugh and said, "Yep, the old man is still there. Anybody else?"

"Inmates or guys with guns?"

"Not inmates. Somebody with authority."

"Probably. What's going on?"

"Well, it does involve Bolton. He's been there for five years and from time to time gets his hands on a cell phone."

"Not at all unusual. In every prison there's a huge black market for phones. Along with drugs and pretty much anything else."

"Right, well, Bolton's got one now, and to be honest, he's driving us crazy with it. Can't seem to keep his nose out of the firm's business."

"What are you asking?"

"Drop an anonymous call to prison security, tell them inmate number two-four-eight-eight-one-three has a cell phone.

They'll find it and slam him into solitary for a month. He's been there before."

"You want your father in solitary?"

"Just for a month or so. He's driving us crazy and causing far too much trouble."

Walt took a bite and started laughing. When he could speak he said, "This is awesome. I love it."

"Just do it, okay?"

"Sure. Who gets the bill? The firm?"

"Yes, but call it something else. You've always been creative when it comes to billing."

"That's because I work for a bunch of lawyers."

"Just get it done. The sooner the better."

"Right away, boss."

(28)

One of the most crucial steps in mounting a successful coup was to cut communications. When they confirmed that Bolton was again in solitary confinement, the next step was to neutralize the opponent's allies. Again, it was up to Rusty.

He barged into the cluttered office of Stuart Broome on the seventh floor, unannounced and ready for battle. Old Stu was caught completely off guard. No appointment had been made. Rusty had not set foot in the office in many months.

"We need to talk," he said tersely, leaving no alternative.

"Well, good morning, Rusty. What's the occasion?" Stu said sarcastically as he stepped down from his motionless treadmill.

"The occasion is this, Stu. It's time for the firm to distribute some of the tobacco money you and Bolton are hoarding offshore. The fees are being paid to the law firm of Malloy & Malloy, a firm that no longer includes our dear father. You have a couple of choices here, Stu, so listen carefully. The first choice is to say no, we can't have access to the money because you're loyal to Bolton and not to us, and in that case I'll fire you immediately and escort you out of the building. I have two security guards in the hallway, armed, I might add, and when you're fired then you will leave without touching anything on your desk."

Stu's face was ashen and he almost gasped. When he spoke his voice was labored and scratchy. "You have guards? It's come to this?" He made it to his sofa and sat down hard.

"That's what I said, Stu. Armed guards. Termination without pay or severance, and if you want to sue us then we'll see you in court. Should be able to keep things tied up for several years while you fork out huge sums of money to your lawyers."

"What's the other choice?"

"Play ball with us and get rich. We're forming a little venture that will be highly profitable for the four limited partners."

"Four?"

"Me, you, Kirk, and Diantha. Equal partners. We'll take our share of the tobacco money now and as it comes in."

"Bolton will kill me, Rusty. And he'll probably take out you three while he's at it."

"Bolton is in solitary confinement right now, Stu. And when he gets out he'll still have five more years to serve. He thinks he'll get parole but that won't happen because he keeps getting caught with contraband and he's even been accused of bribing guards. Same old Bolton. Right now he can't touch us. We're not taking all of his money, so he'll be a rich man anyway."

"How much are we taking?"

"A million each up front for starters. Then half a mil each year for a spell. We'll figure it out later. The money stays offshore so no one knows about it."

Stu scratched a sagging jaw and looked as if he might cry.

He couldn't hold eye contact and stared sadly at his shoes as he said, "I've never been tempted to steal money."

"Steal!" Rusty roared. "Are you kidding me? This money represents honest legal fees earned by our law firm, a firm that Bolton was forced out of in disgrace when he got himself convicted, disbarred, and sent off to prison. So far he's been able to bully us and keep us away from the fees, but that game is over. Bolton can't keep all this money, Stu. Nor can we. What we're proposing is a fair split of the fees, nothing more or less."

"But I'm not a lawyer and I can't split fees."

"True, but you can damned sure take some bonuses, can't you?"

Stu liked this and began thinking of the initial installment. He stood and tried in vain to straighten himself, the hump in his back working at odds against his protruding belly. It would have been a pathetic thing to watch but for the smile on his face, a real rarity. In a lighter voice he said, "You know, if you fire me you'll never find the money."

Rusty was ready for it and shot back, "You think we're stupid? We know a firm of forensic accountants often used by the FBI. They could go to the source of the money, the tobacco companies and their insurers, and track it down. The IRS can do the same, if they want to."

Hemmed in on all fronts, Old Stu grudgingly caved in. "Okay, okay," he said, raising both hands as if in surrender. "Count me in."

"Attaboy, Stu. Good move."

"I can't believe I'm knifing Bolton in the back. I can never face him again."

"Maybe you won't have to. Maybe he'll serve his time, take his money, what's left of it, and ride off into the sunset. He has no friends to speak of around here, Stu. You know that."

"But he thought I was his friend."

"He used you, Stu, same way he used everyone else in his life. Don't shed any tears over Bolton Malloy. He'll be fine. And so will we."

"I guess we will."

(29)

Over the next week or so, Stu met separately with each of his three co-conspirators and explained the impenetrable web of offshore bank accounts and shell companies he had established on behalf of Bolton and his tobacco money. They were duly impressed and even flabbergasted at the intricate maze designed to hide it and keep it away from American tax collectors, or those from anywhere else. As if they had rehearsed, all three were adamant in their desire to move "their" money yet again to foreign banks they could deal with privately and directly. Stu felt a bit slighted, as if they couldn't wait to get the money away from him.

Rusty bolted first. To impress a new girlfriend, he chartered a jet and away they went to the British Virgin Islands where they spent a week in an oceanside villa and lounged by the pool. When she needed time in the spa, he met with his new bankers and verified that the money was in hand. More was on the way, he assured them, and they spent a few pleasant hours devising an investment strategy. With a million in hand and at least half that much due every year, investing was much less complicated.

Late one afternoon, sitting on a shaded terrace with the shimmering indigo ocean around him, and drinking a rum punch, Rusty began to have serious thoughts about quitting the law. He was tired of the pressure, the grind, the hours, the unpleasantness of dealing with his brother, and he was especially tired of getting his ass kicked in the courtroom. He was forty-six years old and wondering if he had peaked at such a young age as a trial lawyer. He had certainly lost his touch with juries. Insurance companies no longer feared him.

Why not take his new money and live a simpler life on a beach?

Diantha and her husband, Jonathan, were not currently living together, but the idea of a trip to Europe sounded good as a way to maybe re-ignite the romance. When the first three days went well and they promised to renew their vows, she finally told him about the new fee-splitting arrangement at Malloy & Malloy. Jonathan was impressed and seemed even more determined to make the marriage work. They met with bankers and planned ways to manage the cash. After a few days in Zurich, they flew to Paris and roamed the streets arm in arm.

Kirk was unable to dash off and check on his new fortune because his wife's divorce lawyers would soon be picking through his pocket change. Every movement and every expenditure would be subject to their scrutiny. Terrified of leaving a phone, text, or email trail, he finally managed to contact a London banker through an encrypted email account. Once their communications were secure, Kirk moved his money to a British bank domiciled in the Cayman Islands. It would be safe there, regardless of how many lawyers Chrissy hired.

The secret infusion of funds actually emboldened Kirk to attempt to settle the divorce and offer her almost everything they owned, plus reasonable alimony. The child support alone would be brutal, but, after all, they were his kids too and he wanted to provide. However, it became apparent that her lead lawyer, the infamous ball-squeezer Scarlett Ambrose, was out for blood and wanted another trophy victim. She wanted a nasty trial with perhaps some press coverage to further boost her oversized ego. Chrissy seemed to have been thoroughly brainwashed by her manipulative lawyer and would not negotiate.

The breakup was caused by the mutual hatred of the parties, not bad behavior by either one. Scarlett, though, needed dirt, and she was unleashing her bloodhounds on Kirk's finances.

Let them sniff, he said to himself. *I have a fresh pile of new money buried under the sandy beaches of the Cayman Islands.*

(30)

It was Rusty's turn for the monthly visit to Saliba Correctional Center. He had made the awful trip at least thirty times in the past five years and dreaded every mile of the journey. He remembered those earlier trips and how his resentment grew the closer he got to the prison. He remembered the struggle to have pity on his father for being imprisoned and wearing fatigues like the common criminals and working for fifty cents an hour in the library and eating wretched food. At the same time he loathed the man for manipulating the lives of so many, especially his two sons. He still chafed at the brutal partnership agreement Bolton had forced Rusty and Kirk to sign, one that bound them together at the hip and forced them to stay together. Most of all, he despised the old man for his greed, his determination to keep all of the tobacco money for his own glorious retirement.

Oddly enough, he did not fault his father for the death of his mother. No one did, really. Rusty and Kirk resented the fact that Bolton had been clumsy enough to get caught and disbarred, and had embarrassed the family and the firm, but no one had missed Tillie, not for a split second.

Today was different. The harsh feelings were gone, because Bolton's fortune was being distributed to deserving people, and he had not a clue. Rusty was almost looking forward to the visit so he could secretly laugh in the face of the greedy old man. For the first time in his life he was getting the best of his father.

Outside the attorney visitation room, the guard asked the usual question, "Sir, do you have anything to give to the prisoner?"

Rusty handed him a large envelope and said, "The monthly financials, that's all."

The guard opened the envelope, removed five sheets of paper covered with numbers, scanned them quickly as if he knew what he was looking at, and placed them back in the envelope. Rusty was amused by this show of security. No one could possibly understand the numbers Old Stu had put together for Bolton this month.

Rusty went inside the booth-like room and took his seat. Ten minutes passed before Bolton emerged on the other side, holding the envelope. He looked tired but managed a smile. They exchanged greetings and Rusty reported that his daughter, and only child, was doing well in boarding school. Her mother, his second wife, had shipped her off years ago.

Bolton said, "I understand Kirk and Chrissy are finally splitting up. How are their children doing?"

Rusty never saw their children and had no idea. Back when he was a free man, Bolton never saw them either. He was asking only to be polite, and Rusty wondered why he even bothered. The Malloy family had never been one to gather by the fire on Christmas Eve and exchange gifts. It was Tillie's fault. She was a cold, hard woman who'd had little time for her own grandchildren and despised her daughters-in-law.

They talked about the law firm and some new cases that looked promising. Rusty was much more like his father than Kirk was. In his day, Bolton loved to brawl in the courtroom and made his mark in personal injury litigation. He despised lawyers who hid in their offices and never went to court.

"So you've lost four in a row," Bolton said with arched eyebrows.

Rusty shrugged as if it meant nothing. "The nature of the game, Dad, you know that better than most." It stung but Rusty tried not to show it. To duck another question, Rusty served up one of his own. "How was solitary confinement this time around?"

Bolton opened the envelope and removed the papers. Without looking at Rusty he said, "I can take anything these assholes dish out."

"I'm sure of that. But why don't you lay off the cell phones? That's the third or fourth time you've been caught. You can forget about parole with a record like that."

"Let me worry about parole. Looks like business was good last month. Revenue up, expenses holding steady."

"Good management," Rusty quipped. The fact that the old bastard insisted on examining the monthly financials for a firm he would never again be a partner in was maddening. At times he had hinted that he planned to return to Malloy & Malloy in full combat mode and run things just like in the old days; at other times he boasted of taking his money and heading for the islands. The truth was that he was permanently disbarred. Old habits die hard, though, and Bolton had kept his eye on the numbers for over forty years.

If he believed that business was good it was only because Stu had finally been persuaded to cook the books in favor of the partners, as opposed to cooking them for Bolton. Old Stu was now a proud member of the conspiracy, and the financials Bolton was so impressed with were about as accurate as an application for a payday loan.

Bolton put down the papers and said, "I'm asking a favor, Rusty."

Rusty immediately flinched. "What is it?"

"I want you to support Dan Sturgiss for reelection."

"He's a Republican."

"I know what he is."

"He's also an idiot."

"Who happens to be in office and will likely be reelected."

"I've never voted for a Republican. That's Kirk's side of the street."

"He's gonna win, Rusty. Hal Hodge is not a strong candidate."

"Weak or strong, he's still a Democrat. Where's this coming from?"

"You boys just don't get politics, do you? You're so hung up on who's a Democrat and who's a Republican, and you lose sight of the real goal. Winning! It's much more important to pick the winners, Rusty, regardless of affiliation."

"I think I've heard this before, at least a thousand times."

"Well, stop hearing and try listening. Sturgiss will win by ten points."

The old man was usually right and had a knack for not only picking winners but worming his way inside their campaigns right before the voting. Cash didn't hurt.

Rusty knew exactly where he was headed. He said, "And you're convinced Sturgiss is your ticket outta here?"

"I'm convinced Hal Hodge is not. I can talk to Sturgiss. As you know, the governor has tremendous influence with the parole board. Let's get him reelected and I'll apply for parole."

Oh, dear Father. If you only knew how many people, including most members of your family, want you to stay here and serve every day of your ten-year sentence.

"I'll think about it," Rusty said, to placate the old man. And he certainly would think about it. He would ponder all possibilities to help keep him locked away.

They spent an hour talking about the old days. Bolton was always curious about what happened to the lawyers and especially the judges he had known back in the day. Only a couple bothered to write him a note from time to time, and visits were rare. He felt abandoned by the bar association he had once proudly served as vice president.

But self-pity was not in his genes. He was a tough old guy who was serving time he deserved. If he stayed healthy he would one day walk free with ten to fifteen years in which to raise hell, travel the world, and try his best to spend his fortune.

(31)

The dinner cost $25,000 a plate and was prepared by a hot new Spanish chef Kirk flew in for the occasion. The setting was the handsome lobby of Malloy & Malloy, decorated with enough flowers for a gangster's funeral. The city's leading event organizer was in charge and had rented the finest silver, flatware, china, stemware, and table linens. Two well-stocked bars served premium liquors and fine champagne. Waiters in black tie whirled about with trays of raw oysters and caviar. A string quartet played softly in a corner as the guests arrived and milled around.

Kirk had promised Governor Sturgiss a million-dollar fundraiser. He had called in all his chips, twisted the same old weary arms, and worked his impressive Rolodex. The result was a brilliant success. He had sold fifty-six places to the top Republican donors in St. Louis, and the event would net at least 30 percent more than the original goal.

The Sturgiss campaign was thrilled. The race was closer than anyone expected and had not gone as smoothly as four years earlier. Fundraising was lagging, though Hal Hodge was still behind in the money hunt. A million-dollar evening was sorely needed, and once again Kirk Malloy had come through.

He was there, the man of the hour, with his staff but not his wife. He and Chrissy were far beyond public appearances.

His crew greeted the guests, chatted with them, laughed at anything remotely funny, drank as much as they wanted, and would recede into the background when the dinner began. The price of a seat was far beyond their pay grade.

Rusty wouldn't be caught dead at a Republican fundraiser, and Kirk always returned the favor. Diantha, of course, was there because she was such a fixture. She was also there because Rusty would want to know the details. When he hosted political parties at the office, Kirk always wanted the gossip.

She was sipping champagne and trying her best to avoid the most odorous person in the room, an operative named Jack Grimlow, better known as Jackal. She had seen several governors come and go and they all had a drudge like Jackal, a henchman adept at the shadier side of politics. Jackal was the bagman for Sturgiss, his fixer, confidant, dealmaker, conspirator, sounding board, and sometimes leg-breaker. Diantha loathed the man because he was so repugnant, and he was also aggressive with women. He touched far too much. His was a position of power and it was well known that the Jackal was always on the prowl. He finally caught her at the bar and she managed to keep her distance. They talked about the race ad nauseam, then he surprised her by asking if she'd seen Bolton lately.

She lied and said she had not. For fun she said, "I hear he and the governor talk occasionally." She had heard nothing of the sort.

Jackal laughed, he was always laughing, and replied, "Seems like I do recall the gov saying something about a chat with Bolton."

"They've caught him several times with contraband cell phones."

"Sounds just like Bolton, doesn't it?"

"It does."

The headwaiter tapped a spoon to a glass and called everyone to order. Kirk proudly stepped forward and welcomed his guests. He thanked them for their generosity, promised a delicious meal, as well as a small number of short speeches, and asked everyone to find their place.

Dinner for the elites was served.

(32)

A week later, Rusty was working from home on a Tuesday because Kirk was in the office. Even though flush with hidden cash, the brothers simply could not let go of their past, or their present for that matter.

Walt Kemp called and said they should meet for lunch. He wouldn't give a reason but said it was important. Of course it was. They'd met for lunch maybe three times in the past ten years, so something was up. Rusty drove to the same Russian deli in Dutchtown, where he found Walt at the same table. They enjoyed the same egg-and-sprat sandwiches with Czech pilsner. Halfway through, Walt finally got around to business.

"So we got hired to watch another cheating husband, big divorce case. Ever hear of a guy named Jack Grimlow?"

"I know him." Rusty nodded with a smug smile. "Sleazy political operative, works for the governor. Nicknamed Jackal."

"Figured you'd know him. He runs the gals pretty hard and his wife is fed up. He doesn't know it yet but she's hired some really sharp divorce lawyers and they're watching every move. We got the call, liked the money, and are now involved. Jackal's got at least two full-time girlfriends and hits on everything else. A busy boy. His wife'll pop him soon enough and he won't know what hit him."

"Terribly interesting and I wish him nothing but bad luck, but why am I hearing this?"

"Hang on. We couldn't pick up his trail online or with his phones, so we hired some hackers to take a look."

"That's illegal in at least fifty states."

"Thank you, Mr. Lawyer. We know that and we're not stupid. The hackers, shall we say, are not U.S. citizens and work from the safety of Eastern Europe. They're quite good, almost got caught when they went trolling through the CIA's super-safe, hacker-proof systems about five years ago. You remember that?"

"No, and I'm barely hanging on here."

"Almost there, Rusty, and it'll be worth it. So, we're watching Jackal's secret emails and tracking him as he bed-hops around the state, always on official business following the governor around. Seems like the gov, too, likes an occasional frolic and Jackal can always arrange things."

"You're kidding?"

"Got the proof, but I digress. Anyway, we found some emails that were unrelated to women but directly related to a scheme of selling pardons."

"Sturgiss is selling pardons?"

"Don't be surprised. It's happened before in other states, not recently and not very often, but it has happened. The governor has an absolute right to pardon anybody convicted of a state crime, and that could be worth some money." Kemp drained his beer and wiped his mustache. "Now, you gotta figure that since most guys in prison don't have a dime and they come from low-income families, the customer base for selling pardons is quite small."

"That's pretty obvious."

"But, for someone who understands politics and whose family can put together some cash, it might work."

"I'm following."

"You also gotta figure that Sturgiss is not a wealthy man and will leave office now or in four years without a lot of assets. Why not make some easy bucks, sign your name a few times, sell some pardons, take the cash and bury it somewhere? With an operator like Jackal doing the dirty work, it's a piece of cake."

"I think I know where this is going."

Kemp looked at his empty plate and then looked at Rusty's. "You finished?"

"I am now."

Kemp glanced around and almost whispered, "Good. Let's walk to my office around the corner and I'll show you an email that might interest you."

"I can't wait."

Kemp's office was an old store on a street lined with the same. It had been gutted and refurbished. With its worn pine floors, brick walls, and high ceilings, it was more attractive than Rusty expected. They walked into a long conference room with wide screens on both ends. Kemp opened a laptop, scrolled and pecked, found what he wanted and looked at one of the big screens.

He said, "This is an email Jackal received on one of his hidden accounts, three weeks ago. His address is MoRam7878 @yahoo.com. The sender is RxDung22steele@windmail.com. Have no idea who the sender really is."

Rusty gawked at the screen and slowly read the email: *"Eyeballs with BM at Saliba CC, confirmed agreement at two mil, full and complete, done after January."*

He was silent for a moment as the reality hit. Kemp finally said, "There are eighteen hundred inmates at Saliba, don't know how many could be BM, but only a handful. The way I read it, the sender met with Bolton in prison and cut a deal for a full and complete pardon, in January, for two million dollars."

"January would be after the inauguration, assuming Sturgiss gets reelected. Any follow-up after this email?"

"No, at least not on any of the accounts we've discovered. Jackal is a smart guy and stays away from email and texts as much as possible. He carries at least three phones in his pockets and he's always talking to someone, but from what we gather he tries to avoid leaving trails."

Rusty shook his head and walked around the conference table. From the far end he asked, "Any indication that anybody else knows about this?"

"Like who?"

"Like the FBI."

"No, none at all. This is collateral damage. We were looking for sex, remember? That's all we're getting paid to do. We stumbled onto this."

"What will you do with it?"

"Absolutely nothing. We're not getting involved. I'm showing it to you because it's your old man and you're my client. And besides, if we took this to the FBI they'd probably bust us for hacking. No sir, we know nothing."

Rusty walked to within two feet of Kemp, pointed a finger, and said, "Walt, as far as you and I are concerned, I never saw this email. Okay?"

"You got it."

He punched a remote and the screen went black.

(33)

About half of the seventh floor of the Malloy building was occupied at the time. The remaining spaces were either awaiting new tenants or being renovated by those who'd already signed leases. Rusty found a small empty office suite last used by an insurance broker. The utilities were on, and most of the furniture was gone. He moved a table and pulled together some folding chairs. No one would ever find them up here. Old Stu was far down the hall and rarely came out.

Diantha approached the meeting with uneasiness and concern. Nothing about it added up. First, Rusty and Kirk were almost never together in the same room. Second, to her knowledge they had never held a meeting on the seventh floor. Third, her little phone chat with Rusty had been cryptic and suspicious enough to set off alarms. He had ducked all of her questions.

They were seated in the room when she arrived, and a quick glance at both of them was cause for even more concern. They had been raised with money and status and had never lacked confidence. They were at times arrogant and condescending. They believed they were a notch above everyone else and expected to get their way, and from their father they had inherited a fearlessness that often bordered on bullying.

One look at them now and it was clear that they were troubled, even frightened. She had never seen them so rattled. There were no greetings. She sat down and pulled over another folding chair for her substantial handbag. She removed her cell phone, turned off the ringer, and placed it by the handbag. Neither Rusty nor Kirk could see her cell phone or were the least bit interested in it.

For reasons she would never fully comprehend, she casually picked up her phone as if to check messages, tapped the Voice Memos app, then tapped the Record button. She put the phone down and glanced at Rusty. His cell phone was on the table.

The deft maneuver, made with no forethought or purpose, would profoundly impact the rest of her life and the lives of so many she knew well.

Kirk looked at her and said, "We're here because the governor has evidently decided to sell some pardons and Bolton has agreed to purchase one for two million dollars."

She stifled a gasp but couldn't keep her mouth closed. She rocked back as if hit with something and repeated the words in a mumble. She looked at Kirk but there was no eye contact. She looked at Rusty and he was nervously chewing a fingernail.

He said, "The deal is being handled by Jackal, no surprise there. A private investigator I know came across some of Jackal's secret emails. I saw one that confirmed the bribe. Two mil for a full and complete pardon in January. Looks like the deal's been cut."

She breathed hard and gawked at both of them. "Okay, is anybody with a badge in on the plot?"

"No, don't think so. My contact has told no one and will stay quiet. Doesn't want to get involved, doesn't want the attention."

"I'm somewhat surprised at Dan Sturgiss. Had him pegged for a stand-up guy."

"He's broke," Kirk said. "And his campaign needs cash."

Rusty said, "And he also listens to Jackal, who'd steal from his grandmother. Bolton's playing them like a fiddle. He'll be out before we know it."

All three took a deep breath and considered that awful scenario. Diantha glanced down at her cell phone. One minute, 52 seconds of a recorded conversation that could roil the state in an unprecedented scandal. What would it mean for her? Should she turn off the recorder? Should she leave the room? Her mind was whirling and her thoughts were muddled.

Kirk cleared his parched throat and said, "We all know what's at stake here. If Bolton walks he'll find out immediately that a chunk of his offshore money is missing. We'll have to confess, there's no hiding it. He'll go nuts on us and evict the law firm from this building. Malloy & Malloy will be history.

He'll hire some tough lawyers and come after us with brutal litigation to recover his money. And he'll likely win in court. And, Bolton being Bolton and a disciple of the scorched-earth theory, he'll probably go to the U.S. Attorney and demand a criminal investigation."

"Is that all?" Diantha asked, as a knot the size of a softball clotted in her bowels.

"That's all I can think of right now. Give me some time."

Rusty was frowning hard. "I'm not sure he'd go so far as to hound us with criminal charges, but nothing would surprise me."

"Eviction?" she asked.

"It's in the lease," Kirk said. "I reread it an hour ago. He owns the building and he can order his old law firm out in ten days. The rest of the tenants get thirty days and there must be good cause. Not so for Malloy & Malloy."

Rusty said, "Eviction will be the first step. Then the lawsuits. And it will not be possible to keep it quiet. Front-page news again as the Malloys slug it out."

Kirk said, "I can see the headline. 'Malloy Brothers Accused of Fleecing Firm While Father Sits in Prison.'"

Diantha said, "Hang on. When we all agreed to take some of the money, we felt as though we were entitled to it. Legitimate legal fees, earned by Malloy & Malloy, right? And Bolton is no longer a member of the firm."

Kirk was shaking his head. "That sounds good in theory, but the truth is that the fees were earned entirely by the old man. We were all opposed to the tobacco litigation, as he has reminded us often enough, and once the tide turned he kept the file to himself. He never talked about it, mainly because he didn't want Tillie to know."

Rusty said, "And don't forget that damned partnership

agreement. Signed the day before he left for prison. We agreed not to touch the tobacco money. I'm not sure that section is enforceable, but you can bet he'll use it like an assault weapon."

A long, heavy pause ensued as the three tried to absorb the unfathomable. Finally Diantha said, "I'm not so sure he'll fight over the money. He still has plenty of it and there's more on the way. A big fight will bring a lot of unwanted attention, and the offshore business could be discovered. Talk about messy. Bolton is in the middle of some serious tax evasion here and it could land him in a slammer where bribes don't work."

"Good point," Kirk said.

Rusty was shaking his head again. "The problem is that we can't predict the unintended consequences. We don't know what Bolton will do, and there will be no way to control him. I for one cannot believe that he'll take this without a big fight."

"Agreed," Kirk said. "He'll come out swinging and then start throwing bombs."

Diantha said, "Okay, but this is a bribery scheme involving Bolton and Governor Sturgiss, right? We have nothing to do with it. What if we play the role of the good citizen and tip the FBI? It'll be a huge scandal, a tsunami, but we'll go untouched. Sturgiss goes down, gets his just rewards. Bolton gets ten more years and dies in prison. The money's ours."

Rusty kept frowning. "Sounds good but it won't work. Any criminal investigation into Bolton Malloy will eventually lead to the offshore money. At that point we're all screwed."

Kirk and Diantha exchanged glances with raised eyebrows, as if to say, *This guy is quicker than we are. Thinks like a crook. Glad he's on our side.*

Rusty cracked his knuckles and raked his fingers through his hair. They could almost hear him thinking. Then he said, "Here's an idea that'll work and everything will be kept quiet. Plus,

Bolton will stay where he is. Let's go to Jackal and tell him we know about the bribery scam with the old man. Since they want a bribe, we'll give 'em one. We'll pay two-point-five million to keep Bolton where he is for the rest of his sentence. Sturgiss gets his money plus a little extra. We keep the bulk of ours. Bolton is told the deal is off and he'll think Sturgiss got cold feet."

Now Kirk's jaw dropped. "You want to bribe the governor to keep Bolton in prison?"

"I thought I was fairly plain. Did you get it, Diantha?"

"I did. I'm speechless."

"Tell me why it won't work," Rusty said with a nasty grin.

They were indeed speechless. Kirk leaned back in his chair and glared at the ceiling as if searching for an answer up there. Diantha pinched the bridge of her nose and felt a headache roaring in from the back of her neck. Then she remembered her cell phone. The recording was now at 22 minutes, 46 seconds, and counting, and it had scooped up a conversation that could land all three of them in prison with Bolton.

It was imperative that she now play defense. "I'm not so sure about it," she said.

Rusty said, "It's beautiful. The more I think about it, the more perfect it becomes. Five more years with Bolton locked away and we'll have most of the tobacco money."

Diantha asked, "What if Jackal says no?"

"Then we tell him we're going to the FBI. He'll back down. I can handle that clown."

Kirk chuckled at first, then began laughing. "It'll work. Jackal will grab it because it's more money but also, and more important, there's no crime. Think about it! Selling a pardon is obviously a crime. But taking a bribe to do . . . what? *Not* sell a pardon? It's never been heard of."

Rusty was revved up and kept going. "You can't find a statute in any state that makes it illegal to not sell a pardon. It's beautiful."

Diantha glanced down: 24 minutes, 19 seconds, and counting and getting deeper. To save her neck, she said firmly, "I'm not in, boys. I don't like it and I disagree. There's got to be something illegal about it."

"Come on, Diantha," Kirk said. "We're all in this together, aren't we?"

"Hell no. We're all splitting the tobacco money because we're entitled to a portion of it. This is something different. You guys are on your own here."

She grabbed the cell phone, dumped it into her handbag, rose dramatically, stood without a word, and left the room. She practically sprinted to the elevator and expected one of them to call her name. She ducked into the stairwell and was halfway between the fifth and sixth floors when she stopped to catch her breath. She pulled out her cell phone and turned off the recorder: 26 minutes, 27 seconds.

Now what was she supposed to do with it?

(34)

Mimi walks to a large window and gazes at the traffic below. It has been a long session, almost ninety minutes, and she is in no hurry because her patient has not been this fragile in many years. Mimi crosses her arms, speaks casually to the glass. "You don't trust them now, do you?"

The answer is slow and deliberate. "No."

"Have you ever trusted them?"

"I think so. We've worked together for eighteen years, got off to a rough start and all, but over time we came to respect each other. Now, though, their worlds are unraveling and they're under pressure. Their problems are self-imposed but then most are, aren't they?"

"Have they ever engaged in criminal conduct before?"

"Not to my knowledge. They may have danced around some campaign finance laws, something they learned from their father, but I have no direct knowledge of it. As I said, they believe they are committing no crime if they pursue this plan."

"And you're a lawyer. What's your opinion?"

"It's bribery, plain and simple, and I can't believe they feel otherwise. They're very bright and they know it's illegal."

Mimi turns and leans against the glass, arms still crossed. She looks at Diantha, who's lying on the couch, heels off, eyes closed. Mimi says, "It seems to me that you're in a dangerous predicament. Are you afraid?"

"Yes, very. There are too many crooks involved and something will go wrong. When that happens, no one knows who'll get caught in the crossfire."

"You've got to protect yourself. And trust no one."

"There's no one to trust."

(35)

Of the many lawyers currently working in the office of the U.S. Attorney for the Eastern District of Missouri, Diantha knew only one. She had served on a committee honoring "Women in the Law" with Adrian Reece, a career prosecutor known for her tenacity in going after sex traffickers. They kept in touch and enjoyed long lunches in which they happily bitched about the clumsy antics of their male counterparts.

Diantha called and immediately had Adrian on the phone. She said they had to meet as soon as possible. She had adjusted her afternoon schedule and leaned on Adrian to do the same.

Two hours later, they met at a busy shopping center, in an ice-cream parlor with a rowdy birthday party in one corner. The racket provided excellent cover.

Over stale coffee, Diantha handed over a letter she'd addressed to the Honorable Houston Doyle, U.S. Attorney for the Eastern District. She nodded and said, "Please read it."

Adrian looked puzzled but adjusted her reading glasses.

Dear Mr. Doyle: I have in my possession a recording of a meeting that took place two days ago. The topic was the selling of pardons by Governor Sturgiss. I strongly believe that an agreement has been made by operatives working on the Governor's behalf and a certain state inmate with access to money.

Attached to this letter is an immunity agreement. It promises my cooperation if there is no threat of prosecution. I have committed no crimes. My identity will remain anonymous throughout any investigation. When this letter is signed by the two of us, I will hand over the recording, the existence of which can never be made known.

Sincerely, Diantha Bradshaw,
Managing Director, Malloy & Malloy

Adrian glanced around and said, "You're not joking."

"Of course not. How soon can you have this in Doyle's hands?"

Adrian glanced at her watch, though she knew what time it was. "I saw him this morning so he's in town. How urgent is this?"

"Very. The election is almost here."

Adrian considered this and seemed somewhat dazed. "Selling pardons? It's just, so, old-fashioned, you know?"

"Wait till you hear the rest of the story."

(36)

In an office overwhelmed with modern variants of bad behavior—cybercrime, terror cells, meth labs, narco-trafficking, kiddie porn, hate groups, insider trading, credit card fraud, online piracy, and Russian hacking, to cite a few examples—the idea of a governor selling pardons was indeed old-fashioned. So simple, so low-tech, so nostalgic. And so irresistible that Houston Doyle dropped everything else on his jam-packed daily planner to welcome the Honorable Diantha Bradshaw into his huge and imposing office in the Thomas F. Eagleton U.S. Courthouse, four blocks from Malloy & Malloy.

He was appointed by a Democratic administration. Sturgiss was a Republican. Not that it mattered. Catching a governor from either party was an idea so delicious that Doyle couldn't believe his good fortune. The publicity would dwarf every other case already on his crowded docket and any that could possibly arrive later.

Diantha and Adrian sat on one side of the rich mahogany table, courtesy of the taxpayers. Doyle sat on the other side next to Foley, a ranking agent of some variety from the FBI. They hurried through the necessary chitchat and got down to business.

"Who is Stuart Broome?" asked Doyle, holding the immunity agreement.

Diantha said, "He's the in-house accountant for Malloy & Malloy. Confidant of Bolton, longtime master of creative bookkeeping, knows everything about hiding money in places most travel magazines have never heard of."

"And why do you want immunity for him as well?"

"Because he's an employee of the firm who's always done what his boss told him to do. Because he's my friend. Because he's not guilty, and even if he has done something wrong it's because Bolton told him to. If he doesn't get immunity, then no deal." She could push as hard as she wanted because Doyle badly wanted a governor.

"Very well. I've reviewed your agreement with our people and it's in order." Doyle signed it, slid it across, and Diantha signed it as well.

Doyle struggled to contain his eagerness. He smiled and said, "Now, let's hear the recording."

Diantha pulled out her cell phone, placed it in the center of the table, and tapped it. The three voices were quite clear.

Since she had listened to it twice, she knew every word, but sharing it with the U.S. Attorney and the FBI was another matter. She had almost convinced herself that she was not stabbing old friends in the back, that her actions were reasonable and justified in light of what the old friends were up to. She had the right to protect herself, and Stu, from consequences that were thoroughly unpredictable. But reality hit hard as she listened to the voices she knew so well. She was ratting them out, and their lives would never be the same. Nor would hers. She was hit with a wave of guilt and kept telling herself to be strong.

Doyle listened with his eyes closed, as if hanging on every word. Foley tried to take notes but gave up halfway through.

At the end, Diantha did a convincing job of walking away from the plot and staying innocent. When she stopped the recording, Doyle asked, "Any indication that the money has changed hands?"

"There has been no exchange. Stu Broome would know it."

"And you're convinced these guys are serious about bribing the governor not to pardon their father?"

"Yes, and I'm even more convinced that Bolton would try to bribe his way out of prison. I'm a little surprised at Kirk and Rusty, but then they're under a lot of pressure. The money has changed everything."

"Do you know how much Bolton has?"

"Roughly. His payout from the tobacco settlement is three million a year and it began five years ago. They run a fraction of it through the firm to make things seem legit, but the vast majority of the money is hidden offshore in various tax havens. Mr. Broome knows where it is."

Foley needed to appear involved, so he said, "Three million bucks a year. For how many years?"

"Depends on how much it's earning, but at least twelve years, maybe more."

"And these fees are not unusual in your business?"

"I didn't say that. The tobacco settlement was a historic bonanza for trial lawyers, but there have been others. Bolton just got lucky and signed on early."

Doyle waved him off and said, "Let's save this for later. The pressing issue is approval from Washington. We need to move fast. I assume the Malloys will be meeting with Jackal in the near future."

"That's a good assumption," Diantha said. "How will I know what's going on?"

"Well, we can't let you in on the investigation, but you can call me anytime. Or Adrian here. I'll keep her posted. I suggest you return to the firm and act as though nothing is going on."

Foley said, "But be careful what you say because we'll be listening."

"Got it."

(37)

The enthusiasm for nabbing a felonious governor, especially a Republican, was shared by those who mattered in Washington. Emergency meetings were thrown together at the Justice Department and the FBI headquarters in the Hoover Building on Pennsylvania Avenue. The Attorney General and the FBI director signed on quickly and fired off orders to Missouri. Important men in dark suits left D.C. on a private jet and headed to St. Louis. By 10:00 p.m. search warrants had been issued and surveillance plans were coming together.

Jackal's three cell phones were tapped, along with those of Rusty and Kirk. Bugs were installed throughout the law firm and the offices of the Sturgiss reelection campaign. Warrants allowed the FBI to monitor the emails of the players. It took an FBI hacker four hours to track down Jackal's secret addresses. When everyone was in place, they waited.

But not for long. As Diantha predicted, Kirk made contact with Jackal. Rusty played the other side of the street and loathed getting near Sturgiss and his gang. The call went from Kirk's cell to one of Jackal's, and since both used the same service provider the eavesdropping was even easier. Not surprisingly, they agreed to meet over lunch the next day at a suburban country club, far away from downtown. It was one of Kirk's clubs and he knew most of the men who hung around during the day, waiting for golf or happy hour. Familiar turf, and if strangers were lurking he would notice them. He also liked the idea of lunching and being seen with someone so close to the governor.

After the club's general manager was served with a search warrant and its attorney arrived to look it over, the FBI descended on the place. There were three dining rooms available for lunch. Mr. Malloy preferred the Mens Grille, near the pro shop. Women were still excluded from the area. There was also the Banquet Room, which was fancier, and the FBI suggested that it should be closed the following day due to problems with the ovens. The GM at first objected, but fell in line quickly when reminded by the lawyer that the club would cooperate fully. The third dining room was called the Patio, and

Mr. Malloy had been known to eat there, though not nearly as often as his wife.

At nine the following morning, Kirk's secretary called to reserve a table for two in the Mens Grille. It was then temporarily closed for an hour, due to plumbing issues, while a team of FBI technicians bugged two tables the general manager selected. When Kirk arrived at noon and parked near the pro shop, no less than eight FBI agents were watching and filming his every move. Same for Jackal, who appeared five minutes later. When they were shown to their table, two hidden cameras recorded their hearty greetings.

Of the ten tables in the grill, eight were occupied. The staff had been warned to carry on as if nothing was unusual.

A federal grand jury soon heard the entire conversation. The indictable portion was:

KIRK: So we know about the plan to spring our father in January, after some funds change hands.

JACK: [*Laughs.*] Oh really. Not sure what you're talking about.

KIRK: Come on, Jack. We're in the loop. Two mil for a full and complete pardon.

JACK: [*After a long pause.*] Well, well, I must say I am surprised. I guess Bolton decided to include his boys.

KIRK: Not at all. Bolton has said nothing about it. We picked it up from another source, verified with an email from one of your secret accounts, which really isn't that secure so you should be more careful, Jack. We know the deal is going down and Bolton plans to walk in January. Not sure where the two mil goes but I guess that's none of our business. So cut the crap and talk to me face-to-face with no bullshit, because we know.

JACK: You gotta problem with the deal?

KIRK: A major problem. Our lives are much less complicated without Bolton sticking his nose into the firm's business. He got only ten years, a rather light sentence for disposing of our mother. He deserved twenty. Bottom line, Jack, is that he's served five years and a pardon now will cause a major shit storm that Sturgiss can't survive.

JACK: [*A grunt, a fake laugh.*] Sturgiss won't care once he's reelected. He can't run again after four more years. He couldn't care less about what the wacky newspapers say.

KIRK: Okay, okay, let's not argue politics. My point is that we are opposed to a pardon.

JACK: [*Another laugh.*] Let me get this straight. You want to keep your old man in prison. Right?

KIRK: Yes, that's correct. And we're willing to pay.

JACK: [*Laughs some more. Takes a long pause.*] Gotta say, Kirk, this is a new one. I just thought I'd seen it all. [*Another pause.*] So, uh, now that we're in a bidding war with Malloys on opposite sides, how much are you willing to pay?

KIRK: Two point five.

JACK: [*Whistles.*] Okay. Plain enough. Two point five to forget the pardon and keep the ole boy behind bars."

KIRK: "That's it. And the gov gets the added benefit of not breaking the law. He's not selling a pardon.

JACK: The governor is not involved, Kirk.

KIRK: No of course not.

JACK: I'll uh, discuss it with the committee and get back. Time is of the essence. What if I pop by your office tomorrow?

KIRK: That'll work. I'll be in.

_____

The following day, the FBI trailed Jackal as he was driven, in a black SUV registered to the campaign, from its headquarters to the Malloy building. He got out on the sidewalk, never bothered to look around, and went in through the front door. Most thugs engaged in a criminal enterprise would at least glance at the surroundings, but Jackal had far too much experience to appear ill at ease.

There were no FBI agents inside the firm because it was deemed too risky, but Kirk's office, as well as the three conference rooms in his suite, were filled with enough bugs to start a plague. Two vans filled with technicians and listening devices were parked at the curb.

Six days later, the grand jury would hear the second conversation.

Again, the indictable portion was:

KIRK: Have a seat.

JACK: No thanks. This won't take but a second. The committee met last night to consider your bid and decided it's a tad low. The price is three mil. Half now, as soon as possible, for the campaign, payable to our PAC, all nice and clean. The other half is due in January, and we'll handle it offshore.

KIRK: [*Grunts.*] Why am I not surprised? You guys raise the price for all your pardons.

JACK: It's not a pardon. It's a non-pardon. In or out?

KIRK: [*A long pause.*] Okay. okay. We can do three.

JACK: And there's the small matter of my broker's fee. Two-fifty, payable up front, offshore.

KIRK: Of course. Anybody else?

JACK: Here are the wiring instructions. Keep this close.

No paperwork anywhere, no emails, texts, cell phone
calls. Everything leaves a trail.
KIRK: That's what they say.

Jackal was trailed back to the campaign headquarters. An
hour later, Kirk called Rusty at home and replayed the conversation. They cursed the governor and Jackal, and struggled
with their next move. Neither wanted to pay the bribe, but the
thought of Bolton out of prison and on the loose was beyond
unsettling. Finally, they agreed to move forward. Kirk would
ride to the seventh floor, have a chat with Old Stu, give him the
wiring instructions, and start the ball rolling.

The conversation was eavesdropped and recorded. When
Kirk entered Old Stu's office, every sound was scooped up by
the bugs. Stu played along, took the wiring instructions, made
a copy for the FBI, and promised to start the two wires: the first
to the campaign for $1.5 million, and the second to a numbered
Swiss account for $250,000.

Kirk had serious doubts if anyone with the campaign, including Sturgiss himself, knew of Jackal's "brokerage commission."

He left the firm for lunch and went to the extended-stay
hotel suite he was renting by the month. He'd been there for two
weeks and was already tired of the place. As cramped as it was,
he was delighted to be out of his house and away from Chrissy.

He stood in a hot shower for a long time, trying to wash
away the grime and filth of dirty politics.

(38)

Diantha met Adrian Reece after work in a wine bar near Washington University. They ordered a half-bottle of a Riesling and

retired to a dark corner. Diantha had resisted the temptation to call Houston Doyle directly because she knew he was a busy man and wouldn't divulge much.

Adrian was cautious with her update. The surveillance had worked beautifully. The three conspirators had said more than enough to get themselves indicted. The grand jury would see the case in three days and everyone expected formal charges. Governor Sturgiss would be investigated soon after the election. Word had come from the highest places in Washington that Sturgiss would not be charged with anything until well after the votes were counted. When and if he were charged, he would be presumed innocent and entitled to a fair trial. A quick indictment just before the election smacked of raw politics, and the Attorney General said no.

Early the next morning, Diantha called both partners at home and said that a meeting of the three was imperative. Rusty declined because it was a Tuesday, a day he avoided the office and his brother. She knew that but didn't care. The meeting was necessary, even urgent. Be in her office at noon.

Diantha assumed that the surveillance extended to her private spaces as well—office, phones, computers—and that was okay with her. The meeting had nothing to do with any illegal activity Kirk and Rusty were cooking up. The meeting was long overdue and she was on a mission.

When they arrived, in various stages of belligerence, she began pleasantly with "This is unfinished business from many years ago, and if you don't do what I ask then I'm walking out the door. I have my letter of resignation prepared and I'm ready to go. As we know, I'll take a lot of valuable information with me."

That startled them enough to get their complete attention. They gawked at her as she picked up a document and said, "This is a new partnership agreement that will go into effect today and shift around the ownership of this law firm. I'm joining as a full equity partner, with equal rights. That'll make three of us."

"You're asking for a third?" Kirk asked.

"Yes."

Rusty appeared confused and said, "Okay, but an equity deal means you have to buy into the firm. If you want to own a piece, then you have to pay for it."

"I know how it works, Rusty. I can argue that I've already bought my ownership here because I should've been made a partner years ago, and because I've been kept on an employee's salary for far too long, and because I have not been allowed to share in the profits, and because I paid dearly a long time ago when I was sexually harassed and abused by Bolton, and thanks to your own dysfunctional relationship with each other I've been the de facto managing partner for years, and the MP in any firm has an equitable stake."

They took this like a slap in the face and both seemed unable to breathe. Rusty finally caught his breath and said, "But a full third?"

"A third of what?" she demanded, ready to pounce on a question she knew was coming. "Right now a third of this firm is not worth much. With our rising debts, bloated overhead, plummeting revenues, and lack of success in the courtroom, this is not exactly an attractive asset."

"We'll bounce back," Rusty said, but only to defend his turf.

"Maybe," she said. "And when we do I want a third of the net profits."

"What about the tobacco money?" Kirk asked.

"We have a deal in place for that money. The four of us. This deal is about the law firm of Malloy & Malloy and who owns it. I should've been cut in as partner years ago. Take it or leave it, fellas. I'm not negotiating."

Rusty said, "Well, can we at least read it first?"

"Sure." She handed both a copy, and of course each tried to finish first. Kirk said, "You cut out the language that prohibited us from hitting the tobacco money."

"Yes, I thought that was a nice touch. This agreement, fellas, is for a future with no Bolton Malloy in it."

Rusty tossed his copy on the table and said, "I'm in." Both signed and gave her a hug.

If you boys only knew, she thought to herself as they left her office.

(39)

The grand jury was confused by the facts and the charges and wrestled with the case for over two hours. It was difficult to believe that the Malloy brothers were willing to spend such a huge sum of money to keep their father in prison. Houston Doyle handled the case himself and patiently explained that first, the firm and its partners were quite wealthy, and, second, the elder Bolton was well along in his bribery scheme to free himself. Doyle was forced to present the theory that the boys missed their mother and held a grudge against their father.

A majority of the jurors were appalled at the thought of their governor being on the take and wanted to indict him as well, forget the election. Doyle assured them that an investigation was underway and the FBI was watching Sturgiss. His day of reckoning would come.

In the end, they returned indictments against Kirk, Rusty, and Jack Grimlow. One count of conspiring to bribe a public official, a Class E felony with a maximum penalty of four years in prison and a $10,000 fine.

Adrian Reece called Diantha that night with the news and

asked her to avoid the office the following morning. Stay at home, don't answer the phone, and watch the news.

At 3:10 in the morning, Rusty's cell phone beeped and he snatched it off the night table. A vaguely familiar voice said, "Rusty, this is an old pal. The FBI has a warrant for your arrest and they're coming to your office this morning. Something about bribery." Before Rusty could say a word, the caller was gone. The line dead.

He sat in the dark for several minutes and tried to gather his thoughts but it was impossible. He threw on a jogging suit and sneakers, tossed some toothpaste in his travel kit, grabbed as much cash as he could find, and went downstairs without turning on any lights. He eased out back, got into his Ford SUV, and quietly left the neighborhood.

The FBI had listened to the call, had stuck a tracking device to his fuel tank, and was watching him as he thought he was making an escape. Rusty was approaching a thoroughfare when blue lights appeared from everywhere.

For Kirk, a Friday morning meant a day away from the office. He had planned to work in his hotel suite for a few hours, then make another painful visit to see his divorce lawyer. Such a visit, though, would seem like a trip to the ice-cream parlor compared to what was about to happen.

At 7:00 a.m., there was an abrupt knock on his door. It did not sound like housekeeping, and certainly not at that hour. He stepped to the door and asked, "Who is it?"

The response buckled his knees. "FBI! Open up. And we're armed."

Jackal was in Kansas City with the governor, campaigning hard with just days to go. He was dragged out of a hotel room before dawn and marched through the lobby. Thankfully, it was empty. An aide sent word to Governor Sturgiss.

By 9:00 a.m., word of the arrests had been leaked to the press and reporters appeared at the Malloy building and also at the jail. When the first bits of information hit the internet half an hour later, Diantha was waiting nervously on the sofa and staring at her laptop. By 10:00 a.m., the story not only had legs but was raging through the cyber world. A local TV station broke for news and weather at 10:00, and there were the first photos of the defendants, or at least two of them. The Malloy brothers in mug shots. As the story grew, Diantha's phone vibrated nonstop.

At 11:00, she instructed her secretary to tell all employees of the firm to go home and lock the doors. She was not coming in. She called Old Stu to check on him and he said he was happily missing the show downstairs, said he was all wrapped up in some new accounting rules for deferred depreciation.

At noon, Houston Doyle held a press conference to chat about the case. Reporters assaulted him with questions about Governor Sturgiss, who, obviously, had not been charged with anything, but it wasn't difficult to add two and two and get four. The alleged crimes involved a public official. Jack Grimlow worked exclusively for the governor. Doyle maintained a solid wall of nondisclosure and would not implicate the governor in any way. More than once, though, he said that the investigation was ongoing and he expected more charges. That drove the reporters crazy.

At 2:00 p.m., away from the stampede of reporters, Rusty and Kirk appeared via remote cameras in front of a federal magistrate. They had not had time to retain counsel, though both were busy trying to do so. They were being held separately and could not compare notes or give each other advice. Rusty requested a reasonable bond but the government objected pending a more thorough hearing. The assistant U.S. Attorney described both men as having access to money and owning vacation homes. Thus they, at least for the time being, should be considered flight risks. It was also noted that just three weeks earlier, Rusty Malloy had chartered a private jet for a vacation in the Caribbean.

The fact that the government knew this stunned Rusty because it proved that the FBI had been digging through his life for some time.

The magistrate, a man Rusty knew on a first-name basis, did not buy the flight risk argument, but was not ready to set a bond either. He ordered a bail hearing for 9:00 a.m. Monday.

Barring some slick end run by a defense lawyer, the Malloy brothers would spend the weekend in jail.

(40)

The slickest defender in town was F. Ray Zalinski, a white-collar-crime specialist Rusty had known for years. F. Ray had begun the day in federal court in Columbia, but upon hearing the news raced back home to St. Louis. At 2:45, he finally made it to the jail and was taken to an attorney conference room where he waited half an hour for his client. Rusty eventually arrived in handcuffs and a faded, oversized orange jumpsuit. When the jailers removed the handcuffs and closed the door, the two awkwardly sat at the metal table.

With a raspy, wounded voice, Rusty said, "Thanks for coming."

F. Ray offered a quick smile and said, "I assume you want me for the defense, right?"

"Sure, thanks. I tried to call."

"So how are you doing?"

"How do you think? Not good. I'm still in shock, you know? Still sleepwalking through this, can't believe it. Every minute or so I have to remind myself to try and breathe."

"I got Doyle on the phone driving in and we discussed bail. Looks like you might be here for the weekend, get out Monday."

Rusty shrugged as if it didn't matter. "Whatever. It's not that bad. I feel safe. A lot safer in here than out there. You seen the news?"

"No, not yet."

"It's awful. Everything's awful. I can't believe it."

"You want to talk about the charges?"

Rusty shook his head and scratched a jaw. A minute passed. "Back when I finished law school, my father made me work as a public defender, said I needed to get my hands dirty, learn what life was like in the streets. I had a lot of clients, all of them poor, almost all guilty, and I learned the lesson that you, the lawyer, never ask a criminal client if he's guilty, if he did the crime. Why? Because they never tell the truth. Second, because you don't want to know the truth."

"I'd like to hear the truth, Rusty. It'll make it easier."

"Okay. The truth is that Bolton had a deal with Sturgiss to buy a pardon for two million dollars. We found out about it. We went to Jackal and offered to top Bolton's deal to kill the pardon. For a lot of reasons, Bolton needs to stay in prison."

"How much?"

"Jackal came back and said it would cost three million, plus a little on the side for him. We agreed to their terms."

"Who tipped the Feds?"

"Don't know."

"Okay. As far as the Feds are concerned, assume they're listening to everything. Do not talk to your brother or anyone at the firm. In fact, don't say a word to anyone period. If you get out Monday we'll find a place to hide. You okay until then?"

"Yes. If Bolton can survive five years in prison, I can handle a long weekend in jail."

"Good. Something else to start thinking about. There are multiple defendants and not all will be treated the same. It's never too early to go to Doyle and get a deal."

"I'm not sure—"

"Cooperate, Rusty. My job is to get you off free and clear, but if that doesn't work, then to get you the best deal. You gotta think about saving your own skin because you can bet your ass the others will try to save theirs."

"Turn state's evidence?"

"You got it. Rat 'em out for a good deal. Play ball with Doyle, make his case easier, and you get off much lighter. The big question, Rusty, is this: Can you turn on Jackal?"

"No problem."

"Can you turn on your brother?"

"Sure."

"Let me hear your best pitch."

"Okay, Kirk negotiated directly with Jackal. I was not in the room. They cut the deal, not me. I thought the whole idea of paying Sturgiss to keep Dad in prison was some sort of a joke. I didn't realize they were serious."

"I like it. Might just work."

(41)

Three doors down, Kirk sat with his new defense team—two lawyers and a paralegal. His orange jumpsuit fit better than his brother's and was not quite as faded.

The lead lawyer, Rick Dalmore, was handling the initial meeting while the other lawyer and the paralegal took notes. Kirk was not as forthcoming as his brother.

Dalmore asked, "Now, who first had the idea of making a counteroffer to Jack Grimlow?"

Kirk replied, "Oh, it was Rusty's idea. I thought he was crazy, still think he's crazy. Someone, I don't know who, tipped him. Rusty claimed he saw an email that confirmed Dad was trying to bribe Sturgiss. Rusty went nuts, got this crazy idea that Dad has to remain in prison and serve his full term. So Rusty came up with the idea of upping the ante, out-bribing Dad. It was insane."

"But you met with Jackal."

"I did. Met with him twice. First time at the country club, second time in my office."

"Why did you meet with him if you didn't trust him?"

"You kidding? No one trusts Jackal, but he's a big man who works for the governor. The governor is my friend. Rusty refused to meet with Jackal because Rusty can't stand the guy. He hates most Republicans. So I had to. By then I was convinced the whole thing was a joke and that Rusty would not go through with it."

"So the conspiracy was Rusty's idea?"

"Every bit of it."

Dalmore smiled at the paralegal, then smiled at Kirk. "This will become a question of survival, and to survive you may have to testify against your brother. Does this bother you?"

"No, not at all."

"So you can do it?"

"Yes, no problem."

"Good. I like your story. We can do something with it."

(42)

Thanks to two martinis expertly prepared by Jonathan, who was now back home and working harder than ever to be the attentive husband, Diantha managed to sleep for seven hours before waking at dawn. It would be another dreadful day.

Jonathan, who had his own bedroom, was already awake and she could smell the coffee. She eased into the kitchen and asked, "How bad is it?"

"Terrible," he said, as he poured her a cup and set it on the table next to the Saturday edition of the *Post-Dispatch*. The bold headline across the front page screamed **MALLOY BROTHERS ARRESTED IN PARDON SCAM.** Just below were three large black-and-whites of Kirk and Rusty, with one of Bolton between them. Halfway down the column on the right side was a photo of Jack Grimlow, identified as a top aide to Governor Dan Sturgiss.

"Oh boy," she mumbled as she lifted her cup. She read the first article, then a second. With the indictment sealed, Houston Doyle saying little, and no word from the defendants or their lawyers, there were not many facts to explore or embellish. The implication, though, was fascinating. It appeared as though the press was initially under the impression that all three Malloys were in cahoots in a conspiracy to purchase a pardon for "several million dollars."

She glanced at Jonathan's laptop and asked, "What's online?"

"Everything and nothing. They're all repeating the same stories."

She looked at her phone and saw a thousand calls. Her mailbox was full and would remain so.

Jonathan said, "Most of the reports are careful not to get too close to Sturgiss, as of now. A few, though, have already jumped

to conclusions. Some of the crazies want him indicted immediately since the election is only three days away. You wouldn't
believe the garbage out there."

"It's always out there."

"Made *The New York Times, Wall Street Journal, Tribune,* half
a dozen other papers. Everyone smells a link to Sturgiss so the
story is raging. Ever hear of *Whacker*?"

"No."

"It's just another online news source, but it has an article
about the history of pardon-selling in America. Pretty good
read. There have been a few cases, usually involving bribery of
parole boards and stuff like that. The last case was in the 1970s
in Tennessee. Governor named Ray Blanton was accused of selling pardons, along with liquor licenses and anything else he
could find around the mansion."

"That's nice."

"Sorry. I'm rambling. Third cup. Is there a link to Sturgiss?"

She glared at him, tapped her lips with an index finger, and
said, "Don't know." He rolled his eyes. He had forgotten her
warning that someone might be listening. She had real doubts
about the FBI bugging her home, but she could not be certain.
She assumed they were listening to her cell phone and covering
every square inch at Malloy & Malloy.

As the sun lightened their breakfast nook, she spent some
time online while Jonathan scrambled eggs and toasted wheat
bread. Their daughter, Phoebe, was fifteen and would probably
sleep until noon, as she did on Saturdays if no one bothered her.

The doorbell rang at 7:05 and Jonathan gave her a look. He
went to the front door, opened it slightly, and had a quick chat
with a reporter holding a small recorder. Jonathan explained to
the man that he had about thirty seconds to get off his property
before he called the police. He slammed the door and watched
through the blinds.

Diantha's favorite associate at the firm was Ben Bush, Rusty's longtime litigation associate. She scrolled through her recent calls and saw four from Ben, all on Friday afternoon. She called him, woke him, and asked him to stop by her house as soon as he was up and moving around.

At 8:00 a.m., she sent an email to all twenty-two associates, seventeen paralegals, twenty-eight secretaries, and a dozen assorted staff, informing them that the office would be temporarily closed. All were encouraged to work from home and stay as current as possible. Those who had court appearances were expected to honor them. The press was to be strictly ignored. Firm business was more confidential than ever.

Ben Bush arrived at 9:00 and was greeted by Jonathan. "Keep your coat on," he said as they entered the kitchen. Diantha was dressed in jeans and an overcoat and shook hands with her friend. She jerked her head to the right and said, "I'd like to show you something." They stepped outside onto the patio and walked slowly across the backyard.

"You got my email?" she asked.

"I did. Thanks. Everybody is panicked."

"With good reason. We'll keep the place closed for a week, maybe longer. Maybe forever."

"That's comforting."

"There is absolutely no reason to feel comfortable or optimistic. I'd like for you to go to the jail and see Kirk and Rusty. Tell them to stop calling me. Both tried last night from the jail. The FBI is listening everywhere—my phone, their phones, your phone, who knows how many, but those two clowns have got to stay off the phone. Got it?"

"Sure. The FBI is listening to me?"

"Probably yes. They got warrants a week ago and it's safe to assume everything is bugged."

"Shit! So that's why we're out here in the cold weather, right?"

"Right."

"Okay, okay. They're getting out Monday, right?"

"That's the plan. They cannot return to the office anytime soon, okay? Convince them of that. They gotta lay low. The press is everywhere."

"I got calls last night."

"Monday morning, I want you to visit, not call, the security company and get the passcodes and key cards changed. For the entire firm."

"You're locking out Rusty and Kirk?"

She turned and managed to offer a tight smile while glaring a hole through his eyes. "Listen to me, Ben. They're not coming back, okay? The FBI has them on tape making the deal with Jack Grimlow to bribe Sturgiss. They're dead guilty. They're going to be convicted, and of course that means automatic disbarment. There goes the firm. Malloy & Malloy will no longer exist, and who would hire us anyway?"

As stunned as he was, Ben's second or third reaction was to ask: "How do you know so much?" Then, "Who tipped the FBI?" But he filed his questions away for another day.

He tried to absorb it all and looked away. "So, we're all out of work?"

"Afraid so. How many good cases does Rusty have right now? I counted eight."

"How do you define 'good'?"

"Potential settlement value of at least half a million."

He closed his eyes and tried to calculate. "Close, but I'd say more like five or six."

"Why don't you take those cases and hit the door? I'll authorize the firm to release the files to you."

Ben smiled and nodded and wasn't sure what to say.

She said, "You've been there for almost ten years, Ben. That's a long time for a Malloy associate. With no chance of becoming a partner, the associates don't hang around."

"Seems like we've had this conversation before. I've been thinking about leaving for some time. Hell, we all think about leaving."

"Well, the moment has arrived."

"Folks are already jumping out of windows. It was always toxic, and now this. You can bet no one will brag about working at Malloy & Malloy."

"It's very sad. Once a great firm."

"I can't believe they're going to prison, Diantha. They don't deserve something that harsh."

"Agreed, but it's out of our control. They're just like their father, Ben. Good folks at the core, but privileged and above the law."

"What'll happen to Bolton?"

"Nothing good. We'll talk about it later. Go see Kirk and Rusty and report back. Can you meet here in the morning? We have a lot of stuff to go over."

"Sure."

"And stay off your phone."

(43)

In the scheme of correctional priorities, libraries were not that important. An old Supreme Court decision decreed that every prison must have one, along with current books and periodicals, so that inmates have access to the knowledge that might help their cases. Those with active appeals used the library and leaned on the ex-lawyers who held forth. There were three of them at Saliba, each with a wide repertoire of colorful stories about where they went wrong and how they got caught.

In his five years at Saliba Correctional, Bolton had become a decent jailhouse lawyer, with two releases to his credit. Two notches in his belt. He had commandeered one cluttered corner of the library, cordoned off with old metal shelves. He even had a desk, a hand-me-down from some state agency, and he kept it spotless.

Saturday morning he sat at his desk, all alone. Before him was the latest edition of the *Post-Dispatch*. He stared at himself in disbelief and asked what went wrong. He had a deal! Why was he on the front page again?

He stared at the faces of his two sons and wondered how in hell those two boneheads had managed to screw up everything.

(44)

By the time the video bail hearing started at 9:05 Monday morning, the legwork had been done by the lawyers and their clients were ready to walk. The magistrate set the number at a million dollars each for Kirk and Rusty and ordered them to surrender their passports. He declined to require ankle monitors but forbade them from leaving the state.

Rusty's fancy condo was tax-assessed at $2.1 million and mortgaged at $1.3. The magistrate allowed him to tender in trust the deed and walk out with no cash involved. F. Ray Zalinski left the jail through the front door for the benefit of the press, while an associate slipped out of the basement garage with their client hiding in the rear seat. Once out of the city, they stopped at a biscuit joint and enjoyed breakfast. From there they drove two hours to a fine rehab clinic for a month's treatment for alcoholism and drug abuse. Rusty had not used drugs since college, nor was he an alcoholic. According to F. Ray, the first trick in a white-collar defense was to get the client clean and sober and use rehab in negotiating for a lighter sentence. Also, any felonious behavior could always be blamed on the substance abuse.

Kirk's morning did not go as smoothly. His fine home in a gated community had sufficient equity to satisfy the magistrate. However, it was still jointly owned with Chrissy, who had no interest in jeopardizing her one-half ownership. She refused to sign anything and told Dalmore, his lawyer, that she didn't care how long he stayed in jail. Dalmore tracked down Diantha, who brought in Old Stu, who finagled a "loan" to Kirk for $100,000, the cash required to satisfy the bail bondsman.

Jack Grimlow's bond was only $250,000, and he paid 10 percent to another bondsman for his freedom. When he walked out at noon, Kirk was still in his cell. Grimlow also managed to dodge the reporters. The election was the next day and he did not want to be seen.

(45)

The nonstop coverage of the Malloy scandal would have continued at full throttle if not for the election. On Tuesday, the voters went to the polls in lackluster numbers. Hal Hodge, the challenger, had failed to inspire anyone outside his base. Dan Sturgiss had begun the race with a commanding lead, then tried several different ways to blow it. The pardon-selling scam still raging around him didn't help, but by ten o'clock on election night he was still 200,000 votes ahead, out of 3,000,000 cast, and it was clear he was on his way to a second term. When he addressed his admirers in a hotel ballroom, he took a few moments to declare his innocence and claimed no knowledge of any bribery conspiracy. He even managed to get choked up and almost cried at the thought that anyone could think such terrible thoughts about him. He vowed to "fight on!"

Houston Doyle watched the vote counting and the speech with his wife at home in their den.

She asked, "Do you believe him?"

"No. But he's a pretty good liar."

"Will he be indicted?"

"You know I can't discuss the case with you."

"Sure, that's what you always say, and then we discuss the case."

"It depends on Jack Grimlow. If he doesn't budge and takes the fall, then it might be impossible to nail Sturgiss. The money never changed hands."

"Okay, got that. So how do you convict the Malloys?"

"We have them on tape conspiring to bribe. Unfortunately, we don't have Sturgiss on tape."

"So he dodges the bullet?"

"Right now, I'd say it's fifty-fifty."

(46)

By Thursday the election was old news and the press was once again enthralled with the Malloy brothers, neither of whom had been seen. Nor were their lawyers saying anything.

News was made anyway, however, late in the afternoon when the Missouri State Bar Association announced it was temporarily suspending the licenses of Kirk and Rusty, pending further investigation.

Kirk got the news while in the conference room of Nick Dalmore, his criminal defense attorney. The suspension meant he could not enter his office, which was locked tight anyway, nor could he contact any of his clients. He left Dalmore's and went to the office of Bobby Laker, his divorce lawyer. Scarlett Ambrose, Chrissy's pit bull of a litigator, was making demands and wanting more documents.

From there, Kirk went to his hotel room and got drunk.

Rusty didn't have access to booze but he would kill for a drink. He was still tucked away in a clinic getting rehab he didn't need, and he was already bored. They took away his laptop, but he managed to cajole them out of it, so he was watching his world crumble on the internet.

On Friday morning, one week after the arrests, his attorney, F. Ray, met with Houston Doyle in the big office in the federal building. F. Ray was ten years older and the two had known and respected each other for years. Normally, Houston would have deferred to his elder and been happy to have the meeting in F. Ray's office, a splendid suite forty floors above St. Louis. But these days Houston was the U.S. Attorney and all meetings were held at his beck and call. Besides, F. Ray needed something, a huge favor, and Houston wanted the begging to be done on his turf.

After sipping coffee and dissecting the election, F. Ray got serious with "Look, I know this is preliminary, but I want to plant a seed. I want you to think about cooperation from my client. If he rolls over, takes a deal, then your case gets much easier."

"Thanks, Ray. I know you're really concerned about how easy my cases are. What can Rusty offer me?"

"Full cooperation."

"You mean he'll squeal on his own brother?"

"There's no love lost. They've been at war since they were kids."

"So what's his story?"

"Bolton had the deal cut at two million for a full pardon. Kirk wants Bolton in prison, so he went to Jackal with a better deal. Rusty thought it was a joke—bribing a governor to keep someone in prison."

"Ha, ha." Doyle stood and walked to the mahogany conference table. At one end was a small audio box with a round speaker wired to it. He pointed to a seat and said, "Please, join me." F. Ray was puzzled but did what he was told.

When both were seated, Doyle said, "There are three tapes. The first was made by a witness who will not be named. The second and third are FBI. I think you'll enjoy them." He tapped a button and the first recording began. "Kirk and Rusty at their office," Doyle said. "The woman's voice has been altered, not that you would recognize it."

Half an hour later, Doyle tapped a button and the third tape stopped. He said, "Your client is lying to you."

F. Ray was shaking his head, deflated. "Well, it won't be the first time."

"No cooperation, Ray, because I don't need it. With these tapes I got both of them by the balls. You want to play these recordings to a jury?"

F. Ray shook his head some more. Finally he said, "What do you want?"

"Unofficially, I'll offer thirty months each, full fine of ten grand, five years before they can apply for reinstatement."

"Ouch."

"Could be worse. We could go to trial and play the tapes. Kinda reminds me of when Bolton took a dive to keep that big snake away from the jury. Sometimes the proof is just too strong."

(47)

Later that morning, Diantha sent an encrypted email to the associates and all other employees of the firm. She explained that the actions of the State Bar in freezing the licenses of Kirk and Rusty gave the firm no choice but to remain closed for an indefinite period. She was optimistic that business "might" resume after the new year. She cautioned that the situation was fluid and nothing was certain. Signing off, she wrote: *"In spite of it all, I wish you Happy Holidays. Diantha Bradshaw, Managing Partner."*

They had always known her as the managing director. Did this signify that she was the sole remaining owner of the firm?

At 2:00 p.m. Friday afternoon, she met Stuart Broome in the lobby of the Robert A. Young Federal Building downtown. He seemed older than ever and was walking with a cane. They rode the elevator to the offices of the IRS and were shown to a small conference room. The appointment with Ms. Mozeby, the field director for the state, was for 2:15. She arrived five minutes late and brought two flunkies with her. No one offered coffee.

In securing the meeting, Diantha had been forced to slog her way through several layers of bureaucracy until she found someone who understood the gravity of the situation. That person, name now forgotten, had successfully lobbied Ms. Mozeby to grant an audience. To expedite matters, Diantha had emailed a secure document, two pages in length, outlining the issues. At least they would not start from scratch, and some of the shock would be negated.

Diantha set the tone by beginning with "I'd like to offer you a copy of an immunity agreement signed by the U.S. Attorney for the Eastern District. It covers both myself and Mr. Broome here."

"I've spoken to Mr. Houston Doyle and am aware of the agreement," Ms. Mozeby said coldly, officially.

Diantha nodded and continued, "The tax evasion involved here is ongoing and we, on behalf of the law firm, want to address it, file amended returns, and pay what is owed."

"How much has Bolton Malloy received in fees from the tobacco settlement?"

"Fifteen million. Three million a year for the past five years."

Ms. Mozeby was impressed and glanced at the flunky to her right. She asked, "And how much has he declared in income?"

Diantha looked at Old Stu who said, "We've run about ten percent of it through the firm. The rest has been kept off the books and hidden in tax havens around the world."

"And who knows where it's hidden?"

"I do. I put it there, at the direction of my employer, Bolton Malloy. He wanted a fairly aggressive evasion scheme."

"And how long will the fees continue?"

Diantha said, "Based on an estimated annual return of four percent, the income stream should last for at least eleven more years."

"And where will these payments go?"

"To the law firm that earned the fees, Malloy & Malloy. Once the current mess is cleaned up, we will declare all income and play it straight."

"Okay, but the law firm appears to have some rather significant problems right now, if you don't mind my saying so. I just read the newspapers. Is it fair to ask how long the firm will survive?"

"Fair enough. I can assure you the firm will survive until all of the tobacco money has been received."

"Eleven years?"

"Eleven, twelve, thirteen. Doesn't matter."

"And you admit that you've known about this evasion?"

"I didn't know the specifics and never saw the money, until this year. I'd like to remind you of the immunity agreement."

"Got it." Ms. Mozeby took a deep breath and managed a forced smile. She glanced to her right and her left and said, "Very well. When do we see the records?"

Old Stu held up a thumb drive and said, "They're all right here. I can go over them with you. Take about an hour."

"Great. Let's get to work."

(48)

The following weeks turned into a nightmare for Diantha. For sixteen hours a day she rarely left the windowless office in the basement of her home. Presiding over the implosion of a sixty-year-old law firm was an impossible task that she was not pre-pared for. Who was? Where was the handbook on how to handle disgruntled clients, desperate associates, demanding judges, missed deadlines, shrinking fees, cash shortages, unreasonable bankers, frightened secretaries and paralegals, a monstrous social media backlash, the ever-obnoxious press, and lawyers circling like buzzards ready to pounce on the carcass? Amid the chaos, she was constantly distracted by the investigations into the Malloys' crimes, as well as the IRS probe into Bolton's tax shenanigans. She stayed at home because she felt safer and did not want to risk being tracked down by Rusty or Kirk, or their lawyers. Both the offices of F. Ray Zalinski and Nick Dalmore desperately wanted to chat with her and resorted to sending investigators to her home. A security guard hired by Jonathan ran them off.

She did talk to lawyers, and plenty of them. Houston Doyle called every other day with an update. Kirk and Rusty had lawyered up in a big way, and it would be weeks or months before a trial date was set. Doyle did not anticipate going to trial, but no meaningful plea negotiations would begin until months passed and the lawyers got fat. She could not comprehend the horror of walking into a crowded courtroom and testifying against her two longtime colleagues, and Doyle repeatedly assured her that it would not happen. He was confident that, in the end, they would plead to thirty months and be sent to a nice federal pen.

She dreamed of that scenario. The longer they were without their licenses, the longer the firm accumulated the tobacco money.

And she, Diantha Bradshaw, was the firm.

She talked to Justice Department lawyers representing the IRS and was pleased with the progress of the investigation. Because of Stu's fastidious records, the money was not hard to find. Early in December, she was advised, confidentially, that Bolton Malloy would soon be indicted on five counts of tax evasion.

She talked to dozens of lawyers with cases pending against the Malloy firm and begged for time. She talked until she was tired of the sound of her own voice.

Sleep was fitful and there was never enough of it. She had no appetite, though Jonathan continued to cook for her. Phoebe, her daughter, shamed her into doing yoga and riding a stationary bike.

She had to get away. When Phoebe's holiday break began, the family fled to New York, then Paris, where they spent the Christmas season at their favorite hotel. From there they drifted by train to Zurich where a beautiful snowfall had just blanketed the city. Diantha met with some bankers. Back home, Old Stu moved some more money around. She met with a lawyer and established a private Swiss office for Malloy & Malloy in the heart of Zurich's financial center.

They took another train up to the Alps, found a quaint hotel in Zermatt, and skied for a week. When they had enough of the slopes, they returned to Zurich with no plans to leave anytime soon. The family had made the unanimous decision to stay in Europe.

They found a spacious apartment on the fifth floor of a new building on the banks of the Limmat River. They leased it for a year and enrolled Phoebe in an international school.

From her narrow balcony, Diantha looked across the river to the gleaming office tower of Föderation Swiss Bank, the new home of her tobacco money.

She wanted to be close to it.